# IF I CAN
# SAVE
# ONE CHILD

# BOOKS BY AMANDA LEES

WW2 RESISTANCE SERIES

*The Silence Before Dawn*

*Paris at First Light*

*The Midwife's Child*

STANDALONE NOVELS

*The Paris Spy's Girl*

AMANDA LEES

# IF I CAN
# SAVE
# ONE CHILD

*bookouture*

Published by Bookouture in 2024

An imprint of Storyfire Ltd.
Carmelite House
50 Victoria Embankment
London EC4Y 0DZ

www.bookouture.com

ISBN: 978-1-83790-630-7
eBook ISBN: 978-1-83790-629-1

*For Delilah*

# PROLOGUE

Outside the cave, the wind howled and screamed, snowflakes whirling like dervishes, a curtain between us and the demons on our tail. In here, it was pitch-black, the walls wet to the touch. I didn't dare try to relight the lantern or even a matchstick. God knows where they were or how close. All we could do was sit it out.

Alice sniffled. 'Elisabeth, I'm scared.'

I reached out to pull her to me. 'Hush now. It'll be alright.'

My whisper echoed off the stone, a sigh that engulfed us just as the darkness did. I could smell the sweet scent of Alice nestling into my side. Heard a stifled cough from Robert. Caught the gleam of Guy's eyes as they met mine.

'Here.'

He shrugged off his coat, handing it to me. I opened my mouth to protest, but he raised his finger to his lips, nodding at the children.

I wrapped the coat around the three of us, pulling them closer, one on each side of me. My eyes were growing accustomed to the gloom. I could make out Guy's profile turned towards the cave entrance, keeping watch. He was massaging his chest and his shoulder now and then, wincing as he did so. How he'd made it this far I would never know. Or perhaps I did. The hand that had been rubbing his chest reached out to touch mine. I smiled through the murk. It was going to be alright.

At that exact moment, the sound of a gunshot ricocheted off the mountainside. Both children flinched.

'Is it them?' whispered Alice.

I shook my head. 'Probably just a hunter.'

A lie that was too close to the truth for comfort. They were hunting us down as they would an animal, a pack armed with a hatred as lethal as any of their weapons. A hatred that had already killed too many. I'd be damned if they'd take us as well.

Another shot resounded.

Trying not to disturb the children, I drew my pistol from my belt, catching sight of Guy's already in his hand. The shots were getting closer. There was shouting now too in German as they tried to flush us out. I could feel the children shrinking against me.

'Not a word,' I murmured.

We watched as shadows passed through the curtain of snow, right in front of the cave entrance.

Not shadows. Soldiers. Drexler's men.

I held my breath, praying with all my might. The ferns covered the entrance but still they might spot it. And then all would be lost.

A final couple of shadows marched past, their guns all too visible. The minutes ticked away, my eyes fixed on that sliver of light, ears straining for any sound. We were once more staring at nothing but snowflakes, dancing now like falling stars. I let out a long, slow breath. They'd gone.

I looked down at the children to see Robert's mouth gaping in fear. Before I could stop him, he let out a shriek of pure terror, his trembling finger pointing towards the entrance. Another shadow filled it, this one more distinct. The silhouette of a man, his familiar outline sending waves of terror through me. As I watched, he took a step inside the cave and raised his weapon.

I pulled my trigger. Perhaps Guy did too.

The world exploded, gunfire drowning out the children's cries, flashes illuminating the ghastly scene. And then all was silent once more.

# ONE

'Come on, you bastard... tell us what you did with the money.'

A whack as Albert's fist connected with Harry King's jaw.

Still, King said nothing, glaring back at the three men confronting him, not bothering to acknowledge my presence as I lurked by the door. Normally, he threw me a contemptuous glance when he saw me. I was too small, too insignificant as far as he was concerned. King liked his women blowsy and as loud as the suits he wore. Too bad he didn't understand it was my ability to blend in that had kept me alive.

More thuds as first Albert and then Captain Grant landed blows, King grunting as he doubled over, each time righting himself to take another. For a lowlife thief and cheat, he was taking this in a remarkably sporting manner, although I suspected it was to try to stop them from going further rather than through any noble instinct.

All of a sudden, Grant stopped and took a step back, signalling to the other men to do the same. You could hear the silence humming in the room, like an electric wire, fizzing with a danger that was palpable, especially to a feral creature like King. He edged towards the open window as if that might offer an escape route, but Albert darted forward, slamming it shut, cutting off King from the rear.

'I think we should take a moment to consider our next steps,' said Grant. 'This is, after all, a very serious matter.'

'I don't need to think about it,' snarled Janek, shooting a glance at King. 'He's a traitor. We shoot traitors. It's that simple.'

Albert folded his arms. 'Yes, but we are civilised people, which means we must give him a fair hearing.'

'Fair hearing? He won't speak. We've been trying to get him to do so for hours,' snapped Janek.

I had to admit he had a point. King was still staring at us all belligerently, a trickle of blood oozing from his nose down into his mouth. He licked at it, his tongue darting like a lizard's. I wanted to wipe that expression off his face, preferably permanently. But the others were right. If we stooped to his level, we would become as bad as he was, betraying not just ourselves but the people we were trying to help, downed aviators and refugees alike, all desperate to reach safety.

With the money King had stolen from us, we could have helped even more. It cost a fortune to run an escape line like ours, not least in bribes. He might try and bluster that he'd used the money to pay off the railway guards and police, but we knew better – he hadn't recognised Albert tailing him on his latest trip north, watching as he pocketed the cash meant for the people who risked their lives running the safe houses; who fed and clothed the escapers as well as providing them with new papers.

Grant came to a decision. 'Janek, you stay and keep an eye on him for a moment. Elisabeth, come with us. We need to discuss what we do next.'

Janek opened his mouth to protest and then thought better of it. We all knew how he felt. He'd have shot King there and then and been done with it. It was the three of us who had to come to a consensus, and that wasn't going to be easy. Spare

King and we ran the risk he would do it again – or worse. Condemn him and we would have his blood on our hands when our job here was to save lives, unless we were dealing with the enemy. Then again, it looked as if King was the enemy now.

His eyes flickered across us, weighing up what to do next, but he stayed mute. He knew the game was up. Say the wrong thing now and he might just seal his fate.

We huddled in the corridor outside the room, keeping our voices as low as we could so as not to alarm the assorted escapers and patients waiting in the apartment to see Dr George. To some he dispensed medical advice, while to others he offered sanctuary. Either way, Dr George was good to his very core, unlike Harry King.

'Do you think he's sold us out?' muttered Albert. 'You saw how much he was carrying. Even more than we gave him to pay the expenses for the last three trips. Where did he get that from if not from the Germans?'

'He's certainly had the opportunity,' I whispered, 'but what's his motive? Is it just the money, or is he an out-and-out traitor? He's been such a loyal member of the escape line. Would he really sell us out to the Germans?'

With a heavy heart, I realised that of course he would. The very qualities that made him such an effective comrade in arms were the same as those that would send him in the other direction. He could lie convincingly at the drop of one of the many hats he wore as disguises, loved fine wines, women and the expensive suits he strutted around in when off duty, not to mention the car he drove too fast whenever he got the opportunity. I'd thought it strange that he could not only find the petrol but had somehow held on to the car when so many were being seized. Perhaps here was the explanation.

It was as if Albert had read my mind. 'A man like that? With his tastes? Of course he would.'

'I agree,' I murmured. 'He's too flash, like a con man, except not a very effective one. If he had any sense, he'd stash it away until it was safe to get it out of the country. Instead, he's constantly spending his money. Our money. And no one appears to have picked him up for it. I smell a rat.'

'A very large one.'

Grant nodded. 'I agree. So what do we do with him?'

'We can't trust him,' I hissed. 'If he'll steal from us like this, he'll do anything. We need to get rid of him. For good.'

A beat passed as we looked at one another.

Just as Grant opened his mouth to speak, we heard an almighty crash from behind the closed door, followed by a bloodcurdling yell. I grabbed the door and flung it open, Grant and Albert hard on my heels.

King was standing by the open window, a gun in his hand. When he saw us, he fired. In the same instant, Grant threw himself across me, but the bullet slammed into the door behind us. King spun on his heel and, in one smooth movement, leaped out of the window, just like a cat burglar. I ran to it, rounding the bed to find Janek slumped on the floor, moaning.

'Are you alright? Did he shoot you?'

'*Kurwa!* He took my gun.'

There was a huge bruise on Janek's forehead, but he looked to be otherwise unharmed.

I stuck my head out of the window to see King jumping from one balcony to another. I aimed my pistol and fired, but King looked up, saw me and made a final leap to the ground. He was running now, racing along the street, disappearing around the corner at the end of it.

'Son of a whore,' I spat. 'He got away.'

# TWO

## 25 OCTOBER 1942

Less than a week later, we were gathered in that back bedroom at Dr George's place once more, this time staring at a message the radio operator had just delivered.

'Another one raided,' said Grant. 'The two agents running it have disappeared. That makes six in two days. At this rate, we won't have a single safe house left along the line.'

Grant's face was twisted in fury and frustration. We both looked at Albert, still clutching the scrap of paper the radio operator had handed him.

'We also received a message from the *comtesse*,' said Albert. 'She's moved all her parcels to another apartment in Lyon. They're targeting the safe houses between there and here. We must warn the others to move their parcels too.'

I stared at him, my mind spinning. This was all happening so fast. 'We need to try and find other places to put them. At least until this dies down.'

My voice tailed off as my eyes met Grant's. We both knew that was practically impossible. It was hard enough finding safe houses in the first place, never mind when the police were raiding them like this. The penalty for harbouring our parcels, as we called the escapers and evaders, was execution. The helpers knew that. And still they volunteered their homes, risking their lives for what we all believed in. Freedom.

Except that many of them would never see freedom again. The airmen were prisoners of war and should be treated as such, although the Nazis considered them spies if they were in plain clothes, as so many were once they started passing down the line. They shot spies too, although not as regularly as they tortured and then killed those who aided the enemy, like the helpers who sacrificed so much. In their eyes, we were all the enemy. Especially people like me.

'Can we head up the line and warn them in person?' I asked. Grant knew where all the safe houses were located. Had been located. In fact, he was the only one who knew. Or so we thought. He'd be the last person to betray the line, which meant it had to be someone who'd worked alongside him and paid close attention. Too close, as it turned out.

Grant shook his head. 'That would be far too risky. They know precisely the houses to target, which suggests they also know the routes we use. They'll be watching those like hawks. Anything out of the ordinary, like one of us knocking on the door of a safe house, and they'll arrest the lot of us.'

'Then how are we going to let them know? If we send messages, they'll almost certainly be intercepted. We might as well hang a sign outside their doors inviting those bastard police in.'

A pall hung over the room, seeping into our spirits. I could smell it – defeat.

No. Giving up wasn't an option. There had to be something we could do to save these people. In the meantime, there was another scent. The stink of betrayal.

'How do they know where to go?' I muttered. 'Who the hell is telling them?'

Albert cracked his knuckles. 'I have my suspicions.'

'Me too,' said Grant. 'But all we can do is sit tight and hope we can somehow rebuild the line.'

A faint hope right now, at the rate it was collapsing – along with everything we'd worked so hard to build. Although nothing mattered as much as the lives that now hung in the balance, airmen and civilians alike, hiding in attics and cellars across the country, their safe havens about to be shattered by a knock on the door.

# THREE

Four days later, they came for Grant. I returned from delivering two more parcels to Dr George's apartment to find Albert hovering in a doorway at the end of our street. He grabbed me by the arm and marched me off in the opposite direction before I could protest, pulling me behind a parked truck just in time to see Grant being escorted out of the building by half a dozen policemen, looking resigned but resolute. There was no point trying to fight them. Knowing Grant, he would do everything he could to persuade them they had the wrong man without betraying the operation.

'*Bordel de merde*,' I hissed under my breath, peering through the truck's window so I could watch them bundle Grant into a car. Two of them got in beside him while the others returned to the building, no doubt to ransack the apartment. The Vichy police were the worst, betraying their fellow countrymen and those helping them to the Germans. 'We have to find out where they're taking him.'

'Agreed. But first, we must get you somewhere safe.' Albert sounded worried as he pointed to a poster on the wall opposite.

I squinted at it, did a double take and looked even harder. 'My God. It's me.'

The pencil sketch was accurate enough that you'd recognise me if you studied my face, although the nose and mouth were a little off. Someone had drawn this from a description, and I'd wager anything it was King who'd provided that. But it was the figure beneath my face that stopped me dead in my tracks: five million francs. The reward for any information that would lead to my arrest. A pretty price to put on my head, and one that most people, suffering as they were, would find hard to resist.

We slipped out from behind the truck, walking at a normal pace along the street, careful not to arouse any suspicion. All it would take was one glance too many, especially with the lure of that reward.

'These posters appeared this morning. Apparently they're all over Vichy France; some in the north too.'

'Do we know who put them there?'

'My guess is the police, but it will be the Gestapo who're behind it. You've ruffled too many feathers there. Shown them up too many times.'

'That's my job.'

'I know. And you do it well. Too well, it seems.'

I glanced over my shoulder. There was an old man standing in front of the poster, staring at it. I ducked my head.

Stupid. He hadn't seen me. But someone else would. I needed to change my hairstyle. My outfit. Adopt a new disguise.

'Come on,' I muttered. 'Let's move a little faster.'

We were nearly at the end of the street, just a few more paces to go. Albert glanced at me then back to where the old man had been standing. I looked too, just in time to see the police emerging from the building. For half a second, I thought they hadn't seen us. Then I heard it. A shout, followed by a whistle.

'You. Stop right there!'

I looked at Albert. 'Run.'

# FOUR

We darted around the corner, legs pumping, no longer even trying to pretend. There was the odd glance from passers-by, who looked hurriedly away again, but no questions. The first rule of survival.

I scanned the street as we ran. There was a passageway on the right somewhere.

There it was. I grabbed Albert by the arm, pulling him after me, and dived through the narrow opening that widened out just enough to fit us comfortably, snaking behind the shops, twisting and turning towards the docks.

Our breath was coming in pants now. Behind us there was the shrill squeal of a whistle. More shouts. Shit. They'd found us.

Boots pounded the paving stones, but the end of the passageway was in sight. We burst through it just as they opened fire, bullets ricocheting off the passage walls. With any luck they would shoot themselves.

'Here.'

We exploded through another doorway, this time into a courtyard. I wrenched the door shut behind us and shoved the bolt into place. Horses looked up, startled, from their stable doors as we scuttled across the delivery yard. On the other side, the office. I prayed under my breath as we thumped on the door.

It opened, and a face peered out. The right face, thank God.

'The police, Eric. They're after us,' I panted.

The door swung wider, and we tumbled through it. Instantly, Eric bolted that too, leading us through into the next room and shoving a desk aside before pulling up a trapdoor. Beneath, there was a crawl space just big enough to contain both of us.

'Quick – get down,' he commanded, shutting the trapdoor the moment we were crouched together beneath it, cutting out all the light. I could hear the scrape of the desk being shoved back into place and then nothing except Albert breathing beside me. I tried to slow my own breathing, to not give in to the claustrophobia that was already descending. What if they took Eric and left us down here? How long would it take us to suffocate? So many thoughts.

More noises. A distant hammering. Raised voices. The clomp, clomp, clomp of boots on the floor right above our heads. It was hard to make out what they were saying. Then silence. I listened, straining; could feel Albert doing the same, my heart doing its best to beat out of my chest.

Finally, a shaft of light fell across our faces as Eric lifted the trapdoor once more.

'They've gone.'

As we clambered out, I spotted the marks of their boots on the floor, the pattern of their heavy tread scoring the dust.

Eric saw me looking. 'Don't worry. I swept away your footprints before they got here.'

I smoothed my hair back, tucking a strand into the victory roll I loved to wear in a silent jibe. 'Thank you, Eric. You saved our skins yet again.'

His lean face creased into a smile. 'As ever, it's my pleasure.'

Eric was one of the best, supporting the line in any way he could. That included moving the black-market goods that helped feed our parcels, all of it passing through his yard on its way to one of the safe houses.

He lit up a cigarette, offering us both one. 'Wait a few more minutes,' he counselled. 'Then I'll drive you out in one of the carts.'

As well as his vans, Eric relied on horses and carts for many of his deliveries, especially now that petrol was so scarce. On occasion, he even delivered the odd parcel from one safe house to another, secreting the escapers and evaders among the crates and barrels atop his cart. A good half hour later, it was where we were hiding too, ducking under the canvas Eric threw down before he arranged his produce on top.

Then we were off, this time to the clip-clop of a horse's hooves, trotting through the streets until we drew to a halt by the docks. I could smell the salt air and hear the gulls even before Eric peeled back our canvas covering and helped us down. We were standing behind a mountain of crates that were waiting to be loaded. The perfect hiding place.

'Thank you,' I mouthed, glancing round to make sure there was no one observing us.

With a brief nod, Eric gathered up his reins and disappeared once more, back to base.

I had to stand on tiptoe to see over the crates. There was just the odd dock worker, who knew better than to notice us. No sign of any police.

I looked at Albert. 'Take me to Dr George's.'

He shook his head. 'Too dangerous. I'm taking you to the Chateau Bleu.'

# FIVE

'The Chateau Bleu?'

'It's just outside the city, owned by a couple who escaped from Paris. They've been helping us out for a while now. Grant knows too much about the safe houses here in Marseille, including Dr George's place. There's always the danger he might crack and talk.'

It was no surprise that I'd never heard of this couple. The tighter we kept things, the safer for everyone. 'Alright, but I seriously don't think Grant will tell the Vichy police anything. It's not as if they're going to torture him.'

He took me by the arm, guiding me out from behind the crates and along one of the streets that led away from the docks. 'Don't you believe it. The police have learned a lot from their Nazi friends. At the very least, they'll beat him up. We can only hope they don't summon the Gestapo from Paris. Or send him up there.'

I gaped at him in horror. 'Can they do that?'

'They can do what they like. Things are changing fast, even here in the south. We need to be prepared. Here we are. Hop in.'

Albert indicated his van, parked at the end of the winding street we'd just marched down, one of the maze of streets around the Vieux Port that helped shield the operation from police raids, so confusing was it to navigate. Dr George's apartment wasn't too far from here but, instead, Albert fired up the engine and drove off in the opposite direction, heading northwest out of the city towards Aix-en-Provence. I tied on a headscarf as we wound through the backstreets, all the better to disguise myself...

As we left the city behind us and drove out into the suburbs, my shoulders dropped, and the nagging sense that someone was right behind me, on my tail, finally began to dissipate. I hadn't even realised how tense I was until that moment. Months of constantly looking over those same shoulders had done that to me, along with the growing sense of fear in the city where so many were gathering, coming from all over the occupied zone and even further, trying to get on board one of the boats bound for freedom in Spain, Gibraltar and beyond.

We did what we could for these refugees, but our focus had to be on our parcels, the airmen and other soldiers, along with agents who'd evaded capture. Get them safely out of France and they would live to fight another day. It was a huge responsibility, and one that weighed heavy. I'd had no idea how much until now.

At last, we turned off the road and along a driveway that wound uphill through beech, pine and oak trees, their twisted branches overhanging the track so low in places that they scraped the roof of the car. The place looked abandoned even before we rounded the final bend and the chateau came into sight through an avenue of cypresses, a gothic pile that appeared at first sight to be half ruined, rising fortress-like against the sky. It seemed at once desolate and welcoming, the walls eccentric rather than ruined now that I could see them better, rambling across the wilderness that ran up almost to the edge of the place.

As I climbed out of the van, the arched front door opened, and a slender woman came running down the steps that led up to it, dark curls bobbing around her face.

'Welcome,' she cried. 'I'm Eliane. Welcome to the Chateau Bleu.'

# SIX

I smiled at this woman, instinctively liking her.

'I'm Elisabeth,' I said. 'What a glorious house you have.'

She flung open her arm as if to encompass it. 'It's all yours. Feel free to roam anywhere. Right now, though, I suspect you'd like a cup of tea.'

Tea. How very English. Yet Eliane sounded as if she belonged somewhere between France and America, her accent overlaid with a soft twang.

'I'd love some tea,' I murmured.

She led us through the front door and into a salon where a fire roared in spite of the heat of the day. I guessed the sun didn't penetrate the thick canopy of trees which overshadowed the house, making it a perfect hiding place. It was an enormous folly rather than a chateau, sprawling as it did like some story-book castle, its shutters painted a Provençal blue in accordance with its name. I looked around the room we'd entered, taking in the faces of the young girl curled up in an armchair, reading a book, and the two men playing chess in another corner.

Eliane waved towards the girl, whose flaxen hair tumbled over her shoulders in a way that tickled my memory. 'Alice here is Charlotte and Matthieu's daughter. You'll meet them shortly. They're staying with us as long as this wretched war lasts. Paul and Walther are some of our other guests who will hopefully be able to leave France soon.'

Alice glanced up, flashing me a wary look before turning back to her pages. I didn't blame her. Strangers now represented potential danger in a France gone mad. The two men, however, rose as one and came to shake my hand.

'It's a pleasure to meet you,' murmured the one called Paul, while Walther raised my hand to his lips, eyes twinkling above a handlebar moustache that was almost snow white.

'An honour,' he declared.

'Elisabeth will be joining us for a while,' said Eliane.

The two men smiled as if this was the most delightful prospect and shuffled back to their game. I noticed that Paul had a slight limp, while both had accents that were distinctly German. Refugees, like all the others, fleeing an enemy that hated who or what they were.

'It's very kind of you to have me,' I said, 'but I really do need to be able to carry on my work, and this place is very remote.'

Eliane placed a hand on my arm, cutting me off. 'Not to worry. I have vehicles you can use that will get you to where you need to go. We know all the safe routes. You'll be absolutely fine, my dear.'

'You're not French,' I blurted, hearing the slight twang in her voice again, and then flushed in embarrassment. I really must be wrung out to be so unguarded.

Eliane simply smiled. 'I'm half French, half American, married to a Frenchman. My name is actually Eileen, but everyone here calls me Eliane. You'll meet my husband François later. He's busy in his studio right now. He's an artist, you see.'

I was beginning to feel as if I'd fallen down a rabbit hole. Except that this was our new reality, people seeking refuge in the most unlikely of places with the most unlikely of people proving to be their saviours. 'I look forward to it.'

Albert gave us all a little bow. 'I must go. I need to get back to the city so I can find out what's happened to Captain Grant. Don't worry – I'll keep you informed and let you know as soon as I know.'

I looked at him, feeling as any one of these displaced people must, with my own world suddenly upended and all my familiar things snatched away.

'I'll go and fetch your belongings once the police realise you're not coming back to your apartment,' added Albert. Like Grant, he had an uncanny ability to read people. It was what had kept them – all of us – alive.

'Thank you. How will you get word to me?'

'We have a telephone,' said Eliane. 'Unlike our one in Paris, it's not tapped as far as we know.'

'Eliane is totally discreet,' said Albert. 'You can trust her judgement.'

I returned her smile, noticing another man out of the corner of my eye, stumbling into the room. 'I'm sure I can.'

Albert gave me a brief hug. '*Sois sage*. Be careful. See you soon.'

'I'll show you out.'

As he disappeared through the door with Eliane, I heard a crash from behind me. Instinctively, I pulled my pistol from my belt, whipping round to see the man who'd stumbled in lying on the floor beside Alice's armchair, the small table that had been beside it now upended, a look of dismay on the young girl's face. It swiftly turned to alarm as she spotted my gun.

The man on the floor peered up at me through narrowed eyes, trying to focus, then sniggered. 'Is that a real gun?'

'Father, for goodness' sake.' Alice sounded surprisingly English, her ringing tones reminiscent of my aunt. 'Of course it's a real gun. You're being embarrassing.'

He stopped giggling and tried to sit up, falling back against the armchair as he did so. The expression on his face was part anger and part something else. 'Maybe it would be better if I wasn't your father then.'

There was a gasp from behind me. I turned again to see a woman advancing, her eyes blazing with fury. 'How dare you?' she snarled. 'How dare you speak to our daughter like that?'

# SEVEN

## 8 NOVEMBER 1942, CANET-PLAGE, SOUTHERN FRANCE

The waves lapped around my ankles, still warm from the long, hot summer, as I scanned the horizon, my gaze travelling along the shimmering swathe of moonlight that lay like a magic carpet across the Mediterranean, searching for the felucca. Beside me, Janek stood ramrod straight, the torch rock steady in his hand. I could hear the escapers behind me, silent as instructed, although their feet still scuffled in the sand. At last it came – a red flash and then another. Janek raised his torch and flashed it in response. Moments later, a dinghy set off from the main vessel, bobbing along the starlit pathway as it rowed to shore.

I turned to Albert. 'Gather everyone together,' I murmured.

The boat was perhaps a hundred feet from the beach now, its passengers clearly visible. I counted four – six including the boatmen. Far fewer than the number we were sending back. We had twelve evaders, thirteen prison escapees and five civilians, men and women. I glanced over my shoulder. So many faces, some alive with hope, others exhausted and resigned.

'Grab it,' Janek commanded in my ear as he waded out, steadying the prow so that the passengers could jump down while I caught the tail end of the rope the crewman tossed me and held fast. They splashed past me in the dark one by one, black woollen hats pulled low and scarves wrapped around their faces, to be welcomed by Albert on the beach. Each nodded a greeting, but the last, taller than the rest, flashed a smile with his eyes. I automatically smiled back, only to see him hesitate. I could feel him staring at me for a second before carrying on to join the rest. Only a second, but it was enough. There was something about him that was at once strange and familiar, almost as if I'd known him in another life.

Janek was issuing orders sotto voce to his crewmen in Polish. A few moments later, he was waving the people on the beach forward while the other helpers marshalled them. It was going to take two trips. Not ideal when the Vichy police could appear at any moment, but we had little choice.

I helped the women in the party aboard, the rope still held fast in my other hand. One lost her footing as the dinghy rocked, landing heavily in it and letting out a small shriek.

'Shhh.'

I glanced back up the beach, towards the road that led down to the port. No lights. No sign of the police descending.

The crewman whipped the rope out of my hand as Janek let go of the prow with a salute. And then they were off, the first boatload heading towards the felucca and freedom.

Janek and I plodded back up the beach to take a breather before the next load.

'Here.' It was him, the one who'd smiled at me. He was holding out a small flask.

I took a swig and then another, gasping as I tried to stifle a cough. Rough Spanish brandy ripped at my throat like paint stripper as it slid down. I could feel it warming my bones.

'There you go,' he said. 'I thought it would warm you up.'

His accent was even odder than Eliane's, not quite French and not quite American. And there was something about his voice that rang a bell, even though it was muffled by the scarf he

still sported across his mouth – standard issue for agents trying
to evade searchlights at sea and torches here on land. My own
was wrapped around my head, matching the black slacks and
sweater I also wore. We even disguised the boats as they passed
through French and then Spanish waters, painting them in the
appropriate colours to avoid scrutiny from each country's navy.
So far it had worked.

I swiped at my watering eyes. 'It certainly did that.'

He was doing it again, looking at me as if I was some kind of
exhibit. I turned away, as much to avoid his scrutiny as
anything.

The dinghy had reached the boat and was already turning
back. I beckoned to those remaining to move forward, ready to
embark as quickly as possible. This had already taken too long.
It only took one person to mention mysterious lights on the
beach and the gendarmes would descend upon us like the rabid
vermin they were.

As the boat again came close to shore, I waded out further,
grabbing at the rope and chivvying the men forward until at last
I could let go and wave them off, watching as the dinghy disappeared once more along its moonlit trail. In a few days, with any
luck, its precious cargo would land in Gibraltar to be evacuated
back to England, although many would return, eager to carry on
the fight. As for me, I wasn't going anywhere. They could try as
much as they liked to order me to leave. I had a job to do, and no
bounty on my head or furious message from London was going
to stop me.

My trousers were clinging to my legs, sopping wet, as I
made my way to the small group clustered by Albert.

'Follow me,' I murmured as I began to lead them towards
the path that snaked through the dunes and on back to the villa
we used as a safe house.

I'd barely taken two or three strides before I stopped dead,
the men almost slamming into my back.

Headlights. Two pairs. Three. Then more lights blaring down the beach, sweeping backward and forward. I could see figures silhouetted against the lights, dressed in police uniform. All except one. He took a step forward, pointing towards us, and that's when the light hit his face.

'My God,' I gasped. 'That's Harry King.'

# EIGHT

I dropped low, running as fast as I could along the beach in the opposite direction to the lights, trying to stay deep in the shadows, hoping and praying the men did too. I could hear their feet pounding into the sand, mercifully muffled by the sound of the waves, and their muttered oaths as they stumbled or twisted an ankle on the unfamiliar terrain. Then other sounds. The ratatat of a machine gun. *Merde.* They were shooting. That traitor King. He'd sold us out.

More shots, the bullets slamming into the sand as we ran. These weren't just French police; that buzzsaw whine sounded like an MG 42. Waffen-SS.

I turned, took aim, but there was no point at this distance. We'd outrun the bastards. Great. Except I'd love to put one between King's eyes.

Another time.

We were between the rocks now at the far end of the beach, scrambling over and through them, my feet fighting for purchase, eyes scanning for lights, ears straining for the sound of engines or gunfire. A couple more metres and we were cresting the last ridge, pushing onwards, over the scrub and on through the darkened streets.

Canet-Plage sat silent, its villas slumbering hulks that peppered the shoreline, the streets that wound through them to the town beyond little more than tracks. It was up one of these that we stumbled, to a doorway that stood open, as I knew it would.

Marie was already there, on the doorstep, urging the men in, closing it behind us before she drew the bolts and led us across the courtyard to the stables. The new arrivals could stay in the loft above until it was safe to move them. Her villa, like all the others, was cloaked in darkness in case the gendarmes decided to come calling along with their German friends. With any luck, they'd have given up by now, but you never knew.

She guided us by torch up the stairs, then handed it to me so I could shine it for the men to climb up one by one while she went to fetch food for them.

I pulled off my scarf and ruffled my hair, my mind churning. How much had King told them? Enough to lead them to us tonight. The operation had been planned for months. Of course King knew about it – he knew far too much. We'd have to alter all the schedules and departure points. I could kill him for this. I *would* kill him for this.

'The Englishman's daughter,' said a voice from behind me.

I whipped round.

'I knew it. You're Elisabeth. The girl who used to play with my sister. You haven't changed a bit.'

He wasn't smiling now. Instead, his eyes were dark with something else, something unreadable. I stared at him, searching his face, his features, trying to remember.

He tugged off his hat and scarf too, and then I knew. It was him. Of course it was him. It was the accent that had confused me, along with his disguise. Now that I could see him clearly, I couldn't believe I hadn't recognised him straight away.

'Guy,' I gasped. 'What in heaven's name are you doing here?'

# NINE

No one came knocking that night. I slept fitfully in one of Marie's spare bedrooms rather than risk the journey back to Chateau Bleu. Janek and Albert bunked down in another room, but they'd already left by the time I emerged, blinking, into the bright sunlight that washed the courtyard, bouncing off the stone walls.

'Good morning.'

Guy was standing behind me, holding two cups of coffee, looking much more like himself now that he'd shaved. With the beard gone, I could see the clean lines of his jaw and the mouth that appeared to be permanently quirked in a half-smile, just like his sister's. Hélène had always been the beautiful one. I was what you might call gamine, not blessed with her curves or her womanly allure. No wonder Guy had always treated me like a kid, even as I'd blossomed into a teenager. Not that there had been much blossoming. You might say I remained permanently in bud.

He held out one of the cups. 'Here. Your friend made us all breakfast.'

Beyond him, I caught a glimpse of Marie bustling backward

and forward with a tray, laying out croissants and fruit alongside a large coffee pot. The courtyard was surrounded by high walls, overlooked only by the house. I was pretty certain King knew nothing about this place, but still I felt a twinge of anxiety. We had to get these men out of here and safely on their way.

I took the coffee from him, noticing the ring on his little finger. 'Thank you.'

He smiled, his eyes crinkling at the corners, and all at once I was back there, on another beach, this time with Hélène and the rest of his family, Guy teasing us as only an older brother could, diving under the water to grab our ankles, pretending to be a shark, making the pair of us squeal in delight. He was always like that, mischief in his eyes as he joked around. Then, as now, there had been a sensitivity behind those eyes, a sweet-ness that belied the devil-may-care attitude.

Once or twice, we'd even come to the beaches here, at Canet-Plage, driving along the coast road with the roof down on Papa's convertible, me singing away alongside Hélène in the back while Mama's scarf whipped around in the wind like a tail.

A sudden flash in my mind's eye of Guy at fifteen, almost a man, as we twelve-year-olds cavorted in the water, pleading with him to play while he pretended to ignore us from behind his sunglasses, his olive skin turning a deeper shade as he tanned. Hélène was as fair as he was dark, her hair white blonde, her eyes azure like the sky. Her curls had darkened into a honey shade as she grew older, with natural streaks from the summer sun that boys found irresistible. She'd been sixteen when they emigrated, but try as I might, I couldn't imagine her all grown up.

Naturally, we'd written to one another, the gaps between letters growing longer as we both got on with our lives, me here and then in England, although I never forgot Hélène. We might have left our childhood behind, but she still held a place in my heart. Then, just before war broke out, I received another letter, an excited missive telling me all about her sweetheart, the one she was going to marry. More letters followed, one asking me to be her bridesmaid, although they grew fewer again as it became harder to send mail across the Atlantic, with German U-boats and battleships attacking convoys and sinking our ships.

'How is Hélène?' I asked. 'I haven't heard from her in a long time.'

A shadow fell across his face. 'Hélène is dead,' he said quietly. 'She was on a ferry that was torpedoed. She'd joined up as a nursing sister and was on her way to Newfoundland when a U-boat got them in the Cabot Strait six months ago.'

'Oh God no,' I gasped. 'Not Hélène.'

It felt as if someone had plunged a dagger into my heart. I'd seen death many times, come close to it as well, but nothing could prepare me for the sheer agony of hearing that someone who mattered so much to me was gone.

Guy looked at me, his eyes seared with a pain that looked almost as fresh as mine. He'd adored his sister, however much he might have attempted to pretend otherwise. I could see how deeply he felt her loss; hear it too in his voice, muffled now with what sounded suspiciously like tears.

'I'm afraid so.' He held up his hand. 'She gave me this ring before I left for Scotland.'

'It's beautiful.'

I stared at it, blinking back my tears, all too aware of the glances our way. Past friendships played no part in this war – we left everything and everyone behind when we were posted. If the Nazis got a sniff of any kind of personal relationship when they had you in their hands, they would use it to extract information. I'd heard of captured agents being tortured in front of one another to try to get the observer to crack too. It was far worse if they were friends or, heaven forbid, related in some way.

I glanced over my shoulder, catching sight of Guy's

companions. It was my job to get these freshly landed agents safely to their new posts. Distractions were dangerous, especially one like Guy.

'Come along,' I said. 'Let's join the others.'

If he was taken aback by the briskness of my tone, he didn't show it. But it was that or break down.

As we approached the table, the others made room, smiling their greetings. One with tufts of corn-coloured hair spoke up, his ruddy cheeks and broad, workworn hands branding him a country boy. 'Will Hammond. Good to meet you. This reprobate is Tom Sefton.'

'Pay no attention to him,' retorted Sefton. 'He's a bloody northerner, for God's sake.'

Their cheery banter took me straight back to the training camps in England, but the other fellow was more reserved. He executed a little bow. 'Lionel Sabourin at your service.'

'Are you Canadian?' I asked.

'French-Canadian. I trained with Guy here.'

He pronounced Guy's name the French way, just as I always had. I noticed he was also wearing a ring on his little finger, engraved with a tiny arrowhead, the exact same as Guy's.

I pointed to it. 'What is that?'

'That is the insignia of the First Special Service. Or, as some call us, The Devil's Brigade.'

I looked from him to Guy. 'You're mad to wear those here. If the Nazis get hold of you, they could cost you your life.'

Guy flashed me that devil-may-care grin. 'The Germans have no idea what that arrowhead means. The Devil's Brigade have yet to be deployed in Europe. Besides, they won't get hold of us, and if by some miracle they do, they'll soon learn how we earned that nickname. Although we're not here as part of the brigade.'

'Then what are you doing here? I was told we were expecting agents, not Special Forces.'

'And that's what we are. Agents working for MI9. Here to carry out a top-secret mission.'

'So secret you can't tell me what it is?'

He looked me straight in the eye. 'Actually, you're a vital part of it.'

# TEN

I could feel four pairs of eyes on me now, watching and waiting. Guy cupped his hand under my elbow and drew me aside, ambling across the courtyard and back towards the stable block as if we were strolling through a park. I had no choice but to fall in with him. That was another thing I remembered about Guy – his ability to charm the birds from the trees. And it was effortless. That smile, his air of complete and quiet confidence – there was just something about him that had all the older ladies enthralled while even the men nodded and shrugged. It was Guy after all. Who could resist?

Me for starters.

I followed him up the stairs, through the concealed hatch and into the attic space. Once we were settled in the eaves, perched on one of the makeshift beds Marie had set up, Guy spoke again. 'They sent me here to make contact with you and Grant. I had no idea you'd be the welcoming committee.'

His face was silhouetted against the shaft of sunlight that streamed in through the tiny square window set high in the apex of the beamed ceiling. The place still had a faint redolence of the horses that had once lived below – an earthy, comforting scent.

'Who's they?'

'My superiors at MI9. They want us to help you rebuild the escape line. Set up new safe houses and find new helpers so we get people moving again. Not just the airmen, although they're our first priority. There's also a little boy among them somewhere, along with the woman who's looking after him. But that's strictly between you and me. No one else must know he even exists.'

I looked at him quizzically. 'A little boy? How come?'

'He's called Robert, and he's the last remaining survivor from an orphanage the Gestapo – led by a man named Otto Drexler – raided. Apparently, he makes it his personal mission to hunt down and destroy anyone he considers an enemy of the Reich.'

'Including children?'

'Including children and people like you and me. They arrested everyone there and transported them to Drancy. All except this child, who'd been taken to the dentist that day by one of the women who ran the orphanage. It seems his toothache saved his life and hers, but if Drexler finds out he's alive, he'll do everything he can to take him too.'

I stared at him. Drancy was a transit camp from where the Nazis transported people to their concentration camps in Germany. Tales of what happened in those camps had filtered out, so awful they could scarcely be believed. Except I had no doubt they were true. 'They transported children? How many?'

'Thirty-three, according to our source. Along with the staff looking after them. The Germans would hate for the rest of the world to hear about it. They like to keep their atrocities well hidden, but they reckoned without anyone surviving to tell the tale.'

No wonder this child was so special. 'How old is this little boy?'

'Six, from what I understand.'

Six years old and the only survivor of such a heinous act. 'We have to get him out of France safely.'

Guy nodded. 'We do. Not just because it's the right thing to do, but the boost to everyone's morale will be incalculable. The war isn't going well for us right now. Bringing him back to England would mean such a lot to so many people. It would also ensure the world gets to hear what the Nazis are capable of. Arresting orphans and sending them off to camps like that is a new low.'

My heart twisted. 'He's a child, not a propaganda coup.'

'I know.'

Our eyes met, and I saw in his the same thing that burned in mine. It wasn't so much revenge we wanted as justice for all those who'd suffered, especially the weak and defenceless, like these children. Like little Robert, wherever he was.

# ELEVEN

It was Guy who looked away first, staring into space as if he was calculating something. Perhaps my reaction. When he looked back at me, his eyes were bleak. 'Do you realise that nearly a hundred escape-line helpers have been arrested so far along with their parcels?'

I shook my head. 'I hadn't realised it was so many.'

'Almost three hundred people taken by the Nazis. Someone must have betrayed them. There's no way they found them all by chance in that short space of time. We need to find out who it was.'

'I think I can help you with that.'

His eyes narrowed. 'Go on.'

'There was a man with those police bastards on the beach last night. Name of Harry King. Long story but we confronted him a couple of weeks back. We were about to shoot him, but he managed to escape. He must have run straight into the arms of the Gestapo.'

'You were going to shoot him? Why?'

'He stole the money we gave him. Spent it on himself and his fancy women rather than the escape line. We knew we couldn't trust him anymore, but I don't think any of us suspected he might go this far. I wish I'd got him that day.'

Guy's expression was grim. 'You think it was King who told the Gestapo where the safe houses were?'

'Absolutely. He probably told them where they could find Ian Grant too. You know he was arrested?'

'I do.'

'Captain Grant welcomed King with open arms,' I spat. 'He gave him the chance to "do his bit", as he put it, and made sure King was well paid for his efforts. I suppose the Gestapo offered to pay him even more.'

'I have no doubt that was the case. I'm also sure, from what you've said, that it was King who gave them our routes, including the one you used last night. We're going to have to set up new ones along with safe houses and the people to run them.'

I felt another lick of anger, this time for a different reason. 'Why you? Captain Grant set up the escape line, and I helped him. We know the helpers personally, and he knows where all the safe houses are located. Or at least where they were. I assume none of you are acquainted with either.'

Guy's gaze was steady. 'You're absolutely correct. We don't have your knowledge or experience. What we do have is the money to pay off the right people and set others up so they can start passing people down the line. MI9 is authorised to meet all the line's expenses. You need us, Elisabeth, as much as we need you.'

He was right. So far, we'd kept the line going through the generosity of the people who helped run it, but it cost a fortune to feed and house the fugitives until we could bring them to safety, as well as bribing the right people and paying off the wrong ones. Too bad we hadn't paid off King before now.

With a bullet to his head.

Guy was looking at me expectantly. He knew I didn't have a

choice, the arrogant bastard. How dare he turn up and expect to take over? I swallowed hard. 'You said you want me to join your operation.'

'I do. At least part of it. I have a particular mission in mind.'

'I see. And you would be in charge?'

A glint of acknowledgement. He knew what I was thinking. 'For now.'

'What do you mean "for now"?'

'You'll understand when I explain the mission.'

He hadn't changed – he was still as infuriating as when he was a teenager, lording it over us with that superior smile. 'Alright then, what exactly is this mission?'

'We're going to liberate Captain Grant from Fort St Hippolyte where he's being held. For that, we need your help. We want you to get in there and make contact with him. That's the first stage in getting him out.'

It took a moment for his words to sink in. 'Have you lost your mind?'

His smile had returned. 'Not at all.'

'Captain Grant is being held in solitary confinement, as far as we know. That fort is impregnable. You can't even get close enough to recce it.'

Guy nodded. 'That's where you come in.'

'What do you mean?'

'I mean that we want you to pretend to be Captain Grant's cousin so you can take him in a food parcel and recce the place without anyone getting suspicious.'

'You're completely mad,' I said. 'As if the guards will fall for that.'

'Why not? Prisoners are permitted family visits under the Geneva Convention, and you're as English as he is. There's no reason to suspect that you're not, in fact, his cousin.'

'Half English. And I look nothing like him.'

'So? Isn't that what you're famous for – being so wily you

keep outfoxing the Germans? In fact, isn't that what the Gestapo call you – *Kleiner Fuchs*? The Little Fox?'

I stared at him, playing dumb. 'I have no idea what you're talking about.'

'Yes you do. You're so good at evading them, the Nazis are offering five million francs to anyone who can help them arrest you. How many times have you gone in and out of the occupied zone without getting caught?'

So he knew. Of course he did. MI9 and SOE shared intelligence when it suited them. It evidently suited them in my case. 'Too many to count.'

'Exactly. And yet here you are, still alive and doing what you do best. I have to hand it to you – I never thought the little girl I remember would grow up to be someone like you.'

His face was turned towards me now, the sun streaming through the window onto it, bleaching everything out save his eyes and the contours of his face. They might have had different colouring, but their faces were the same shape more or less, his and Hélène's, high cheekbones punctuating an otherwise perfect oval, each with a slight indent in their chins, and as I gazed at him, it seemed for a moment that I was looking at her once more, her face transposed over his, her eyes meeting mine. Then I blinked and shook my head, trying to banish the stabbing ache in my chest at the same time. So many dead. Yet Hélène was more to me than most. She had been my friend, my confidante, my twin soul in many ways.

'Why not?' I asked. 'You told me Hélène had joined the nursing sisters. She was off to war too. We always did things together, she and I. You think I would sit at home and knit socks for the troops rather than do this?'

Maybe it was a trick of the light, but his eyes appeared to mist over. 'I would never think that,' he murmured. 'I just never thought you would have grown to be the Gestapo's most wanted agent. Or that you would be so beautiful.'

I was still staring at him, dumbstruck, when I heard a shout from the courtyard. Then another followed by the crack of a pistol and the thunder of boots on flagstones. A storm that was growing louder.

Then came the slam of the stable block door as it was kicked open. Someone barking orders so close now we could hear him urging his men to search for anyone they might have missed.

I held my finger to my lips, my eyes fixed on the concealed trapdoor, blood rushing in my ears. Had we closed and covered it properly? Would they spot it? It was too late now to do anything. Another slam as they marched out of the stable block, leaving a silence pregnant with so many questions. All I knew was that my luck had held. For now.

# TWELVE

Dr George shot the bolts on the apartment door and ushered us through the patients crowding his corridor, patiently waiting their turn to be seen by him, as his wife Fanny hurried forward to greet us. Once we were safely in his spare bedroom with the door shut, I introduced Guy. He shook his hand warmly, his moustache practically bristling with pleasure. It was part of what made him both an excellent doctor and a vital member of our organisation – the bedside manner that put everyone at ease.

'Welcome,' he said, beaming. 'It's an honour to have you in our home.'

Guy withdrew a thick envelope from his pocket and handed it to him. 'Thank you. It's a pleasure to be here, Doctor. I've heard a great deal about your good work. With the compliments of our chief in Lisbon. It's to help cover your expenses.'

'You're very kind,' murmured George, handing the envelope to Fanny. The two of them spent all they had looking after our parcels. I was glad to see that MI9 recognised the fact. I was even happier that we'd made it here unscathed. George might have escaped scrutiny until now, but every delivery increased the risk, as it had done for poor Marie.

I looked at George and Fanny, as resolute as ever. 'You heard what happened in Canet-Plage?'

George nodded. 'We did. I'm sorry about your men and Marie. Unfortunately, so far there's been no word of where they've taken them. The Vichy police have a nasty habit of handing such prisoners over to the Germans. We can only hope they desist or at least delay in this case.'

'What do you think the chances are of rescuing them?' asked Guy.

'Very slim.'

There was a glint in Guy's eye now, one I knew well. 'But not impossible?'

'Nothing is impossible, as you know.'

'I do.'

It had all happened so fast. When we finally emerged from the stable block, we found the place deserted, coffee cups and croissants still sitting, untouched, on the courtyard table. The shock had almost wiped out what he'd said. Almost. I kept running his words through my mind, wondering what he meant. I was still wondering as I met his eyes now. Guy might appear relaxed and at ease on the surface, but still waters ran very deep in his case. I never knew what he was really thinking. All I knew was that we had to find his men and Marie before they were turned over to the Nazis as well.

I could feel George's eyes on me and hastily remembered why we were here. 'And now,' I said to Guy, 'we must take you to be photographed for your new papers.'

George glanced at Fanny. 'My wife will escort you so that the concierge doesn't pay too much attention. Did they see you come in?'

I shook my head. 'There was no one around.'

Today, my newly chestnut hair was tucked under a hat that

also obscured my face, while the shapeless dress I wore made me look bigger than I was. Even so, I avoided making eye contact with anyone in the street. Those damn posters were still everywhere. In fact, they seemed to be proliferating.

'Good, good. Every day we try to be more careful. There are whispers, you know. People talk. I worry that the concierges see too much, although there are people in and out of here all the time. Still, you never know.'

His beetle brows drew together as he put his fist to his chest, wincing.

Fanny moved to his side, gently taking him by the arm. 'Is it the pain again? Here, George, sit down.'

He brushed her off, but not unkindly. 'I'm fine. Really. We have work to do. We must get this gentleman his papers so he can help us put the line back together.'

'If it helps at all,' I said, 'we know who betrayed the line. It seems Harry King is now working for the Gestapo.'

At this, George clutched his chest once more, his face reddening with the effort of fighting off the pain. 'King? That bastard. You should have shot him that day.' He straightened, the effort of doing so visible. 'It was in this very room they interrogated him, Elisabeth here along with Captain Grant and the others. He somehow managed to escape, but then he would, the slippery son of a whore.'

For a gentle doctor, George could certainly break out the oaths when he needed to.

'There, there, George,' soothed his wife. 'What's done is done.'

'I wish we'd done for him.'

'Don't you worry,' I said. 'We'll catch up with King sooner or later. In the meantime, we need to get Guy his papers.'

'Before we do that,' said Fanny, 'I'll show you where you're going to stay.'

Guy smiled down at her. 'That's very kind of you.'

'Once you're organised,' I said, 'we can start with breaking Grant out of prison. If anyone can rebuild the line, it's him.'

'And you.'

Guy was looking at me as he'd once looked at Hélène and I, urging us to jump off a high rock into the water, assuring us we would be fine. I remembered it as if it was yesterday, closing my eyes as I leaped, my arms and legs flailing, hitting the water harder than I expected, the air punched out of my lungs as I sank down and down until, finally, I kicked hard and broke the surface, spluttering and laughing, although deep down I was shaking like a leaf. Beside me, Hélène too was shrieking in triumph while Guy grinned at us both. 'See? I said you could do it.'

He had the same expression on his face now.

'You think so?'

He smiled. 'I know so.'

If I hadn't known better, I would have sworn that he was remembering along with me. But I did know better. This was the real world. A world at war. And if I was to do my job, there was no room for sentiment or superstition, not even when it came to Guy.

Especially not when it came to Guy.

# THIRTEEN

## 11 NOVEMBER 1942, CHATEAU BLEU, SOUTHERN FRANCE

'The Germans have crossed the demarcation line.'

Everyone in the salon froze, Walther's fingers dropping from the piano keys, Eliane's knitting sliding from her hands to the floor. She grabbed it, gaping up at her husband. 'How do you know?'

François moved to the couch where she was sitting and took her hand. 'Because, my dear, Albert has just delivered the bad news.'

I glanced at the doorway where Albert was hovering, the rain dripping from his hat onto the hall floor. It was pelting down outside, one of those fierce winter storms that raged across the south, although it was no match for the maelstrom inside my head. 'How dare they?' I snapped, jumping to my feet. 'They might as well have torn up the Armistice agreement and stamped on it too.'

'That's exactly what they've done,' drawled Matthieu.

I looked at him, seeing the sharp intelligence that was so often drowned in a sea of alcohol.

'It's retaliation for our troops landing in North Africa.

Hitler was never going to take that one lying down. Any fool could see that.'

'What, even you?' jeered his wife.

Her words sliced like a poisoned sword across the room, scattering droplets of acid over all of us, stinging her daughter in particular as they landed, although Alice tried her best to mask it. She sank deeper into her armchair so that she was scarcely visible, burying her nose in her book. Charlotte stared at her for a moment then dropped her eyes, shame flitting across her face. Or so I liked to think. Her hair was a darker gold than her daughter's, her features perfect. At least, they would be if they weren't constantly twisted in hatred. I could only guess who or what had caused her to be so consumed with it, my gaze sliding to Matthieu as he got up and moved to the drinks trolley, pouring himself a large cognac.

'We should turn on the radio,' said Eliane.

'Is that wise?' asked François. 'The Germans are here now. They might pick up the signal.'

Eliane tossed her hair and marched over to the radio set. 'What tosh. They can't move that fast. Besides, we'd see them coming.'

She had a point. We'd see any vehicle approaching up the drive long before it got here.

'Perhaps we need to institute some kind of watch system,' I said above the crackling of the radio. 'So that someone is always keeping an eye on the front of the house.'

The cut-glass accent of the announcer drowned out my words. 'This is the BBC in London. Here is the news...'

Even the wind seemed to drop outside as we listened in absolute silence to the report of the victory at El Alamein and Churchill's speech. 'Now this is not the end. It is not even the beginning of the end. But it is, perhaps, the end of the beginning.'

Not the end. Not even the beginning of the end. My heart

sank like a lead weight. He was right, of course. But when would it ever end? I could hear Godfrey Talbot now with one of his recorded dispatches from the front. Finally, the announcement we'd been waiting for: as a result of the victories in North Africa, Hitler had violated the 1940 Armistice, his 7th Army advancing on Vichy and Toulon while the Italian 4th Army occupied the Riviera. German tanks were now stationed along the Mediterranean coast.

'Turn it off.'

We all looked at Paul, who was cowering in his chair, his hands over his ears. Walther rose from his piano stool and went to place an arm around his friend's shoulders, which were shaking.

'Turn it off,' sobbed Paul. 'Please. Turn it off.'

Eliane twisted the radio knob until, once more, there was silence apart from Paul's heart-wrenching sobs.

'Oh for God's sake,' snarled Charlotte. 'Pull yourself together.'

My fingers itched to slap her. 'Paul knows better than most of us what Hitler is capable of. You might care to remember that before you speak.'

Her eyes glittered as she turned her gaze on me, feverish in its hatred. 'Who the hell are you to tell me what to do?' she hissed.

'She's someone who's actually doing something to fight back,' jibed Matthieu. 'Unlike you, my darling. But then, isn't that what you do best? Getting others to do your dirty work?'

With a howl of outrage, Charlotte leaped up. 'How dare you?'

Matthieu smiled, a slow, nasty smile laced with pure malice. 'Oh easily, my love. As easily as you destroy lives. In fact, you and Hitler should get together.'

The door slamming behind her was evidently Charlotte's last word on the subject.

Matthieu gulped back his cognac and refilled his glass, raising it in a toast to the rest of us. 'She'll go with anyone, you know,' he hiccupped. 'Well, anyone but me.'

I heard a tiny sigh from Alice, still buried in her armchair. There was so much wrapped up in that sigh. Fear, loneliness. Despair. She was just a child, after all, and the only people she had in the world were at war within a war.

'What are you reading?' I asked, perching on the edge of her armchair.

'*The Secret Garden*,' muttered Alice.

'I love that book. I read it too when I was about your age.'

She looked up at me. 'Did you really?'

'I did, and it made me want a secret garden of my own.'

'Me too.'

'Why don't you make your own garden here?' said Eliane. 'There's so much land for you to choose from. I'll help you explore. We can find you a plot.'

Alice's face lit up. 'My own garden?'

I could feel Matthieu's attention turning from the bottle to us. 'I'll help too, if you like,' I said.

The expression on Matthieu's face stopped the breath in my throat. It was a mixture of pity and pain, almost as if he couldn't bear to look at Alice. But she was just a child. His child. Although he seemed to regard her more as an enemy than as a beloved daughter. Not for the first time, I wondered what was really going on.

# FOURTEEN

## 13 NOVEMBER 1942

Two days after the Germans had marched into Vichy France and Guy was still at George's apartment, hovering as the radio operator messaged London and Lisbon, trying to get some intel about his men. I glanced up at the kitchen clock. Nearly three. The hours were crawling past, as they do when you're waiting. I glanced down at the gun in my hand then up as the back door swung open.

'There's a man in the woods. You must come. Quickly.'

I hastily thrust my pistol back in my belt, crumpling up the cloth I'd been using to clean it. I doubt Alice even noticed. She was panting, her pretty face pink with effort.

'The woods? Where?'

Beyond the kitchen door, I could hear nothing save the birds in the trees. Eliane was in her study somewhere in the depths of the house. The rest of the inhabitants were taking their siesta, while I was filling the hours checking my weapons. At least they were locked and loaded, ready to be used if necessary.

'I was trying to find the right place for my garden. I ended up by the hut. That's where I saw him, sitting outside. Don't worry – he didn't see me. I made sure of that.'

I gave her what I hoped was a reassuring smile. 'You did well. Now, why don't you take me there?'

I'd never heard of a hut in the woods, never mind seen one. But then, each day I spent at the Chateau Bleu turned up a different surprise. The place seemed endless, myriad rooms opening off the corridors and staircases that ran apparently at random up, down and through the various wings while the grounds went on for what felt like forever. It was what made it so safe in many ways and yet vulnerable to someone hiding out there, as this man apparently was. He could be anyone. A local itinerant, a refugee or escaper – even a German spy. It was that last which prompted me to pat my pocket down, making sure my knife was in there as well. If it came to it, close and silent killing might be the only option.

I glanced at Alice as we walked together back towards the woods. 'Tell me where this hut is, and I can take it from here.'

She shook her head. 'You'll never find it on your own. It was Eliane who showed me where it was. She said I could use it as a den if I wanted, although Mother wasn't keen. She thinks it's a bit too far from the house. That's why I like it.'

I was only half listening, trying to work out a way to get Alice to stay safely behind while I located this hut. Maybe I should go and find Eliane after all. And risk him disappearing? No. If this man was some kind of agent or spy, I needed to track him down before he could make his way out of here to report back to his superiors.

Alice tugged at my hand. 'I said it's this way.'

I glanced at her hand in mine, so trusting. 'Alice, I'm perfectly serious. You must go back to the house now. Just tell me the way, and I'm sure I can find it.'

In answer, she tossed her hair and pushed ahead of me, striding so fast I had no choice but to follow. I had to hand it to her, she was moving like a trained operative, her footsteps all but silent, not saying a word.

A sudden flash of déjà vu again – Hélène and I playing in the woods near her house. This was exactly how she'd moved as we pretended to be on the trail of the cowboys, stalking Guy and his friends, who were kicking a ball on the lawn beyond, unaware that we were about to stage a raid.

An unearthly shriek brought me back to the present – a peacock, darting through the trees ahead of us, calling out to its mate.

'Come on,' whispered Alice, gesturing ahead to indicate we were nearly there.

Instinctively, I dropped my hand to my pistol, reassured by its presence.

She was moving ahead more carefully now, trying not to step on a twig or dislodge another creature. I could make out the bulk of a building through the trees, the size and shape of a bothy or a shepherd's hut, branches poking from its mossy roof, the stone walls crumbling in places. The door looked solid enough though, and it was firmly shut. There was no sign of anyone sitting outside.

I drew level with Alice who was half-crouched behind one of the twisted trunks, peering out from behind it.

'He's gone,' she breathed.

I placed a cautionary hand on her arm, putting a finger to my lips. There was the slightest crack and rustle, then a man appeared from around the building carrying what looked like a water canteen. He stopped just as we had, listening hard, looking, or so it felt, straight at us, although the trees were obscuring his face.

'Who's there?' he asked.

I stepped out from behind the tree, gun raised. Then lowered it again, my mouth dropping open. 'Captain Grant.'

# FIFTEEN

He set his cup down with a sigh of satisfaction. 'Proper tea.'

Eliane beamed as she put bread and jam on a plate and placed it before him. 'You must be starving. Eat up. This should keep you going until dinner.'

I studied him as he ate. He looked gaunt but healthy, his eyes as bright as ever. Grant was indefatigable, but even he must have suffered from the privations of prison. 'How on earth did you get here?' I asked.

He took another bite before answering. The poor man must have literally been starving. 'Bloody compass of course.'

At that, I burst out laughing. Eliane looked at me, wondering what the joke was. I wiped the tears from my eyes.

'It's what he always says,' I choked out. 'Use your bloody compass. That's what he tells the escapers and evaders. They all have one, you see. It's in the escape kit they're issued, although some are better at using it than others.'

It wasn't that funny – I knew that. My tears were a mixture of mirth and relief. I still couldn't believe he was sitting here with his cup of tea as if nothing had happened. But that was Grant for you.

'It wasn't the bloody compass that got you out of the fort,' I said.

He happily accepted a refill and took a slurp of his tea before answering. 'No. It was an Italian bus.'

'What?'

'As soon as they took the Riviera, the Italians started shipping prisoners out and over the border. They were transporting a group of us on a bus when they stopped to refuel. I took the opportunity to hop out the back door and into the woods. As it turned out, we were still in France. I stopped off at a couple of farmhouses on the way here where they gave me food and shelter. When I found the hut, I holed up there for a day or so to make sure the Germans hadn't requisitioned the place.'

'I didn't realise you even knew Chateau Bleu existed.'

Grant tapped his nose and winked. 'I know more than you could ever imagine.'

Except one thing: the existence of a little boy named Robert. The child had been preying on my mind. Six years old and still out there somewhere. I glanced at Grant. No. I'd promised Guy I'd keep quiet about him, so that was what I would do.

'Would you like anything else to eat?' I asked Grant.

He patted his stomach. 'Thank you, but I'm not used to such a feast. Those prisons aren't exactly famous for their food.'

'I can only imagine. Well, if you're sure you don't need anything else, perhaps we could talk in private.'

'Why don't I show you to your room?' said Eliane, ever tactful. 'Elisabeth, maybe you could accompany us? You'll find it more private there.'

I rose from my chair, as did Grant. 'Of course.'

We'd just stepped into the hallway when Alice came hurtling round the corner, almost running slap bang into us, her face streaked with tears. She tried to swipe them away the moment she saw us, dropping her head just as her mother appeared. 'You come back here this minute,' she snapped. 'I'm not done with you yet.'

Her eyes swept over me, coming to rest on Eliane. 'Good afternoon,' she cooed. 'Please do excuse my daughter.'

Eliane smiled sweetly. 'She's a wonderful child. Why would I ever need to excuse her for anything?'

Charlotte tutted and turned on her heel, clicking her fingers at Alice as if she was meant to follow. Alice stayed rooted to the spot, looking up at us beseechingly.

'How about a nice cup of milk and some bread and jam?' said Eliane. 'Cook will get that for you as a reward for finding Captain Grant here.'

Alice's face lit up. 'A reward?'

'Yes. Captain Grant is a very important person. Without you, we would never have known he was there.'

Alice's eyes flicked to me, and I nodded. 'It's absolutely true. We're all very grateful to you, Alice. You're a heroine.'

'Just like in my books?' she whispered.

My heart splintered into a thousand pieces. 'Just like in your books.'

# SIXTEEN

Eliane threw open the curtains so that the light bounced off the faded wallpaper with its gilded curlicues. 'I hope you'll be comfortable here.'

Grant looked around in appreciation. 'I can assure you this is paradise. Thank you so much.'

He placed the small bag he had with him on the end of the bed and wandered over to the window, throwing it open and taking several deep breaths of the cool, damp air. 'That's what I missed most in that bloody cell,' he said. 'Fresh air and light.'

'It must have been ghastly,' I murmured.

'Not so bad compared to some. Now what was it you wanted to discuss?'

I plonked myself down in the chair beside a small writing desk. 'While you were away, four MI9 agents arrived at Canet-Plage. Three were arrested almost immediately, along with Marie at the safe house, but their leader, Captain Guy Larose, is safe and eager to find his men.'

I could feel myself flushing as I said this.

Grant looked at me keenly. 'He's French?'

'He is originally, yes. As a matter of fact, he grew up here in

Marseille with me. That is, his sister was my best friend. He's her big brother. Or was.'

'Was?'

'Yes. Hélène, his sister, was killed six months ago when a U-boat torpedoed the ferry she was on. She'd joined up to serve as a nursing sister. I only found out when Guy landed here.'

I gulped back a sob. It was still so raw.

'I'm sorry,' said Grant. 'That must have been an awful shock.'

I nodded. 'It was. It was also a bit of a shock to see Guy and to hear what he had to say. He and his men were sent to restore the line, you see. And rescue you as part of the mission.'

Grant smiled thinly. 'Well, at least I spared them that part.'

'I think we all know that you're completely burned now. Otherwise, it would, of course, be you in charge of things. The thing is, Guy can't restore the line without knowing where the safe houses are as well as the remaining helpers. Apparently, nearly a hundred have been arrested along with their parcels.'

Grant bowed his head for a moment, his face stricken. 'A hundred? Good God. The problem is, Elisabeth, if I give you this information, then it places you in immense danger.'

'I'm already in immense danger. The Nazis have put a five-million-franc price on my head. There are posters everywhere now with my picture on them.'

He stared out the window for a few seconds, a muscle going in his cheek. 'You can't do this on your own, Elisabeth. Not even with Guy and Albert. You remember how long it took us to build the line in the first place and how many people we had to recruit to help."

'I remember. We'll find a way.'

'Very well,' he said finally. 'I already mentioned the *comtesse* in Lyon. At least, she's there as of now. Her full name is the Comtesse de Moncy, although she is, in fact, English.

MI9 trained her when she had to go back to London for a while, so your friend should know about her too.'

'He's not my friend,' I muttered through gritted teeth.

Grant raised an eyebrow. 'Whatever you say. In any case, the *comtesse* can connect you with the next in the line and so forth. It would be foolhardy of me to give you all the names and addresses, and potentially lethal for you to have them.'

Ever protective. I got it even as it galled me. 'What happens if I can't find this *comtesse*?'

'Then you need to go to the café at Avignon station. The patron there can help you. Albert will be able to assist.'

'Is he part of the line, this patron?'

'He is, and that's all I'm saying. It's for your own good, Elisabeth. You know that.'

I did. I also had my own secrets to keep. Or rather, a secret in the shape of a little boy called Robert. I hadn't asked Guy why I couldn't tell anyone else about his existence, but I could guess. It was for the same reason Grant was being so careful with me. Knowledge could be a death sentence, not just for those it might compromise but for the person carrying it. Although not for people like Harry King. Not yet, at any rate. One day I would catch up with him. It might take weeks, months or even years. It might not even be until this war was finally over. But catch up with him I would. And when I did, I'd make him pay for every single person he'd betrayed, including me and Grant, though at least we were still alive.

For now.

# SEVENTEEN

## 14 NOVEMBER 1942

As I came downstairs next morning, I could hear someone playing the piano. Not Walther – the notes were too hesitant. This was a beginner picking their way around a keyboard. Curious, I poked my head around the salon door to see Alice perched on the piano stool, Walther beside her, showing her what to do.

'You place your hand like this, you see,' he said. 'Imagine you're holding a ball.'

Alice's brow was furrowed in deep concentration. She did exactly as Walther said, the notes sounding sharper now, flowing from under her fingers.

'Bravo,' said Walther. 'Much better.'

The door squeaked as I leaned against it, and they both looked up. Alice beamed. 'Look, Elisabeth, I can play a whole song now. Walther has been teaching me.'

'So I see.'

'She's a natural,' said Walther. 'And a very good pupil.'

A sudden thought struck me. 'Alice, do you have any of your schoolbooks with you?'

She shook her head. 'There wasn't time to bring them.'

More likely, her parents simply couldn't be bothered. They never rose before midday, leaving Alice to her own devices every morning. 'Tell you what,' I said. 'I'll see what we can rustle up. You like learning, don't you?'

She nodded enthusiastically. 'I love it. I was top of my class at school.'

'I bet you were.'

My eyes met Walther's, and it was evident we were thinking the same thing. 'I'll have a word with Eliane now. Find out what she already has here. I'm sure we can all teach you something. François is an artist, for example. Do you enjoy art?'

Another nod, shyer this time. 'I do, but I'm not very good at it.'

'Nonsense,' said Walther. 'You simply have to learn the correct technique, as you've just discovered. You played a whole song, didn't you?'

She glanced at him then at me. 'I did, didn't I?'

'You did. Now let's carry on. We need to practise some scales.'

I left them to it, the waft of coffee from the kitchen drawing me in. It smelled like the real stuff too, which meant a fresh delivery had arrived from town bearing black-market supplies. And not just groceries as I discovered when I walked through the kitchen door to find Guy sitting at the table with Eliane, steaming cups at hand. I felt a lurch and a sudden fluttering in my belly as if there were a thousand butterflies trapped inside it. Ridiculous. It was only Guy.

'Good morning. This is a surprise. Any news?'

The tiniest shake of his head. 'No, but I hear you have some.'

My face broke into a smile. 'Isn't it marvellous? Alice found Captain Grant in the grounds, up by an old hut he was using to shelter. Apparently, he managed to escape when they were transporting prisoners from the fort over the border into Italy and found his way here.'

Guy didn't look quite as delighted as I'd expected. 'That is, indeed, marvellous, but we must get him out of France as quickly as possible. Now that the Germans are here, he's high on their wanted list. Do we know how much he told them?'

'Almost nothing.'

I swivelled in my seat to see Grant striding through the door, offering his hand to Guy. 'Ian Grant. Captain Larose, I assume?'

Guy rose to shake it. 'I am indeed. It's an honour to meet you, sir.'

'Nonsense. The honour is all mine. I understand from what Elisabeth tells me that you're here on behalf of MI9 to rebuild the line and get people moving along it again. That's excellent news.'

'I am, and one of the first people we're going to get moving is you, sir. But first we need to iron out a few problems. No doubt Elisabeth also told you that my men were arrested almost as soon as we landed. We have to find them so we can get them out of whatever hellhole they're in. There's also the issue of Dr George's apartment. I've just come from there, and he's worried that he's under surveillance.'

My pulse quickened. 'Do you think that's true?'

Guy shrugged. 'Could be. The concierge certainly seems to have sharp eyes.'

Eliane looked concerned. 'Why don't you come and stay here? Bring whoever else is staying with Dr George right now. We don't want to compromise him or put any of you in danger.'

'I appreciate the offer,' said Guy. 'First, we have to get Captain Grant here over the mountains. I guess there are no boat evacuations planned?'

I shook my head. 'Not for several weeks. We have to wait for the ship from Gibraltar. I'll ask Albert to get in touch with his people in Perpignan. We should be able to get Captain Grant to the border from there. I can accompany him over the mountains.'

'No way,' said Guy.

I glared at him. 'What do you mean "no way"? I've gone across many times, sometimes as far as Figueres and once even Madrid. I know the route almost as well as some of the smugglers.'

'In that case, I'll come with you.'

My temper flared. This really was too much. 'There's no need for you to come. I'm perfectly capable of looking after myself as well as Captain Grant.'

'I'm sure you are, but you forget that MI9 are running the lines now. I want to learn the route too, just in case. Don't worry – I won't tread on your toes.'

He really could be insufferable.

'Fine,' I snapped. 'But if you get in the way, I'll...'

'You'll what?'

My fingers twitched, automatically reaching for my pistol.

He caught the movement and laughed. 'Go on then – shoot me. You always wanted to. Remember when we played cowboys and Indians?'

'If I remember, I had a bow and arrow.'

'Same difference. Although you might find a pistol works a little faster.'

'Oh for goodness' sake,' cried Eliane. 'Will you two stop it?'

Captain Grant wisely kept his own counsel, sipping on his coffee, apparently wrapped up in his thoughts.

I'd quite forgotten they were there, so annoyed was I with Guy. 'You're right. Forgive me, Eliane. Old childhood hostilities.'

'Well, maybe it's time to bury the hatchet. And not in his brain.'

At this, we both burst out laughing. She had a talent for

that, Eliane, defusing any situation. It was no doubt one she'd honed harbouring all these fugitives at her chateau. I loved her for it, as I did her kindness and generosity. In those ways, she reminded me of Hélène. I could see that on Guy's face, too, as he looked at her, the memories flitting through his eyes like so many ghosts.

I reached out and touched his arm lightly, an olive branch. 'She'd have insisted on coming too,' I said. 'Hélène.'

He smiled again, although this time there were shadows at the edges. 'I know,' he said. 'That's why I'm coming. She'd never forgive me if anything happened to you.'

Present tense. A momentary slip. Or perhaps not. It really did feel as if Hélène was right here, with us.

I heard a tiny cough behind me, starting as I turned to see Alice. For a moment there, I thought it was her, Hélène. Then I shook my head, clearing away the cobwebs that obscured time and place. Hélène was dead. This child simply bore a fleeting resemblance. Although, as I looked at Guy, I knew he'd seen it too. More than that, there was something darker behind his eyes.

Not just a memory this time. A question.

# EIGHTEEN

## 18 NOVEMBER 1942, PERPIGNAN, SOUTHERN FRANCE

The tombs stood stark in the moonlight, their white walls gleaming at us like gapped rows of teeth, the spires and statues surmounting them adding a sinister touch. Beyond, I could see the outlines of the cypress trees that guarded the cemetery, looming like sentries over us as we huddled beneath a tomb shaped like a small chapel, the gate in its fence unlocked.

I peered at my watch – nearly eight o'clock. They would be here soon. I patted my haversack, feeling the reassuring outline of my kit box inside, neatly packed with survival essentials. Beside me, Grant crouched. I could sense his every muscle tensed for action. On the other side of me, Guy seemed completely relaxed, although I knew he was listening out for every little sound.

Sure enough, they appeared dead on the hour, two men treading so softly that at first none of us heard them. They rounded the tomb and were on us before I could draw my breath, never mind my pistol.

'Follow us,' whispered one, already heading for the opposite end of the cemetery, out of the rusting far gates and through the quiet streets, each of us keeping the requisite distance from the other, although Guy insisted on walking with me as he had all the way from the station, dropping his arm across my shoulders when a couple of policemen appeared ahead.

Our leader seemed to have melted into the darkness. Behind us, Grant had time to step into a doorway and hide. The policemen were striding towards us, their pace quickening. There was nowhere to go and nothing to do but brazen it out. We carried on sauntering towards them, Guy's arm tightening around me. They were a few strides away when he suddenly spun me round, pushing me up against the wall and smothering me with kisses, apparently overcome with desire.

I began to protest, giggling, playing the coy French girl, but as I watched them approach through half-closed eyes, smirking at our display, my breath caught in my throat. This didn't feel like pretending.

We carried on for a few more seconds, Guy's hands still exploring, his mouth pressed to mine, sending thrills through me. His fingers trailed fire as they ran up and down my sides, reaching around my waist, moving dangerously higher until I slapped my hand down on his. 'I think they've gone,' I gasped.

His lips didn't lift as he murmured, 'Are you sure?'

Part of me wanted to stay there forever, pressed against that wall, succumbing to sensations I'd never imagined, let alone felt. The saner, stronger part knew we had to get going – that this was all an act.

I took a step back, smoothing myself down, glimpsing Grant emerging from the doorway where he'd hidden and our guide ahead, lingering, waiting for us to catch up.

'Perfectly sure,' I said. 'Come on.'

I could swear Guy was smiling under that moustache of his as we set off once more, following our guide all the way to the outskirts of the town where we stopped by a small stream bordered by a reed thicket.

'This is the Well of the Grass Snakes,' he said, sticking two fingers in his mouth then whistling long and low.

At this signal, two more figures stood up from the reed beds where they'd been hiding. Smugglers, no doubt wanted on both sides of the border. The men who would be escorting us over the Pyrenees and taking Grant on into Spain for a price.

Our guide duly handed over the money while we clustered round, one of the smugglers patting his chest as he announced his name: 'Pedro.'

The guide spoke to him in Catalan. I caught most of it. 'These two are coming with you as far as the border. This one is going over.'

Pedro looked at his pockmarked companion, coming to some kind of silent agreement. Apparently, that would cost extra. We had no choice but to hand over more money. These men knew the routes over the Pyrenees better than the lines on their palms. We had to rely on them or risk perishing on our own, halfway across the treacherous mountains. But that reliance came with caution. It was one of the reasons we never sent someone on their own with these guides. Their motive wasn't patriotism but profit. And everyone had their price.

'Good luck,' said our guide as Pedro motioned to us to follow him.

I wondered then if he was trying to tell us something.

'He's taking a shortcut,' I muttered as Pedro suddenly veered from the normal route, heading straight for the Gorges de Lavall instead of taking a more circuitous path. His chum parted ways with us here, disappearing into the woods that fringed the foothills of the Pyrenees. The prickling on the back of my neck told me something was up.

'Let's keep a close eye on him,' murmured Guy as we trudged side by side.

Grant was a few paces ahead, directly behind Pedro. If necessary, we three could take him, although I hoped it wouldn't come to that. Pedro's route was taking us away from the mouth of the Tech river upstream. The moment I saw the swollen, raging waters, I knew there was no hope of crossing here.

'We need to go downstream,' I said to Pedro in Spanish. He pretended not to understand, so I pointed in that direction. He shook his head, indicating instead that we should go even further upstream.

'This is crazy,' I muttered. 'The river will be even more swollen further up.'

Guy looked at Grant, who nodded. 'Agreed. Tell him we won't go that way.'

Pedro was adamant. 'No, no. I know this route. I am your guide, and you do what I say.'

It was a stand-off, and by now, the day was drawing in.

'We need to get across before nightfall,' I said to the other two. 'Otherwise, we won't make it to the hut, and we'll have to sleep out here in the open.'

'I guess we'll have to trust him then,' said Guy. 'Although frankly, I don't.'

'Nor do I, but we have little choice.'

Pedro was already heading off upstream, following the river. We fell in behind, casting glances at each other as we went.

Two kilometres further along, Pedro stopped again. Sure enough, the waters were churning even more madly here, surging over treacherous rocks.

I glared at Pedro. 'If we try and cross that, we'll all be swept away.'

Even he looked nervous, his eyes darting everywhere, looking for some way out of this. Eventually, he muttered, 'I will go and fetch a rope.'

'A rope? From where?'

He waved vaguely down the mountain. 'I have supplies hidden. Wait here.'

Before I could stop him, he was off again, scrambling back down the slope, vanishing into the mist that was creeping up it. I stared at the other two.

'Do you think he'll be back?' asked Guy.

'He's a fool if he doesn't come back. The Resistance would shoot him for not delivering on his contract, and he knows that.'

'I have no doubt they would,' said Grant. 'Now, why don't we make ourselves comfortable while we wait?'

I gazed at the mist rising ever closer, the bare rocks and exposed mountainside all around. 'The best we can do is huddle between those,' I said, leading the way.

Guy crouched beside me, his warmth a welcome buffer against the cold and damp. Grant half-curled into a ball beside him, his head resting on his knees.

As the moon rose higher in the sky and the stars shone above the clouds, I felt my head fall sideways onto Guy's shoulder. I have no idea how long I drifted into a half slumber. All I know is that I woke with a start when he stood up.

I could see him silhouetted against the mist, an eerie figure standing stock-still, evidently listening. Then he turned to me, slumping back into position.

'I thought I heard Pedro coming back.'

There was a lump in my chest that was growing bigger and bigger. A hot, hard lump of fury. 'He's not coming back.'

# NINETEEN

'We need to move. Now.'

Grant blinked up at me, still half asleep. 'How are we going to find our way in the dark?'

'Same way we always do. We'll follow the river.'

Fury had given way to a cold, hard certainty. I was going to have to get this man across the border, come what may. Make that men. Guy was matching me stride for stride, but he had no idea where we were going. Grant was dragging his feet, depleted as he was from the past few weeks. It was all up to me now. I kept mentally running the route through my mind. I might have trodden it many times, but the smugglers were the ones with the intimate knowledge of these mountains. One slip could turn out to be a fatal error, as Pedro had proved.

Following the river to its mouth meant heading downhill once more, through the valley it bisected, towards the sea. I silently cursed Pedro. His miscalculation on the crossing point had cost us hours.

At last, the terrain began to slope more gently, and I could see the wider gleam of the estuary far below. The water here was flowing steadily into the Mediterranean. Across, to our left, the lights of Argelès twinkled. We were miles off course.

'I'll go first,' insisted Guy.

'It's better I go. I'm the smallest, so if I can make it, you can as well.'

I stepped into the water before Guy could object further, feeling it seep over my ankles and into my boots. It was shallow enough to wade right across to the far bank, although it soaked me almost to the top of my thighs.

The night air hit as we heaved ourselves out of the river, chilling me to my core. It was at least two or three degrees colder up here, and we had nothing with which to dry ourselves. I pulled off my boots and poured out the water that had been swishing around my feet.

'We have to go back up and over the mountain pass,' I said. 'The coastal route is too dangerous now. Far too many patrols and the fascists control it on the Spanish side.'

Grant raised a weary smile. 'Whatever you think is best.'

I could see he was exhausted. The man had been on the run for days and in prison before that. 'I promise I'll get you to Spain,' I said. 'Whatever it takes.'

What it took was several more hours hiking back up the mountain in silence, ever fearful of patrols, until at last I spotted the remote hut where we could rest. Unlike many dotted across the Pyrenees, this one was in good shape. There was even a full canteen of water inside left by the last inhabitants, probably evaders or escapers too.

With the first fingers of daylight filtering through the small, cobweb-covered window, I decided it was safe enough to light a fire without being spotted. There were remnants of the last one in the grate, which I managed to get going, along with some scavenged twigs. Tucked beside the matches in my kit box were my precious teabags, along with the tin mugs I'd packed. I boiled up some of the water in my trusty can and dropped them in.

'There you go,' I said, pulling off my boots and socks and setting them by the fire to dry before pouring the tea into the mugs. We drank it as if it was nectar, the hot liquid permeating our cold, tired bones, filling my stomach with a warmth that was as comforting as a hot-water bottle.

'I suggest you get some rest,' I said. 'I'll take first watch. We leave again as soon as it gets dark. This next bit is the most dangerous. It's heavily patrolled.'

I could feel Guy looking at me over his mug of tea. Let him look. I was in charge here, especially now that Pedro had disappeared. I knew these mountains far better than he did, certainly when it came to the freedom trails. All Guy knew were the campsites and cols he remembered from his youth. 'The Guardia Civil are out there too,' I added. 'We have to be on red alert.'

The Spanish were as keen as the French on catching those attempting to escape France, not just carrying out frequent patrols but opening and closing the borders as it suited them. As soon as they got to know of a route, we had to find a new one. So far, this one had remained one of the safest, although, as we moved closer to the border, things became more perilous.

I studied Grant as he slept, his mouth half-open, snoring softly. He was normally fit and strong, but his time in solitary confinement then being passed from place to place, always looking over his shoulder, had taken its toll. It wasn't always the physically fittest who made it. You had to have the right mindset as well. Above all, you had to believe that you could do it, and I wasn't convinced Grant felt like that anymore.

'Don't worry. We'll get him over that border,' murmured Guy.

I flicked him a glance. 'I thought you were asleep.'

He stretched, yawning. 'I can't sleep. Not while you're awake.'

'Don't be ridiculous. I'm fine. Just go to sleep. You're useless to me if you're too exhausted to walk.'

His eyes flashed. 'You don't hold back, do you? OK, fair enough. I'll be a good boy and go to sleep.'

'You do that,' I muttered, averting my gaze.

Ever since we'd pretended to be lovers in front of those policemen, I'd found it hard to look at him. Stupid. We were play-acting. He was an agent, and so was I.

Without thinking, I put my hand to my lips then pulled it away the moment I realised what I was doing. Still, they tingled, a resonance that rippled through me. For God's sake, this was Guy. I knew him almost better than I knew myself. Or I had done. A lot had changed in the years since I'd last seen him, including me.

What would Hélène have thought? Good question. Another pang shot through me. How I wished she was here. She'd have laughed and told me that it was just Guy, her brother, up to his old tricks. Yes, that was it. Guy the charmer. The boy who could win over the older ladies with that smile of his and woo the girls with it too. Well, I wasn't falling for it. Not now and not ever. This was strictly business, and our job was to get Grant over the line to safety, come hell or high water.

We'd managed the high water part. All we had to do now was navigate through hell.

# TWENTY

## 19 NOVEMBER 1942

Guy shook me awake as the sun was slipping beneath the horizon. We'd swapped watches hours before, leaving Grant to sleep. Now, as I rubbed my eyes, I saw him twitch and then waken too. He blinked, looking around, obviously trying to work out where he was.

'It's alright,' I said. 'You're with us, remember? We're getting you across the Pyrenees to Spain. Now, how about another cup of tea?'

Fortified, we set off once more, treading as silently as we could along the mountain pass, veering off into the trees when a wooded area rose to line it, conscious that a patrol could appear at any moment. We were resting in a clearing between the pines when I held up my hand, motioning to the other two to stay silent, sniffing the air as I did so.

Cigarette smoke.

I sniffed again to make sure. More of it now, drifting our way, accompanied by voices. There were three, maybe four of them, laughing and joking. It sounded as if they'd stopped for a rest too, accompanied by a cigarette break.

Holding my breath, I padded towards them, placing my feet

carefully on the forest floor so as not to alert them, slipping through the trees as silently as a woodland creature, until I was close enough to see them through the branches.

There they were – German soldiers. The first I'd seen out here. Four of them, three smoking while the other passed around a flask of what was probably brandy. They'd set their torches at their feet, illuminating their faces from beneath so that they appeared eerily ghoulish, mountain demons sent to hunt us down.

I considered my options. Shoot them and there would be vicious reprisals, not just for us but for anyone trying to cross in the future as well as those they suspected of helping evaders and escapers. Shoot out their torches and there was still a chance they would have some kind of backup light. The only thing to do was hold fast and hope they went on their way without spotting us.

I stayed rooted to the spot, staring at them, hoping with all my might that Guy and Grant would follow suit. Mercifully, they did.

The four men stubbed out their cigarettes, slung their rifles back over their shoulders and picked up their torches, ready to march. That was when I heard a sharp intake of breath, followed by an oath. Shit. The torch was shining directly in my face. One of them had spotted me.

At the very moment he yelled, I was already racing back through the trees. 'Four-man patrol,' I gasped. 'They've seen me.'

At that, Guy drew his weapon, as did Grant.

We began to back away through the forest as they came crashing towards us, our weapons raised.

'There they are! I see them,' cried one in German. 'Put your hands up and come on out.'

We fired almost simultaneously, one of our bullets finding its target. A cry and then a shout. Bullets whizzed towards us now, slamming into tree trunks, burying themselves in the dirt. I could see the whites of their eyes as they burst into the clearing we'd just vacated. Pulled my trigger. Another one down. Then another as Guy's bullet found its target too. The fourth hit the ground still firing, his rifle flying into the air as he fell backward into the mud.

I'd long ago learned why they called silence deathly – it hung over us now like a shroud. We kicked their weapons away even though it was obvious they were all dead. Bile rose, bitter, in my mouth. I gulped it back. No time for revulsion or regret.

'We need to bury them,' I said. 'If anyone finds them, there'll be hell to pay.'

We scanned the forest floor for anything that could be used as an implement. Nothing. The best we could do was drag them deeper in among the trees, scrabbling aside as much of the dirt and leaves as we could before covering them with it.

When we were done, I stared at the mounds that had been living, breathing humans a short while ago. Just what kind of cold-hearted monster had I become? Except it was kill or be killed – those were the rules of the game.

'Let's go,' I said, turning my back on them. 'We've already lost enough time.'

With that, I started to push my way once more through the trees, back towards the path. We had to take the quickest route now, come what may, and that meant the most direct one. With any luck, this was the only patrol out here this high.

Luck. Not the best thing to rely on, but it was all we had.

Above us, the moon sailed across the sky towards the dawn. Ahead of us, the Spanish border. *Keep going, Elisabeth* – a drumbeat in my head. The rhythm to which I marched. Or maybe that was my heart, leading me onwards, ever onwards while a tiny part of it walked behind me, filling my footsteps with his own.

# TWENTY-ONE

## 20 NOVEMBER 1942

I tapped on the farmhouse window twice, then once more. We waited. It was well after sunrise. Someone should be about. Sure enough, I caught a glimpse of a face behind the lace curtain, staring out at us. A few moments later, the front door swung open, and the farmer bade us enter. Inside, a man was waiting at the kitchen table. He rose when he saw us, holding out his hand.

'Miguel Garcia,' he said. 'I work for the British consulate. Please sit down.' He adjusted his spectacles as the farmer's wife appeared bearing coffee. 'Which of you is the parcel?'

Grant raised his hand. 'I am.'

Garcia shoved a piece of paper and a pen towards him across the table. 'Please write down your name, rank, regiment and serial number. Tomorrow, you'll be taken to the train station, but for now, you must eat and then rest.'

His gaze included all of us. I liked Garcia on sight. He had a calm efficiency coupled with the compassion that shone from his eyes. A rare quality in an official like this.

'Thank you,' I murmured as the farmer's wife reappeared with bread and mutton stew. I glanced at the clock. Past noon.

The delay with burying the patrol meant we were several hours behind schedule, but Garcia had patiently waited. I felt a prickling behind my eyes. There were so many good people out there. It helped outweigh the bad.

Dropping my head, I addressed myself to my stew, swallowing each pungent mouthful as if it was my last. Now that we were here, safe, I could feel all the adrenaline draining from me. I'd done it. Got us all across. Now all I had to do was get us back.

'Go and sleep,' muttered Guy as Garcia made his farewells. 'I can keep watch.'

'No need. These people are utterly trustworthy. They've never once let us down. I suggest we all go and get some shuteye. You and I need to leave just after sunset, and Captain Grant has a long journey ahead of him tomorrow.'

Guy looked unconvinced. 'If you say so.'

'I do.'

'I want to thank both of you,' said Grant. 'And to say goodbye for the moment.'

'In that case' – I smiled as I hugged him – 'it's *au revoir*. I just wish we could have restored the line together.'

'Me too,' murmured Grant as he hugged me back. 'You'll do it, Elisabeth. I have every faith in you.'

If only I could be as confident. There was just me, Guy and Albert now. Not enough of us to set up new safe houses and helpers while still running the fragment of the line that remained. The one we'd just used to bring Grant here, to safety.

He shook Guy's hand. '*Au revoir*, and I hope you find your men.'

'Thank you. Sefton and Hammond are very capable. With any luck they'll manage to escape too. We can't rebuild the line without them so we can only hope. As for Lionel—'

Grant cut across him. 'Did you say Sefton?'

'I did. Lieutenant Thomas Sefton.'

'There was a chap of that name brought to St Hippolyte, but they transferred him to Mauzac prison camp from what I heard.'

I looked at Guy. 'It's an unusual name,' I said. 'Worth checking out.'

'Absolutely.' Guy pumped Grant's hand again. 'Thank you, sir, and bon voyage.'

This time, it was I who woke Guy, tiptoeing into the room where he was buried under the covers, only a few tufts of his hair visible above the blankets. Seeing them, I hesitated. It was as if the little boy he'd once been was snuggled under there, safe in his nest.

*For goodness' sake, woman, get a hold of yourself.* He was a man, not a child. And I had to get us both back over those mountains without being arrested or killed.

'Time to get up.'

He tugged the blanket more firmly over his head.

'Guy, I said wake up.'

This time, I grabbed a hold of the blanket, pulling it off him before he could grab it back. He was in his underwear, the muscles in his back rippling as he groaned and rolled over. I averted my eyes. 'I'll meet you downstairs in five minutes.'

'What, no cup of coffee?'

I snorted and turned on my heel, but not before I caught a glimpse of him laughing.

I had to admit, that irrepressible spirit of his came in handy as we embarked on the long trek back, this time taking an even higher route to avoid any extra patrols out looking for the one that had disappeared. By now, they would have expected them to report back to base; at first light, they'd start sending out search parties. We were walking by night, but there was no guarantee they wouldn't be out there too with their torches, so we kept off the main tracks, marching parallel to them through any cover we could find, sharing a glance or a brush of our hands now and then, although we didn't dare speak for fear of our voices travelling in the clear mountain air.

Cresting the ridge that ran between the mountains was the hardest part. Here, there was no cover, and we were completely exposed, easy pickings for anyone with a weapon, although the patrols rarely came this high.

Descending once more, I kept my eyes peeled for shelter. I was busking it, and we both knew it, following my nose back towards the French border. Out here, in no man's land, anything could happen. Once or twice, I thought I saw lights moving, far below.

As we paused to catch our breath, Guy nudged me, pointing towards some kind of building far in the distance, its windows glowing orange, the lights on inside. A farmhouse maybe. Or a station for the guards who were no doubt scenting blood. There was nothing they hated more than to lose some of their own. I understood how they felt.

'It's nothing,' I murmured. 'Let's keep going.'

Still, I kept it in my sights until it disappeared behind the trees, the forest closing around us, a labyrinth of endless pathways to nowhere if we chose the wrong one.

By luck rather than skill, we emerged from the forest unscathed onto pastureland. Tucked into the lee of the hill, beside a stream, stood one of the stone shepherd's huts. It was so low that even I had to stoop to enter, but inside there was the traditional bed platform piled with pine leaves. They were brown with age and dried to a crisp. No one had used this place in a very long time.

'We must have gone further west than I thought,' I said. 'You only find this type of hut in Ariège.'

'I remember we camped out in a cluster of them one summer,' said Guy. 'A bunch of us boys. We must have been around fourteen.'

I smiled as I slumped against the stone bed platform,

stretching my legs out in front of me. 'You were a devil at fourteen.'

'You think?'

He was building the fire this time, expertly piling up handfuls of the dried-out pine needles under a pyramid of the twigs that lay scattered across the floor. 'Maybe not a devil but certainly capable of mischief.'

'You're a fine one to talk.'

I watched him blow on the twigs gently as he held his lighter to the fire; a wisp of smoke rose, and then the whole thing caught light. 'Well, if you can't be mischievous when you're a kid, when can you be?'

His eyes met mine across the flames. 'How about right now?'

My breath caught in my throat. The moment hung in the air between us, dangling a promise of something so terrifying I could barely look. 'The sun's nearly up. I'll take the floor. You can have the platform.'

'Don't be silly. We can share it. Unless you're scared to, for some reason.'

There was a challenge in his voice now. A teasing note. If there was one thing I couldn't resist, it was a challenge, and Guy knew it. 'You're the one who should be scared. I talk in my sleep.'

'I know.'

'What do you mean, you know?'

'I've heard you, many times. When we were kids and even now. You were muttering something when we were in the other hut. I'd love to know what you were dreaming about.'

I could feel the colour rising in my cheeks. 'Whatever it was, it certainly wasn't about you.'

'More's the pity.'

I jumped to my feet, making great play of patting down the pine needles before curling up on them close to the rough stone wall, my back turned to Guy. I could feel him settling down beside me on his back, his shoulder against mine. Within seconds, or so it seemed, he was breathing deeply and evenly. The bastard. How dare he fall asleep so easily?

Just as I was cursing him, his maleness and everything about him, I thought I heard him murmur, 'Goodnight, sweetheart.'

# TWENTY-TWO

## 22 NOVEMBER 1942

'Good morning.'

I glanced up from the plan I was poring over to see Guy shaking the rain from his hair. 'Good morning.'

Four and a half days since we'd left with Grant, and it felt like I'd never been away. The chateau hummed with life, its inhabitants going about their day as if there was no war raging just a few hundred kilometres from here. This place was an island, a sanctuary for those seeking it. People like Walther, tinkering away on the piano in the salon, or young Alice, curled up in an armchair here in the library, immersed as ever in a book, although this time it was one Eliane had found for her, all about the botany of the area so she could apply what she was learning to her little garden.

She unfurled herself as Guy strode over to the table where I sat, studying the plans Albert had brought. As he, too, appeared from the kitchen where Cook was doling out brioches along with what passed for coffee, Alice got to her feet and slipped from the room. She was wise beyond her years, that one, able to read adults in a way most kids her age couldn't. A skill no doubt acquired navigating the complicated relationship between her parents. I could hear Charlotte most days berating Matthieu. It made absolutely no difference. He drank anyway, his eyes glazed over long before noon.

Guy glanced at Alice as she glided through the door like a will o' the wisp, and I wondered if he saw what I saw, if she reminded him of Hélène as much as she did me. It wasn't just the hair but the air of self-containment. Alice was her own person, fully formed. She might have learned to vanish into the background, but that only gave her even more opportunity to observe. I caught her sometimes, watching everyone else in the salon of an evening, her book the perfect prop. It was also her sanctuary, in a way, the story taking her away from the tensions all around her, immersing her in a world that made sense. I suspected it had long been that way. Charlotte and Matthieu brought chaos wherever they went.

'Is that Mauzac?' asked Guy, leaning over to look at the rows of neat oblongs marked out, one labelled 'North Camp' and the other 'South'.

'It is,' said Albert, setting a plate of brioches beside the plans.

I reached for one. 'Did Cook see you take these?'

'No. Or she'd be in here beating me over the head with a pan.'

I doubted it. Cook might look fierce at times, but she had a heart of gold, forever finding ways to feed her flock, as she saw us, with black-market treats.

'We can park up here,' said Albert, indicating a bridge that looked to be around four hundred metres from the main entrance.

I peered over his shoulder at the spot he was indicating. 'So the Red Cross have confirmed that he's definitely in there?'

'The Red Cross have confirmed that a Lieutenant Thomas

Sefton is being held in Mauzac, but he's due to be transported to Germany any day.'

'Then we have to move fast,' I murmured. "We need him back here safe and helping us to rebuild the line."

Guy, too, was studying the plan in front of us. 'This place is vast. Do we know exactly where he's being held?'

'He's in the north camp. But that's all we know. It's up to Elisabeth to find out the details for us once she's in.'

I nibbled at my brioche. 'What's the drill?'

'Same plan as the one we were going to use for Grant. You play Sefton's cousin. Once you announce yourself to the guard, they'll check the register and then pass you on to be searched along with your parcel. We'll make absolutely sure there's nothing incriminating in the parcel, at least to the naked eye. Your job then is to get the message across to Sefton as soon as they leave you alone. You must insist upon that. Tell them it's his right under the Geneva Convention. Keep mentioning it. Most of the guards are so poorly educated they've never even heard of it. They employ the lowest of the low to work in these camps.'

I wasn't too convinced about that. 'I'm sure if I sound confident enough, I'll be able to persuade them. Once I'm alone with Sefton, I'll get as much from him as quickly as I can so we can agree an escape plan.'

I was also sure that Sefton would already be thinking about that day and night. It was every prisoner of war's duty to at least try to escape, a fact that even some of the camp commanders respected. 'So all we're waiting for now is that letter of permission.'

Guy nodded. 'Correct. And it could come at any time. We need to be prepared to move the moment it does.'

Something had shifted between us in the mountains, and it wasn't just a new respect for one another. I was beginning to trust him. It wasn't something I gave lightly, and in his case, I did so more cautiously than ever. I wasn't quite sure why. History probably. Or perhaps a deep-seated sense that once I opened up to Guy, I could never go back.

# TWENTY-THREE

## 2 DECEMBER 1942, MAUZAC PRISON CAMP, THE DORDOGNE, SOUTHERN FRANCE

Prison huts ran before us as far as the eye could see, rows and rows of them behind the barbed-wire fence, matching the oblongs on the plans.

'It was built as a gunpowder factory,' said Albert as we huddled in his van, peering out through the rear window. 'But when we signed the Armistice, it was no longer needed.'

It must have been quite some factory. The place was huge. 'So instead of making weapons to beat the Germans, they house their prisoners for them?'

'Exactly.'

Guy looked at his watch – it was five minutes until my allotted appointment. 'Time to go. Good luck.'

I picked up the parcel we'd prepared with the name of a fictitious charity on the side. 'I'll do my best.'

Guy pushed the door open for me and grinned. 'Of course you will.'

We were parked in the spot we'd pinpointed, four hundred metres from the main entrance. I didn't look back once I'd set off in its direction, my new hat pulled low enough that it almost touched the top of the glasses I also sported. My hair was now a dull brown, my lipstick a dark red that made my lips look thinner, while I walked with a pronounced limp thanks to one heel being shorter than the other. I had no idea what awaited me, my trepidation growing as I approached the guard's hut. The worst thing I could do was arouse suspicion, especially as our previous attempt to recce the place had failed.

All we knew was that Mauzac housed political prisoners such as *résistants* and communists alongside the ordinary prisoners brought in by the French police, although that would no doubt also change now that the Germans were here in the south. Luckily for Sefton, he'd been arrested before they arrived, or he would almost certainly be in the hands of the Gestapo by now.

The parcel was packed with the food and clean clothes Sefton was permitted, although secreted within were items including a map of the area printed on a handkerchief and a compass hidden in a shirt button. I not only had to get those past the guards but indicate to Sefton where he could find these escape tools. As I drew close enough to see the prisoners through the fence, though, my heart sank.

So many of them were stick thin, their cheeks hollow, bodies swamped by their clothing. The interned soldiers and airmen were wearing their uniforms, while the civilians sported threadbare outfits which were evidently all they'd been allowed to bring with them to wear day after day. If Sefton was in the same state, we'd need to feed him up before we made any attempt at escape.

I smiled at the guard, who looked me up and down, evidently unimpressed.

'I'm here to see Lieutenant Thomas Sefton,' I simpered. 'I'm his cousin. I have a parcel for him. Here's my letter of permission.'

'Papers.'

So much for my simpering. Sometimes it worked; sometimes, as now, it fell flat. Maybe the hairdo and the limp were having the desired effect.

I handed over the false papers Dr George's forger had prepared, bracing myself for the challenge that never came. The guard glanced at the letter and then my ID before looking at me with an inscrutable expression.

'Madame Elspeth Sefton?'

'That's right.'

'One moment.'

He picked up the telephone in his guard hut and dialled through as I did my best to hide my impatience. The van was invisible around the corner, hidden among the trees that lined the road leading up to the camp. If asked, I would say I'd walked from the bus stop, but the guard didn't seem too interested in how I'd got there or even in me. With a bored sigh, he signalled to the guards the other side of the visitors' gate to let me through. I was in.

It took them no more than a few minutes to rifle through the parcel. I stood to one side as they gave the tins and jars no more than a cursory examination, throwing one a stern glance when he lingered a little too long over the bar of chocolate.

'My cousin is a prisoner of war,' I said. 'I'm fairly sure the Geneva Convention also covers that bar of chocolate.'

He dropped it back in the box, handing it to me. 'You can go.'

His mate signalled to another couple of guards, who led me to a hut that was separate to the others, next to what appeared to be the medical block. On the way through the camp, I passed men playing boules while others sat around chatting or smoking, scanning every face that I could, trying to see if I could recognise any of our agents. I knew there were at least six in here, possibly more. If I could smuggle more items to Sefton, perhaps we could help them too.

'Sit here.'

The guard indicated a hard wooden chair inside the hut. There were a couple of others in the room, set around a scratched and worn table. Aside from the furniture, there was a portrait of Pierre Laval on the wall. I contemplated spitting at it but thought better of it as the door opened once more, and the two guards led Sefton into the room. I wondered if he'd even recognise me. After all, we'd met just once before.

He looked at me blankly and then again, a tiny spark lighting up his eyes. So he did remember me. That was one hurdle cleared. He didn't look as bad as some of the other prisoners, although he was considerably leaner than he'd been in Canet-Plage. I smiled and half rose from my chair, but the guard gestured to me to stay seated, so instead I pushed the parcel across the table to him.

'For you, my dear. It's so good to see you.'

One of the guards left, while the other stood just inside the door. I gave him my frostiest stare. 'I wish to speak to my cousin alone. That is also his right.'

I wasn't too sure if it was, but I was banking on the fact that the guard wouldn't know either, especially if I spoke with enough authority. Sure enough, he looked confused and made to protest but then thought better of it, backing out of the hut with a final slam of the door.

I waited a second then murmured to Sefton. 'We're going to get you out of here. The Germans have invaded the south, which means they'll be taking over this camp, so we need to spring you before they do. You'll find a few items in here that may help.'

He stared at me. 'So it's true then? We heard rumours but nothing more.'

'It's true. The Nazis have occupied the south. They marched over the demarcation line a couple of weeks ago.'

'My God,' muttered Sefton. 'What about the others, ma'am? Hammond and Sabourin?'

'We haven't heard anything. When was the last time you saw them?'

'They put Sabourin in a separate cell at the police station when they arrested us. We didn't see him again after that. They were taking me and Hammond by train to be interrogated when he jumped.'

'Hammond jumped from a moving train?'

'Yes, ma'am. We'd made a plan. Said we needed to have a smoke in the corridor. I was going to jump with him, but at the last minute, one of the guards appeared. I managed to distract him long enough so Hammond got away. They gave me an extra beating for that.'

'You're lucky you weren't shot.'

I leaned forward, lowering my voice so it was barely above a whisper. 'I need to know everything you can tell me about this camp. Weak spots. Guard shift patterns. Everything.'

Sefton sat a little straighter, speaking even more softly. 'There are watchtowers all around the perimeter. Two sets of fences to get over or through. We may be better off trying to bribe one or more of the guards, especially now that the Germans are here. No wonder they've been so jumpy. They're probably fearing for their jobs. Most of them drink at the local inn after their shifts. Find the right one and I'm pretty sure they'll do what you ask in exchange for a price.'

He glanced towards the door. Sefton might be wan and undernourished, but the fight was still in him.

'This inn – does it have rooms?'

'Yes. Some of the prisoners' wives stay there.'

'Then I'll take one and see what I can do. In the meantime, you must eat. Get some flesh on your bones. There's plenty of food in that parcel along with those extra items.'

He nodded, hearing the inflection in my voice and raising his slightly. 'Thank you. I'll digest everything, I can assure you.'

The guard rapped on the door. 'Time's up.'

At least he'd done the decent thing and given us a moment before he burst in. I rose as he entered, stepping forward to engulf Sefton in a hug so I could whisper in his ear. 'What about this one?'

Sefton squeezed me in assent and then stepped back, a fond cousin bidding farewell. 'I'll see you soon.'

'Be good and remember that England expects every man to do his duty.'

'And every woman.'

'Roger that.'

The guard had no idea why I was smiling so broadly as I left the hut. Mission accomplished. Game on.

# TWENTY-FOUR

The inn was a cheerless place, but we weren't there for the ambience. I swilled my wine in its glass, watching the rough ruby liquid swirl, while Albert and Guy watched me in turn from a corner of the dingy saloon. I'd deliberately installed myself close to the door so that anyone entering or leaving had to pass by my table. There were a couple of what looked to be guards supping their drinks in silence, but it was hard to tell for sure when they were out of uniform. The only other customer was a woman of around fifty, her mouth set in what appeared to be a permanent grimace. She could be a prisoner's wife or mother. Then again, she might simply be a local in need of a drink at the end of her day.

I looked over at her as she signalled to the landlady, trying to catch her eye, but she settled her bill and departed upstairs without a second glance.

The landlady paused by my table. 'Can I get you something else?'

I looked up into her tired face. The light in her eyes had gone out long ago. This war did that to you. Or perhaps life had got there first. I smiled, trying to rekindle it. 'Another glass of wine please. And a menu, if you have one.'

She nodded and drifted over to where Guy and Albert were sitting. I averted my gaze, not showing any particular interest in them or anything else save the tabletop, pretending to examine the cracks and whorls that scarred its surface. We'd checked in separately a good half hour apart, although, fortuitously, my room was right next to theirs. It was as functional as the rest of this place, the blankets on the lumpy bed thin and worn. Still, it was a darn sight more comfortable than the hut in which Sefton had to bunk down each night. With any luck, we'd have him out of there as soon as possible, although luck appeared to have deserted us for now.

It was only after I'd wolfed down the thin stew that masqueraded as cassoulet that I felt rather than saw the man staring at me from the table nearest the bar. Flicking him a glance as I wiped my lips with my napkin, I recognised him at once. It was him, the guard who'd knocked on the door to tell us the time for visiting was over. Perhaps Lady Luck was smiling upon us once more. I did the same as he studied me more openly this time, raising his glass in a gesture of acknowledgement and then, after another moment, rising to move to my table.

'May I join you?' he asked.

I waved at the empty chair opposite. 'By all means.'

'You are here alone?'

I sighed. 'Unfortunately, yes. It's a long way from where we live, and there was no one else who could make the journey to visit my cousin. It was so good to see him alive and well.'

A pause as he digested this, evidently weighing up what to say next. 'Things might become tougher for him. We heard today that the Germans will be taking over the running of the camp.'

I widened my eyes, attempting both astonishment and distress. 'Do you have any idea when?'

'Only that it will be very soon.'

'I see.'

I let a silence fall between us, hoping he might rush to fill it. In my experience, people generally did, especially when they wanted something in return.

He didn't disappoint, looking right and left before leaning across the table, speaking now as quietly as Sefton and I had only hours before. 'It might be a good idea to try and get him out of there.'

Another sigh. I shook my head. 'If only I could...'

The silence elongated until, finally, he blurted, 'I could help. Maybe.'

I added hope to the widened eyes now, along with a dose of wonder. 'You could? Really? I would be so grateful, *monsieur*. You have no idea how much.'

He cleared his throat. 'That is the question. How much?'

I carried on looking at him, playing dumb, waiting for him to name a figure. When he finally did, it was less than I'd expected.

'Fifty thousand francs?' I whispered in response. 'I... I'll have to see what I can do. If you could permit me a little time to contact my family. We're not rich, you see, but of course we will try and do what we can.'

Pink stained his cheeks. So he was a little embarrassed by his own greed. Good. Although I couldn't blame him. It was all a question of survival, and his wages were no doubt barely enough to feed him and his family. Now that even they were threatened by the arrival of the Germans, his need was as pressing as ours.

'Don't take too long,' he murmured. 'The Germans could be here tomorrow.'

'I can get you an answer by later this evening, so long as there's a telephone in this inn.'

'There is. Why don't I meet you outside by the stables in a couple of hours?'

The stables were situated across the yard at the back of the inn, offering plenty of cover for Guy and Albert to hide and keep an eye on proceedings. 'Perfect. I'll be there at ten o'clock on the dot.'

He stood, smiling at me as if we were old acquaintances, and made his way back to his own table. The other two men had long since vanished, and the landlady was busy polishing glasses behind the bar. I waited a few more minutes then gathered my things, making my way upstairs to my room.

I'd barely pulled the bag containing our funds from under the mattress before there was a knock on the door. The moment I opened it, Guy and Albert slipped into the room.

Guy looked at the open bag on my bed. 'He took the bait?'

'He wants fifty thousand francs. I told him I had to contact family first and that I'd meet him by the stables at ten o'clock to give him my answer.'

Albert moved to the window, gently tugging the curtain aside to peer out. 'There's plenty of cover. We should be in place a good half hour beforehand just in case he tries any funny business.'

'I don't think he will. They're expecting the Germans to take over the camp any day. The man is obviously worried he might be out of a job. He's not going to risk losing out on some money too.'

Guy cocked his head. 'What was that noise?'

Albert tweaked the curtain aside once more. 'I can't see anything,' he murmured. 'Wait. There are lights. A jeep. Shit, it's a German one.'

I snapped the bag shut and stowed it back under the mattress. 'Quick. Back to your room. It might just be an inspection. Or they could simply want a drink. Whatever it is, we can't be seen together.'

'If you need us, shout,' muttered Guy.

'If I need you, I'll use a code word.'

'Good idea. What will it be?'

'Hélène.'

# TWENTY-FIVE

I hadn't meant to use her name; it just slipped out. Guy barely faltered – just nodded and disappeared back out the door, Albert in tow. I checked it was shut tight, turning the key in the lock, then I sat on the edge of the bed and waited. Sure enough, there was another knock. This time, the landlord stood there, twisting his hands, his face an agony of mortification and fear.

'Everyone is to come downstairs with their papers.'

I raised my eyebrows. 'Why?'

His voice dropped to a whisper. 'The Germans are here.'

'I see.'

Downstairs, the saloon was busier than I'd seen it over the last few hours, the woman I'd spotted previously standing, clutching her robe around her, while two younger women huddled by the bar and another, older man, sat at the table Guy and Albert had occupied, a set expression on his face. In the centre of the room, a German Sturmbannführer, or major, was inspecting the landlord's papers while his lieutenant and a soldier stood by. Satisfied, the major waved the landlord and his wife aside and pointed to the middle-aged woman. 'You.'

She stared at him in quivering indignation, mouth pursed, then swept over and slapped her papers down on the table beside him. I wanted to applaud. Instead, I watched as he spent what felt like an age scrutinising her identity card, glancing at her and then at it.

'It says here you live in Lyon,' he snapped.

'That is correct.'

'Then what are you doing here? This is a long way from Lyon.'

She folded her arms, pulling her robe tighter around her as she did so. 'I'm visiting my husband. He's in the camp here at Mauzac.'

The major glanced at his lieutenant. 'Why is he in the camp?'

'My husband is a political prisoner.'

'What is he? A dirty communist? A filthy Jew?'

She drew herself up. 'He's the editor of a newspaper.'

The major thrust her papers back at her. 'Like I said, a dirty communist.'

'My husband is no more a communist than you or I.'

For s second, I thought he might strike her, then he threw back his head and laughed. 'You are joking, aren't you?'

She glared at him. 'No, I am not.'

I felt the sudden frisson in the room like an icy blast, saw the expression on the major's face darken in the split second before he raised his pistol.

'You are joking, aren't you?' he repeated, his finger on the trigger now.

The lieutenant looked at him in alarm, but he was already past the tipping point. As he opened his mouth to protest, the major fired straight into the woman's heart. She stared at him in surprise, her hand clutching at her chest, then her eyes fixed and she slumped to the floor, her leg twitching once, twice before she was completely still. The major gave her an idle kick and then waved his pistol at the rest of us.

'Anyone else want to make a joke?'

I could feel Guy and Albert behind me, their hands no doubt itching, as mine was, to pull their own weapons, but to do so would have been suicidal. I glanced at the clock on the wall – nine fifteen. The guard would be back soon, expecting me to meet him. I didn't look at the woman on the floor. It felt indecent.

The major beckoned to me. 'You. Papers.'

I shuffled forward and handed over the false papers Dr George's contact had created, keeping my hand and my gaze as steady as I could. They were perfect fakes – I knew that. He'd also created the papers I used to get in and out of the occupied zone, along with hundreds of sets for our escapers. Even so, this German was capable of anything. The slightest suspicion from him or slip from me and I could be lying next to that woman or chained up in the back of their jeep.

'You live near Toulouse. What are you doing here?'

I took a breath. 'Visiting my cousin in the prison camp. He's a prisoner of war. A British officer.'

A beat as the major stared me down. 'You are British?'

'I'm French. I was born in Marseille.'

We'd stuck as closely to the truth as ever when it came to creating my story. It wasn't only easier to remember; it prevented stupid mistakes. I wondered if I'd made one now as the German looked at me more closely, his eyes narrowed. 'He's your British cousin and yet you are French?'

'That's right. My father is English, my mother French. I was born here.'

He grunted and thrust my papers back into my hand. 'Next.'

It was only as I walked away, towards the door, that I felt the tension draining out of me.

'Halt!'

Damn. I slowly turned to see the major glowering at me. 'Did I say you could leave?'

'No. Sir.'

Out of the corner of my eye, I saw Guy stiffen, his fingers reaching towards his belt. Beside him, Albert already had his hand in his pocket.

The German raised his hand and pointed. 'You sit over there until I have finished.'

I responded meekly, as would the shopgirl I was supposed to be. 'Yes, sir.'

He gestured to Guy to approach, snatching his papers from him. It felt like an age before he passed them to the lieutenant, pointing to something on the page. The lieutenant stared at it then passed the papers back with a tiny nod. All at once, all three Germans had their weapons raised, pointing them at Guy.

'No!'

I yelled at the same time Albert fired. Perhaps a millisecond later. The major's knees sagged, and then he, too, crashed to the floor. I thrust my pistol into the back of the lieutenant's skull, while Guy shoved his into the soldier's temple.

'One move,' I snarled, 'and you're a dead man too.'

# TWENTY-SIX

You could hear every heart beating in the room, so complete was the silence. Eyes were darting everywhere, although mine remained fixed on the lieutenant's skull. The smell of death permeated the fug of alcohol and cassoulet, its metallic stench rising from the blood and matter that was spreading around the major's head. He was sprawled face down, arms outstretched as if in supplication, although he'd been dead before he hit the floor, the bullet exiting his brain through his forehead. I kicked his gun towards Albert as Guy disarmed the other two.

'Easy now,' he said. 'That's right.'

The walls and doors were thick, the windows shut against the cold evening air. Still, anyone outside could have heard the shot. There was no sign of the camp guard. Even if he had heard something, I reckoned he'd be smart enough to ignore it.

I looked at the landlady, rooted to the spot in shock. 'Where's your cellar?'

She pointed to the door beside the bar. 'Down there.'

I shoved the lieutenant in the back with my pistol. 'Hands above your head. Move.'

'Allow me,' said Albert. 'You have a rendezvous to attend.'

I looked at him, hearing the steel in his voice and knowing what would happen next. He was right. It was almost ten – I had to make it out to the stables or miss the opportunity. Without another thought, I slipped out the door, dodging around the jeep to cross the yard, making a mental note that we had to get rid of that too.

The guard was lurking in the lee of the stable block, the only indication he was there the glow from the end of his cigarette. He scurried forward as I approached, keeping to the shadows.

'You have the money?'

No mention of gunshots. Good.

'I do, but first I want to know what you can do for me.'

He stifled his disappointment with a sigh. 'I have a spare uniform here. It's about the right size. I can smuggle it into his cell and make sure he walks out at the right time wearing it so that no one will notice. The guard changes shift twice a day, first thing in the morning at seven o'clock and then again at five in the afternoon. If he leaves just after the rest of us at five tomorrow, and you have a car waiting, there should be no problem.'

I peered at him, trying to ascertain his sincerity. He sounded confident enough, but you could never be too sure. 'Fine. You get half the money now and the other half when he's safely in the vehicle.'

He made to protest then thought better of it. 'It's a deal.'

I pulled the notes from my pocket, where I'd already secreted them. 'Here you go. Half now and half when the job is done. I'll be waiting near the camp from quarter to five tomorrow.'

'How will I know you'll stick to the bargain?'

'The same way I'll know you'll stick to your side of it. You won't. You'll have to trust me. Frankly, you have little choice.'

He flung his cigarette stub to the ground, crushing it under his heel. 'See you tomorrow then.'

I thought I heard a faint popping sound from the inn. The muffled noise of a pistol perhaps. It came again and then a third time. I held out my hand. 'See you tomorrow.'

He shook it reluctantly and sloped off into the shadows, every line of his posture screaming resignation at his fate. I waited a moment then headed back to the inn to face mine, bracing myself for what I'd find. You never got used to death or the cruelty of this war, no matter how many times you witnessed it. I'd seen my fair share of corpses, and their faces still haunted me, enemies and our own alike, forever frozen in time. One day I'd be free of all this, but today wasn't that day.

I pushed open the inn door to find the saloon deserted. The major was still sprawled on the floor, although someone had covered the woman with a sheet.

Guy appeared from the cellar as the door banged behind me. 'Everything alright?'

'All set for tomorrow, just before five. We need to park up near the prison camp and wait until Sefton appears in a guard's uniform. I paid him half now with the other half once we have Sefton safely in the van.'

Guy looked at me, his eyes glinting with what appeared to be a new respect. 'Bravo.'

I gestured towards the cellar. 'What about the Germans?'

'We've taken care of it.' He grimaced slightly.

'We need to take care of their jeep too before someone comes looking for them.'

Guy waved the bunch of keys in his hand. 'Already thought of it. I'll be driving it into the river. We'll stick this bastard here in it too. With any luck, it'll sink like a stone.'

My heart was plummeting the same way as I stared at him, taking in that dimple, the tilt of his head that was so like Hélène's. Her boat would have sunk like a stone too, all the way to the bottom of the cold Atlantic. She never stood a chance. I swallowed. 'Sounds like a plan.'

He stayed where he was, eyes brimming with pain. 'She'd have been so proud of you,' he whispered. 'Hélène.'

'She'd have been proud of you too.'

His fingers brushed my cheek. 'I hope so.'

'I know so.'

The moment was broken by the sound of footsteps clumping up the cellar stairs.

'Want a hand with him?'

Albert emerged from the cellar, wiping his hands on his trousers, streaks of what appeared to be blood remaining. I didn't ask; I didn't want to know. Together, he and Guy heaved the major out the door while I grabbed a bar towel and started to mop up the blood that was already congealing. The landlady slipped into the room with a mop and bucket that smelled of bleach, silently taking over from me, her eyes still dark with shock, working around the body of the woman, the sheet affording her some dignity.

Guy reappeared, taking in the scene, telling me with his eyes that they'd accomplished their grisly task. 'We'll be back in an hour or so. Don't want to be too close by.'

Another fleeting smile and then he was gone once more, the sound of the jeep's engine dying away as they drove off, the only sound I could now hear the beating of my heart and the insistent whisper in my head.

*No, Elisabeth. Don't even go there. He's Hélène's brother, that's all*. The boy who used to tease us mercilessly. The man who was all I had left of my friend. I shook my head, trying to dispel those thoughts, the echoes that resonated down the years. *Forget the past*. We were here, now, in the middle of the maelstrom that was this war. Tomorrow we might be dead, just like Hélène. We certainly would be if I didn't concentrate on my job.

With a sigh, I made my way up the stairs. Tomorrow was still another day. One I intended to get us all through alive.

# TWENTY-SEVEN

## 3 DECEMBER 1942

He strode out of the gates in his uniform just as we'd planned. I held my breath. Sefton was so tall, so obviously not French that I steeled myself for him to be challenged. Even the trousers of his uniform were slightly too short. Someone was bound to notice.

One stride. Another. He was almost at the van when I heard a shout. A guard horsing around. Something and nothing. Still, we had to get out of here.

I flung open the door as Guy gunned the engine. 'Get in!'

Sefton didn't need telling twice. We roared away from the prison camp, racing down back roads, doubling back until we were sure there was no one in pursuit. It was only when we reached the outskirts of Marseille that we began to relax, although there were new dangers ahead.

Albert pointed to a pharmacy on a street corner. 'Pull in here.'

Guy shot him a look but said nothing, parking up behind another van so we were concealed from the road.

Albert scrambled out. 'I won't be a minute.'

Five minutes later, he was back. 'Change of plan. We're taking you all to Chateau Bleu.'

I stared at him. 'Why?'

'Dr George's place is no longer safe. The Gestapo have been spotted watching it. We'll have to shift the entire operation to Chateau Bleu. The pharmacist here is one of us. He says the Gestapo have been cracking down heavily since they arrived, probably acting on the information Harry King gave them.'

I tried to digest this, my mind working at the speed of knots. 'What about Dr George and his wife?'

Albert's mouth was compressed in a way that spoke volumes. 'They're alright. For now. But there are even more posters of you everywhere, Elisabeth. It seems you're public enemy number one as far as the Nazis are concerned. Apparently, they found the bodies of four of their soldiers up in the Pyrenees. They were on patrol near the route they know we use. A smuggler described a woman who was leading a group over not long before they discovered the bodies. They seem convinced that woman was you.'

I curled my lip. 'I bet I know who that was. A lowlife called Pedro who abandoned us up by the Tech river. Said he was off to get a rope. Evidently, he was off to earn his thirty pieces of silver instead. Or maybe five million francs.'

Guy fired up the engine once more. 'Whoever it was, we need to get you to the chateau. Both of you. Five million francs is a hell of an incentive for someone like Pedro. It's a hell of an incentive for anyone.'

As we drove up to the house, under the branches that seemed to hang lower than ever, I cast a surreptitious look at Guy in the driver's seat, his profile so familiar but still so incongruous. I couldn't get used to him being here, not just back in France but working alongside me. It felt wrong and yet so right. As if he'd come home to help when and where he was needed most.

If only he could have been there for Hélène. I was sure he felt the same. It was the deal with the devil we all made, going off to fight where we were sent, not knowing if we'd ever return, leaving our loved ones to their fates. Hell, Guy had even trained with the Devil's Brigade, although that wouldn't prevent other demons from torturing him. He'd always protected her when we were kids. He must torture himself every day wishing he could have been there to save her.

My eyes drifted to the mirror and locked on his, looking back at me. In them, I could see the agony that would never leave; the agony I felt too. Another thing we shared. It was good to have him here, if only as a friend. Especially as a friend. Right now, I needed all the friends I could get.

# TWENTY-EIGHT

In the short time I'd been away, the chateau had filled up with new arrivals, including a party of airmen who'd been sheltering in the mission in Marseille until the Gestapo arrived. They were billeted in the ballroom, mattresses now strewn around what had once been an echoing space, their kit neatly stacked at the end of each bed, the air redolent with the sweat of men above the lingering scent of beeswax and lavender polish.

I stood in the doorway with Eliane, surveying the scene. A group were playing cards, while others sat around, chatting. These were evaders, men who'd managed to avoid capture after crashing or bailing out over France. Some of them looked to be barely out of their teens, although all had that gaze I'd come to recognise, a look that said they'd already been through far too much, although most remained cheerfully defiant in spite of the odds.

'Come and join us, miss,' one of the card players called out, his grin cheekier than all the rest.

I walked over to them, smiling. 'I'm afraid I can't. Duty calls. Do you boys have everything you need?'

'Everything except a nice kiss and a cuddle,' retorted the cheeky one.

'That will do, Greenwood,' snapped the older man standing a few feet away. He strode over to me, holding out his hand. 'Flight Sergeant Bill McGrath. Good to meet you.'

'You're Irish?'

'I am. An Ulsterman.'

'It's good to meet you too. All of you. My name's Elisabeth. I'm here to help you get home.'

They nodded respectfully, even the cheeky one cowed by the sergeant. They might all be in the same boat, trying to escape, but rank still counted, as did discipline. We'd had a few too many incidents with high-spirited airmen getting overconfident, some even publicly drinking with the locals who were supposed to be hiding them. It meant certain death for the brave souls who risked their lives to help the escape line and quite possibly for the airmen as well.

'Here, miss.' The cheeky one was back, standing by my side. 'Can I show you something?'

He pulled a photograph from his pocket and passed it to me. I studied the figure in it – a pretty young woman, blonde curls framing a freckled face which was lit up by a gorgeous smile. 'She's lovely,' I said. 'Is this your girl?'

'My fiancée, ma'am. We're going to be married just as soon as I get back.'

'Well then, we'd better make sure you do just that.'

He looked at me, his eyes suddenly serious. 'If we don't – make it back I mean – can I ask you a favour? Can you make sure she knows that I love her? Her name is Dorothy, ma'am. Dorothy Purkiss. She lives in Luddenden. That's a village near Halifax.'

'Is that where you're from?'

'Yes, ma'am. Proud Yorkshireman, me.'

'And what's your name?'

'Richard Greenwood, ma'am. Air gunner, Bomber Command.'

'Well then, Richard Greenwood,' I said, handing him back the photograph, 'you can tell her yourself when we get you safely home.'

He tucked it away in his pocket, that cheeky grin back in place. 'Tell her? I'll show her, ma'am.'

I smiled. 'You do that.'

Eliane took me by the arm, steering me away from the group. 'Come,' she said. 'Let me show you where your friend can sleep.'

I glanced at Sefton hovering behind us, still dressed in his guard's uniform.

'I can sleep in here with the other men,' he declared.

'Nonsense. I have a room upstairs you can use. Besides, they'll be on their way soon enough, although I fear more will be arriving.'

Eliane sounded weary. The chateau was bursting at the seams in spite of its vastness. It was going to be very difficult to get all these people safely out of France, even with Sefton to help. Through the French windows, I watched children darting through the wild scrub outside, too delighted at being able to play to feel the cold and too used to darkness to care, while their parents watched or strolled together under the winter stars, arm in arm, in a bizarre semblance of normality. Across the room, François was watching them too, quietly sketching, absorbed in his task. I moved closer so I could see what he was drawing, making out the faces of each child, their parents looking on.

'That's so good,' I breathed.

He glanced up. 'Thank you. I do it for them. To remember. I try to sketch each and every person who spends even a little time with us. It's important.'

'It's for our book,' said Eliane. 'I write their stories, and François illustrates them. One day, perhaps, these people will want to know their own stories, especially if they're too young now to remember. Of course, we change their names in case the book falls into the wrong hands, but I keep a coded list of their real names. It's their legacy, you see.'

Both their faces were shining with a sincerity that touched me to the core. They were such good people, noble as well as brave. It took real courage to hide and house these fugitives from the Nazis, knowing they would be executed if they were caught.

'How did all these people get here?' I asked. 'The line is still broken beyond here. They must have made their own way south.'

'They did, but, like all the others, they were brought by your people from Marseille, most before they even reach the city. The Germans are everywhere now, and still people keep arriving. They're desperate; you can see that, but we simply can't take them all.'

I glimpsed more of them over her shoulder, clustered in the salon where Walther and Paul were hunched over their perennial chess game.

'Hello.'

I turned. 'Hello, Alice. How lovely to see you.'

It truly was a delight to look at her sweet face smiling up at me, an antidote to the most recent horrors I'd witnessed. Now that we were safely here, they'd begun to crowd my mind, flashbacks of that poor woman lying on the floor, then the German major slumped there too, his heart still pumping out blood although his eyes were fixed and staring. It was the eyes that got me the most, the life snuffed out, devoid of anything. Empty. One minute you were here, the next gone. Forever. Life became so precious in the face of constant death. Especially a young life like Alice's.

'What have you done to your hair?' she asked, gazing at my dyed tresses.

'This? I fancied a change. What do you have there?'

She held out the sketchpad in her hand. 'I've been drawing. François's been teaching me.'

I bent over her work, exclaiming at the delicacy of the lines, the way she'd captured Walther and Paul in just a few of them. 'Alice, you're so talented. You should be an artist.'

'Don't be ridiculous, ' said a voice from my left, every word frosted with contempt. Charlotte swept forward, snatching the sketchpad from my hand. 'It's time for your dinner, Alice. It's getting late.'

I could see the other children running in, summoned by the cook. A motherly woman from the village, she beamed at the young faces, scarlet with the cold but wreathed in answering smiles as they raced to wash their hands and sit at the kitchen table.

'Run along, Alice. I'll see you later,' I said, my smile stiffening as my eyes swept over Charlotte. She gazed at me coolly in turn.

'You have a beautiful and talented daughter there. You're a lucky woman.'

She sniffed and swept past me without another word.

I could hear Guy and Albert coming towards us along the corridor, voices raised in cheerful banter. All of a sudden, Guy fell silent. Then I heard him say, clear as a bell: 'Charlotte.'

# TWENTY-NINE

So much resonated from that one word. Recognition. Surprise. No, shock. Charlotte was rooted to the spot, her mouth agape as she stared at Guy. Then she collected herself, tossing her head in that way she had. 'Guy. It's good to see you.'

It sounded anything but. I glanced from one to the other, observing the panoply of emotions playing across Guy's face. Then he, too, gathered his wits about him. 'I wish I could say the same.'

A sticky silence spread like a pool between them, not so much water as the spilled blood of a thousand remembered cuts.

Charlotte emitted a tinkling laugh. 'You always were one for plain speaking.'

He carried on looking at her, his expression closed now, shut down so that not even a flicker betrayed him. Watching them, I felt a churning low in my stomach, that sense that something was very wrong, that there were secrets here I didn't want to know, an unsavoury whiff of things best left buried. Or at least unspoken.

'Ah, there you are, my dove,' slurred Matthieu as he blundered into view, descending the stairs behind the pair of them. Albert reached out a hand to steady him just in time, his feet missing the final steps. 'Whoops.' He giggled. 'Silly me.'

Charlotte snorted her derision. 'Matthieu. I thought you were staying in the room.'

Her words were laden, her tone even more so.

'I was, but then I heard all these voices. So nice to have company.' He rested his blurred gaze on Guy, his smile as slack as the limbs that barely supported him. 'Good to meet you. Matthieu Bachasson de Montalivet at your service.'

He attempted a flourish as he bowed, tipping off balance so that Albert once more reached out to grab him.

Charlotte rolled her eyes. 'For God's sake, Matthieu. Go and lie down.'

Guy was studying him with one eyebrow raised, that half-smile tugging at the corners of his mouth. Except it wasn't a smile of amusement. It was one I'd never seen before in all the years I'd known him, devoid of any mirth. 'Guy Larose,' he said. 'It's good to meet you too.'

Matthieu did a double take that was almost comic in effect. He pointed from Guy to Charlotte, a chuckle rising from his throat that swiftly turned into a cackle. 'This is him?' he managed to choke out. 'Well, this is a surprise, my darling, isn't it?'

Charlotte stalked off without another word, Guy's eyes following her. A couple more children bustled past us into the kitchen, calling out their apologies to Cook. I caught a glimpse of Alice through the door, looking like an apparition in the dim light. For half a second, I thought it was Hélène, so confused was I by all that had gone on. Stupid. Of course it wasn't Hélène; she was dead. It was the shadows playing tricks on me, that was all. Those and the memories that lingered under the surface, stirred up by Guy's presence.

I could feel him now, staring in the same direction. I turned back to see the crease between his brows as he, too, seemed to be wrestling with a memory. Then he shook his head, looking so utterly lost that my heart ached for him. I wanted so much to ask him about Charlotte, to hear that story. Because there definitely was a story behind the look on his face when he'd seen her. But this wasn't the time. I wondered why and what ghosts she'd stirred up too. So many ghosts, some of them scarcely in their graves.

But it was the living we had to think about now, especially the children who darted up and down the corridors, laughing in spite of everything. The same children we had to send on a perilous journey out of here and on a boat to freedom. If we still could.

# THIRTY

I stared up at the ceiling, watching the shadows chase across it, forming and reforming into faces I knew. Outside, the wind howled, tossing the trees so that they, too, cast their long fingers into my room, their silhouettes a whirl of outrage. Or perhaps that was me.

I couldn't get Charlotte's voice out of my head. The contempt in it. The spite. And that undertone that told me there was so much more I didn't know. All of it churning around in my mind along with the ever-present voice that whispered at me in the dark, telling me that it would all go wrong, that there would never be an end to this war or the lives it destroyed. Never mind mine – what of all the others here?

Not just the airmen we had to get out of the country, but the innocent children caught up in something they barely understood. The children François and Eliane were capturing for posterity. Then there were people like Walther and Paul, on the run from people who hated them simply because of their race or their beliefs. So much hatred. Ringing in my mind was one question: why?

It was no good – I would have to get up. I couldn't lie here another minute itching to do something, anything to make it all stop.

I threw on the light-blue silk robe Eliane had given me and crept down the stairs to the kitchen, intending to make myself a cup of tea. Such an English solution to everything, tea. My Spanish mother preferred hot chocolate and, truth be told, so did I, but that would have been an inconceivable luxury right now. I set a pan on the stove to boil and reached for the packet Eliane had secreted behind an empty biscuit tin. The revolting chicory substitute for coffee had become our daily drink, but that little packet of tea was there for those in need. I reckoned I qualified as one tonight.

My mother's words about watched water never boiling popped into my mind while I stood there, doing just that. Above the faint hiss as it began to simmer, I thought I heard another sound, one that appeared to come from the salon. I held my breath, reaching for one of the knives on the counter. It was two o'clock in the morning, a time when everyone should be in their beds, however makeshift, although it could just be someone like me, unable to sleep. Even so, I tiptoed towards the salon, holding the knife down by my side.

The door was ajar. I pushed it as gently as I could, but it still creaked. I heard a tiny cough, almost an intake of breath, and whipped around the door, knife raised.

Walther was sitting by the embers of the fire, stirring them with the poker. He coughed again, into his hand, and glanced up, smiling when he saw it was me. Instantly, I dropped the knife to my side, feeling foolish.

'Come and sit,' he offered, gesturing to the armchair opposite him.

'I'm just making tea. Would you like some?'

His smile broadened. 'You sound like my wife. I would love some tea, thank you.'

By the time I returned with two cups, the knife safely back

in its place, he'd stoked the fire and added a couple of logs so that it roared, obliterating the shadows that had writhed across the ceiling and in my heart.

I looked at Walther as he sipped from the cup I'd given him. 'Your wife likes tea?'

'She did.'

I could have kicked myself for the way his eyelids drooped as he hunched over, staring now into the cup.

'I'm so sorry,' I said. 'That was tactless of me.'

He looked up, his eyes once more brimming with life. With memories. 'Not at all. I like to talk about her. It's my way of keeping her alive. She was a lot like you, you know. Strong when she had to be, but underneath... well, my Rosa, she was so kind. She would give you the dress she was wearing if she thought you needed it. And stuff you with as much food as she could get you to eat. I'm so thankful she never had to see all this. People here starving. The Germans growing fat on the food they steal from them. The killings. Families ripped apart. And for what? To fulfil the desires of a madman who destroys everything in his path.'

He shook his head, more in sorrow than anger.

'She died before the war started?'

'Before the Germans took Paris, thank God. She'd been suffering with these stomach pains for months. Wouldn't listen to me when I told her to go and see the doctor. She said it was indigestion. Of course, by the time she did see the doctor, it was too late. But you know what, in a way I'm glad. It was better she went before they started to treat us as they had in Berlin. That was why we left, you see, in 1934. It was impossible to stay.'

That explained the German accent, although there were so many now like Walther it hardly surprised me anymore. People fleeing their homelands from across Europe, only to find the Nazis were on their heels. Now they were here, across the

Vichy line in the south, and our lives would only get harder. For some, like Walther, it could be a death sentence.

I leaned forward, poking at the fire so that sparks flew from a log. 'How did you and Rosa meet?'

His smiled broadened, his eyes again taking on a faraway look. 'At rehearsal. I walked in on my first day with the orchestra and there she was, this beautiful violinist. I kept looking at her rather than the conductor. They almost threw me out there and then.'

He laughed, a rich chortle that echoed across the years. I could imagine him laughing as he strolled with her through the streets of Berlin, young and carefree. 'How long before you two got together?'

Another chuckle. 'Oh, a very long time. She led me a merry dance, Rosa. She came from a good family, you see, while I was what you might call respectable but poor. My father was a tailor and my mother a seamstress. I got a scholarship to study music at the academy and practised on the piano there as we didn't have one at home. Her mother wasn't at all impressed.'

'It sounds to me as if you worked very hard to succeed so, frankly, her mother was a fool.'

He wagged his finger at me. 'She was no fool. I worked hard, yes, but I played hard too. With Paul, at times, when we were both students. We go back a long way. Still, Rosa saw something in me I suppose. In any case, she eventually agreed to have a coffee with me, and one thing led to another. The entire orchestra played at our wedding. Her mother's idea of course.'

The naughty twinkle in his eye didn't belie the sadness in his voice. I touched his arm. 'Memories can be so bittersweet.'

He stared into the fire. 'They certainly can.'

We sipped our tea in companionable silence until he broke his reverie with another of his glorious smiles. No wonder Rosa gave in – I would have too.

'But what about you?' he asked. 'How did you come to be here?'

I laughed. 'Good question. I can only say that London saw some use for me here because I grew up in Marseille. It made sense that I would help in an area I know like the back of my hand. Plus, I speak the language like a native even though I'm not actually French.'

'You're not?'

'My father is English, my mother Spanish. He was a businessman based in Marseille. They're both in England now, safe, although they worry about me all the time. I can't receive letters from them, but the odd message gets through.'

'You can't? Why not?'

'It would compromise my safety and that of the operation. There are so many lives at stake here, Walther. Including yours.'

He met my gaze. 'I don't care if I live or die. My life ended with Rosa. But our children, they care. It's for them that I carry on.'

'Where are they now?'

'In the United States. My son emigrated there in 1937 and my daughter the year after with her husband. They're musicians too, my son in Chicago and my daughter in New York. She has a baby now.'

The pride in his voice only matched the heartbreak. 'Is that where you want to go? To the United States?'

'They're all I have left, and I'm longing to see my granddaughter. I've only seen one picture of her. She looks like my Rosa.'

'Who's Rosa?'

We both looked to the doorway, where Alice stood in her nightgown, clutching a teddy bear to her chest. She looked younger and more vulnerable than I'd ever seen her, her hair falling, tousled, around her bleary face.

'Alice, what are you doing down here at this hour? Can't you sleep?'

She shook her head, and I thought I detected a quiver in her normally resolute chin.

'Come,' I said, patting the armchair beside me. 'Sit with us.'

She scampered over and climbed onto it, curling her feet under her, the teddy still clutched tight. 'I had a dream,' she whispered.

'A bad one?' asked Walther.

I could imagine him with his granddaughter. He exuded gentle concern.

'Yes.'

'Well, it's gone now. You see, that's the thing with bad dreams. They're not real. They disappear as soon as you open your eyes. My Rosa used to say that. She was my wife.'

Alice blinked. 'Your wife. Oh, I see. May I stay with you a while?'

'Of course.'

We sat there, watching the flames, again in that companionable silence, until I tapped Walther on the arm. Alice was fast asleep in her armchair, her head pillowed on her teddy bear.

'You're so good with children. We must get you out of here and on your way as soon as we can so that you can see yours. Hopefully on the next boat.'

He gave me another smile, this one of infinite resignation. 'I've learned not to make plans. It's better that way. Man plans and God laughs – isn't that what they say?'

The fire spat, its pop and crackle sounding like a gunshot in the silence. I could feel my heart twisting even as I spoke. 'Trust me, we'll get you on that boat. You'll be seeing your granddaughter before you know it.'

Words I would remember. Words I would live to regret.

# THIRTY-ONE

## 24 DECEMBER 1942, CHATEAU BLEU, SOUTHERN FRANCE

The men hauled in the Christmas tree they'd cut down and set it upright in the salon while the children gathered round, squealing in delight, clutching their home-made decorations. I could see Alice among them, her face flushed with excitement. As one of the tallest, she was carefully placing paper chains and painted pine cones on the highest branches, arranging them with her usual artistry, smiling and chatting all the while.

Walther walked over to the piano and opened it, perching on the creaking stool as he ran his fingers up and down the keys. A few more notes and then a familiar tune began to rise from the yellowed ivories. 'Silent Night' – the sound of Christmas. Drawn by the music, people began to gather around the piano, voices lifted in song, the airmen standing proud, thinking no doubt of home.

I glanced to my left and saw Guy singing in his fine baritone, his face glowing with something more than the candlelight. An inner fire. The same one that had been lit within everyone's hearts thanks to the music, the words we'd known and loved in better times filling us up once more. Walther segued from one carol to another until, finally, the music died away, and he took a little bow to wild applause.

I saw Eliane slip into the room and hand Guy a piece of paper. He read it, his brows drawing together, then moved to my side. 'A word?'

'Of course.'

I followed him to the library where Sefton and Albert were deep in conversation by the fireplace, heads bent so close they were almost touching. They looked up as we entered, both their faces wearing such grave expressions that my heart skipped a beat.

I turned to Guy. 'What's happened?'

'We received a message from one of our helpers in Lyon,' he said. 'It's Lionel. He's turned up at a safe house there, badly injured.'

'What are you going to do?'

'I'm heading to Lyon tonight,' said Guy. 'I'm taking Albert with me. At the very least, we have to get Lionel back here so he can get the medical attention he needs. It's too dangerous there.'

'But it's Christmas Eve,' I blurted.

Guy shrugged. 'War doesn't stop for Christmas.'

'I know. Stupid of me. I'm so sorry. I know Lionel is your friend.'

'I consider all my men friends,' he said with a nod to Sefton. 'At least we got you out, although God knows where Hammond is. You're all brave men. The best of the best.'

Guy's voice was bleak, his face etched with worry. He was their leader. He'd sent them all into this.

'We all knew what we were getting into, sir,' said Sefton. 'And we'd do it all over again.'

'I know. But it doesn't make me feel any better.'

It was the price of leadership. I felt responsible for every single man and woman lost under my command, and I was sure Guy felt the same.

I touched his arm. 'I'll carry on running things from here. We have a boat leaving in a few days. We need to get as many people on it as possible.'

Guy nodded gratefully. 'Sefton can stay and give you a hand. The news from Marseille isn't good either. From what George says, the Gestapo are stepping up their efforts.'

'Apparently, the Gestapo have a new man arriving from Paris,' added Albert. 'Name of Otto Drexler. From what we hear, he's even more of an animal than most. His job is to crush the Resistance, just like Klaus Barbie, who he very much admires. Marseille is all but finished for us.'

Drexler. The name rang a bell. Then I remembered – the man who'd led the raid on the orphanage, and the child, Robert, that we had to find before he did. I glanced at Guy, who almost imperceptibly shook his head. Another of the many secrets in this war. All of them necessary to keep someone like this little boy safe.

In the momentary silence, I could hear the fire crackling and hissing as it ate up the logs, consuming them just as the Nazis destroyed the lives of millions. It only made me burn all the more to stop them and to get as many to freedom as I possibly could. Marseille might be finished, but we weren't, not while there was still breath in my body.

'When do you leave?' I asked.

Guy glanced at Albert. 'In a couple of hours, as soon as it begins to get dark. We'll take the back roads and try to get to Lyon before sunrise. With any luck, the Germans will just have a skeleton presence on the roads on Christmas Day.'

'Fingers crossed.'

It would take a whole lot more than that, as we all knew. The risks grew bigger by the day now that the Nazis were here in the south too.

Guy strode over to the small bureau which housed a couple of bottles of cognac. He poured the amber liquid into the glasses provided then handed them round. 'A toast. Godspeed and good luck to all of us. And Merry Christmas.'

I gulped down my cognac. It scorched the back of my throat, a river of fire that rippled down to my stomach and set it alight with renewed courage. Out the corner of my eye, I could see Guy staring now into the flames, swilling his cognac around in its glass, which glowed a deep orange in the firelight.

I touched my glass to his. '*Pour les absents.*'

For absent friends.

His gaze caught mine and held it as he solemnly repeated the words, the flames dancing in his eyes, setting them aglow too. I hoped he could take that fire with him, that it would keep him going on the arduous journey ahead. I didn't think I could bear to lose him as well. Not now that he was here, a part of me in the way that Hélène had been, the memories of childhood wrapped up in every smile and glance, in the way he spoke. In every breath he took.

I stepped back abruptly, suddenly aware I was teetering on the edge of the absurd. The past was just that. Gone. As dead as Hélène in her watery grave. I could no more conjure her back than I could those carefree days on the beaches here. The same beaches that were now the door to freedom for the people in this house as well as those trapped in safe houses further up the line, unable to get here until we repaired the escape route. Despite rescuing Sefton, that felt further away than ever. There were so many people to help and so few of us. We needed to get more helpers on board and more hands on deck but, right now, that seemed as likely as bringing Hélène back.

'I'd better go and help the children with their tree,' I said. 'Some of them are leaving on the next boat, and I want them to have something good to remember.'

Guy carried on looking at me from under his lashes, the same damn lashes Hélène and I had envied so much. It wasn't fair that a boy should be blessed with eyelashes like that while we girls had to make do with the ordinary kind.

'You do that,' he murmured, his eyes raking my face. 'I'll have this to remember.'

I could feel the heat rising in my cheeks as I bade the men farewell and hurried from the room, desperate to hide the tears that were turning my eyes pink even as I tried to hold them back.

Outside the salon, I was so blinded I almost bumped straight into Alice, who looked at me and asked, 'What's wrong? Why are you crying?'

'I'm not crying. It's just the smoke from the fire.'

I dashed my arm across my eyes, aware she was still staring at me, obviously not believing a word.

I heard the library door open and shut along the corridor and then footsteps receding – Guy and Albert no doubt off to make their preparations. I wanted to run after them, to beg them to stay, to send someone else. To do anything but head into the danger that awaited them. Instead, I smiled as brightly as I could.

'Why don't you show me this tree?' I said. 'I can't wait to see what you've done with it.'

Alice didn't look at all convinced. 'Alright. But you have to close your eyes.'

I obeyed, feeling her slim hand wrap around mine, tugging me forward. All at once I was back there, with Hélène, on another Christmas Eve as she led me forward to find the gifts she'd placed for me by the fire while Guy watched from an armchair, the flames setting his eyes alight just as they had a few minutes ago. Eyes I might never see again, just as I would never see Hélène's.

When I opened my own eyes, I was unashamedly weeping.

# THIRTY-TWO

Eliane found me in the kitchen, making up packs of supplies for Guy and Albert. She took one look at my face and began to pull packets from the pantry and shelves, adding them to the neat parcels of dried meat and cheese I'd wrapped in waxed paper and string.

'Captain Grant told me you grew up in Marseille,' she said, handing me a saucisson to add to the selection.

'I did.'

'But you went to live in England?'

'After school here and in Spain, my father thought it would be a good idea if I learned about business. He's a very forward-thinking man, and he wanted me to take over our family firm one day, so he sent me to work for a friend of his in London. Now our business in Marseille is no more and our home gone, but I like to think I still belong here anyway.'

'Of course you do. I feel like I do too now I've been living here for so long. We foreigners need to stick together.'

She had such an infectious spirit to match the smile that never faltered. I'd liked Eliane on sight, and that feeling hadn't changed. 'How long have you been here exactly?'

'In France? Eleven years, ever since I came here to study and then met François. But that was in Paris, where we were living until the Germans arrived. We came south shortly after.'

She made it sound as if they'd merely set out on a day trip, but I knew it couldn't have been easy. 'You managed to escape then?'

Her dark ringlets danced as she nodded. I couldn't imagine Eliane in Paris. She was so elemental, as wild in her way as the tangled branches and untamed lawns that surrounded this place and yet as gentle as the deer that roamed the land. 'We made two bicycles and used those. The Germans were already seizing cars, you see. We knew we wouldn't make it otherwise, especially as the Nazis hate artists like François. He was already on some list those evil swine had for his work. Our work.'

'You made bicycles?'

'We did. Out of anything we could find. François thinks like that. He's an inventor as well as an artist. The Nazis consider our work seditious.'

The few times I'd glimpsed François, he appeared lost in thought, his mind focused entirely on his subjects as he sketched, now and then stopping to exchange a smile or a kind word. 'They think your art is seditious?'

'Not so much our art as our books. We create them together. We share everything – the words and the illustrations. I discovered that I prefer to write than paint or draw. That's why François has the studio now while I work in my office. Though there's not much time for that these days.'

She carried on packing the food parcels into the two knapsacks I'd laid ready as she spoke. There wasn't a trace of resentment in her voice; Eliane obviously saw this as her duty too. I could feel myself warming to her more and more. 'I'd love to see them some time. Your books.'

'They're only little things really.'

Somehow, I doubted that. She didn't strike me as a woman

who did anything on a small scale. This house, for instance, sprawling as it did, was pure Eliane, as eccentric and yet welcoming as she and her husband, a haven for so many lost souls right now.

I could hear Guy's voice outside the kitchen door, Albert's rumbling in response. As I glanced towards the sound, I caught Eliane's eye.

'You like him, don't you?' she said.

'Who?'

'Oh, come on. The handsome Canadian.'

Handsome? I suppose he was. 'Actually, he's originally French. He grew up here too, with me. His younger sister was my best friend.'

She must have heard the catch in my voice because her eyes softened. 'Was?'

'Yes. She was killed seven months ago when her ship was torpedoed by a U-boat. I didn't know until Guy told me after he landed here. I was part of the reception committee that met him and his men.'

'How awful for you. That must have come as a terrible blow.'

I blinked. 'It did. We hadn't seen each other for a while, not since their family emigrated. But we wrote, and I always thought of her as my best friend in the way you do when you've shared everything. She'd even asked me to be her bridesmaid.'

Eliane threw me a shrewd glance. 'And her brother? Were you close to him as well?'

'Good heavens, no. He was just her big brother, you know. Annoying.'

'I had no idea I was such a pain in the ass,' said Guy as he came through the kitchen door, Albert right behind him.

'You were, believe me.' I smiled shakily at him.

'Are these for us?' He picked up the knapsacks and handed one to Albert. 'Thank you, ladies. And now we'll be off.'

I felt a gentle shove in my back. 'Elisabeth, see them out. Good luck, boys. May God go with you.'

As Guy opened the heavy front door, another voice sliced, acid sharp, through the air. 'Leaving so soon?'

Charlotte was leaning against the salon door, arms folded, a peculiar gleam in her eye.

Guy ignored her, shouldering his knapsack, while Albert made for the outbuilding where the cars were hidden. 'I'll see you soon,' he murmured, brushing my cheek with the back of his hand. It was the lightest of caresses, but it reverberated deep.

'I hope so.'

We both knew that could turn out to be a lie. Better, though, to lie in hope rather than give in to fear.

I watched him walk down the steps, saw Albert drive round, half raised my hand to wave and then dropped it again. What was the point?

'*Pauvre petite*,' someone murmured. I turned to see Charlotte staring back at me, her eyes hard as glass. 'You poor little thing.'

I stalked past her. 'I have no idea what you mean.'

Her laugh rang hollow in my ears all the way along the corridor. 'Oh, but I think you do.'

# THIRTY-THREE

## 28 DECEMBER 1942, CANET-PLAGE, SOUTHERN FRANCE

Three days after Christmas, we were standing once more on the sand, spume-tipped waves roaring towards the shore, foaming with the beginnings of a storm. Walther and Paul stood just to my left, each holding a single brown leather suitcase, while the others were clustered around, parents clutching their children's hands. The airmen waited to one side. Twenty-seven people. That was all we could manage on this trip. Even so, I wondered if anyone would make it off this beach. The felucca was scarcely visible through the lashing rain, the children's eyes wide with fear as they stared across the sea.

No matter how much their mothers murmured reassurance, one or two whimpered in terror, while the rest stayed stoically silent in the face of their fate. I held my breath as the small boat began to make its way towards it, two pinpricks of light appearing and disappearing as it was almost consumed by the waves.

'This is madness,' I hissed. 'They'll never make it.'

'They have no choice,' muttered Sefton. 'This could be the last boat out.'

Janek was standing at the ready, water pouring over the tops of his galoshes, staggering now and then as a wave threatened to knock him off his feet. A couple of his men grabbed for the dinghy as it finally made it to shore, hauling at the rope with all their strength. My job was to help carry the children one by one and deposit them safely on board while the men did the same with the women. I gripped tight to one cherub as I battled through the waves, holding him as high as I could while he struggled and shrieked for his mama, who was already aboard.

'Hush now. Mama's there. See? There you go, sweetheart.'

He was having none of it, squirming as hard as he could until I finally managed to place him in her arms and go back for the next one. Women and children first, that was the rule, and the airmen were helping us get them in the boats as best they could. The trouble was that there were so many of them now, and time was running out. Sefton was right – this might be the last shipment, provided we even got away with this one. The Germans were patrolling these waters with increased frequency, looking for fishing boats just like this along with the larger ships that carried our precious cargo to Gibraltar and further afield. Any day now they might close off the passage completely, and then we would have to find another way. There was always another way. At least, that's what I told myself.

The boat was back. More little ones to lug through the water, chatting as brightly as I could to try to keep them calm. Walther and Paul clambering in once all the women and children were settled along with the remaining men. The boat was already taking them out of reach as the currents tugged it out to sea, so I blew them a kiss. They waved as the boat headed towards the felucca, dipping so low at times that it disappeared completely from view, overloaded as it was with the people we'd crammed on board. Each time, I held my breath, only letting it out when I caught sight of the bow once more, the heads of those aboard crowded together.

'OK. Let's go.' Janek signalled to his men to retreat up the

beach, where we all stopped again, scanning the horizon, trying
to spot the ship which had been deployed to meet the felucca.

'There she is.'

I looked where Sefton was pointing, peering through the
unrelenting rain. Just when I was able to make out the blurred
hulk of its hull and the smaller fishing boat chugging towards it,
there was an almighty flash followed swiftly by another.

'Oh my God, no. No!'

I was already running, uselessly, towards the shoreline,
watching the sky explode in flashes so bright they seared my
eyeballs, lighting up the horror that was happening right in
front of us all. The Germans were firing at the felucca, though
from where I had no idea. And then, as I made out the sleek
vessel streaking towards the others, I knew. An E-boat, a
German speedboat, unleashing its torpedoes on the felucca,
which didn't stand a chance. As the flames started shooting
from its deck, I sank to the wet sand, moaning.

The children. Their parents. Walther and Paul. Those
young airmen with their swagger and cheek. All of them being
consumed by the fire that was ripping the boat apart, its decks
already starting to sink beneath the storm-tossed waters,
smashed to pieces by Nazi rockets.

A final lurch and she was gone, the sea swallowing her up
along with all the souls on board. Souls we'd put aboard that
boat – the tiny children I'd carried to their deaths.

Above the roar of the wind and the sea, I heard another
sound. It took me a moment to realise those howls were mine,
torn straight from my heart.

# THIRTY-FOUR

I dreamed of them that night. All of them. That young airman, Richard Greenwood, who would never see his girl again. The children, their faces bright with excitement at Christmas, staring at the tree as if it was a thing of wonder, adorned with the decorations they'd helped to make. I could hear their voices too, raised in song, as we carolled by firelight, Walther wringing some life out of the old piano, Guy's face alight, his eyes reaching for mine and holding them as if he would never let go.

Tearing through the sound of their singing, their screams as one scene gave way to another, waves roiling now, firelight morphing into the flames engulfing the boat, the deck breaking up, all their faces submerged under the freezing water, sinking down, down just as Hélène must have done. She was there as well, holding out her arms, beseeching. The children, too, scrabbling, trying to swim, to reach me as I was trying to reach them. Except I couldn't, hard as I tried. The more I kicked out and tried to swim, the harder the waves pushed me back.

All I could do was stare helplessly across the water, tears streaming down my face, my own mouth open in a silent scream as they were all torn away from me by the relentless sea, disappearing down into the depths from which they would never return. It was the same scream that woke me, only it wasn't silent. It brought Eliane running into my room; the one she shared with her husband was only doors from mine.

'What is it? What's happened?'

I screwed up my eyes against the torch in her hand, which she was shining around the room now, searching for an intruder.

'I'm alright. Really. I was dreaming – that's all.'

I tried to sit up, but my legs felt like lead. I was sobbing and gasping for breath, still half back there, in that water, seeing them all drowning before my eyes.

Satisfied there was no one else in the room, Eliane opened the door and murmured to someone outside it before sitting beside me and switching on the bedside light. 'I told François to go back to bed. We were terrified they'd somehow found you. The Gestapo. Stupid, I know. As if they could track you down here.'

She was gabbling, talking as much to reassure herself as me.

I could feel the terror receding. It was just a dream after all. Just a dream. 'I'm so sorry,' I said. 'The nightmare... it felt so real. I must have been screaming in my sleep.'

Eliane looked at me more closely. 'It doesn't surprise me after what happened at the beach. Those poor children.'

I heard the catch in her voice. She, after all, had known them as well as I had, perhaps better as she doted on each and every one of them. Eliane and François had no children of their own, but they made up for it by lavishing love on everyone they met.

'It was,' I whispered. 'I can still feel them, you know. The weight of them in my arms. Them clinging to me. Handing them over to their mothers. To their deaths. Oh God, Eliane. We should have tried some other way. We knew the Germans were patrolling those waters. It was too much of a risk. But we still took it. And now they're dead, all of them.'

The sob tore from my throat, and I sank my face into my hands. I could feel her hand between my shoulder blades, soothing and warm. As warm as their little bodies had been against my chest.

'Come now,' she murmured. 'It wasn't your fault, Elisabeth. You had to do it. You needed to get them out of France the best way you could. You couldn't have sent little children like that over the Pyrenees, never mind old men like Walther and Paul. They'd have perished before they reached the border. If the Germans had caught them, they'd have sent them to the camps. Don't blame yourself. Blame those bastards. They're the reason people are running for their lives, leaving everything and everyone they've ever known. We can't stop now. There will be more tragedies. There will also be more triumphs, and every person you save can be chalked up as one of those.'

Her words filtered through the miasma of despair, touching a chord deep within me. It was why I did this after all. To save lives when so many had already been lost.

I raised my head. 'Thank you,' I muttered, taking the hand-kerchief she was holding out to me and blowing my nose.

Another image came back to me – Guy's face seconds before the scene changed, changing also, disintegrating as if he'd been dead for days, his eyes sinking into their sockets, lifeless and sightless. Was it an omen? I had no idea.

'I'll try and sleep now,' I said. 'Thank you. For everything.'

Eliane stayed where she was a moment longer, studying me with an intent expression I'd never seen before. 'It is we who should thank you. You risk your life every day simply by being here. Five million francs is a lot of money, Elisabeth, especially to people who are starving. Someone might literally sell you out for a loaf of bread, and yet you keep going.'

'It's what you said. We can't stop now. *I* can't stop. For those children. For all those people. We can't let the bastards win.'

She rose then, smiling as she tucked the blankets around

me. 'We won't. Now get some sleep, darling girl. Tomorrow is another day and all that.'

She slipped out the door, blowing a kiss as she went. Yes, tomorrow was another day. And the day after that. On and on. When would it ever end?

When the last person was saved. When we found that little boy, Robert, and saved him too. He was more important to me than ever now, a symbol of all the ones we'd lost. Reparation, maybe, for those other children, at least on my part. The Nazis had no remorse. They were merciless in their pursuit of those they considered their enemy. Top of that list, it seemed, me. Well, let them do their worst. I'd find him. *We'd* find him – me and Guy.

We'd save that child, whatever it took.

# THIRTY-FIVE

## 3 JANUARY 1943, CHATEAU BLEU, SOUTHERN FRANCE

Eliane burst into the salon where I was doing a jigsaw with Alice, the picture of Montparnasse almost complete. 'Here they come!'

I gaped at her. 'Who?'

She tutted and grabbed me by the hand, pulling me to my feet. 'Come see.'

In true Eliane fashion, she flung open the front door and half dragged me down the steps, pointing along the drive as we reached the bottom. 'There.'

I could make out a car winding its way up to the house. As it drew closer, I recognised the battered Citroën Guy and Albert had driven off in over a week before. By the time the car swept to a halt in front of us, my heart had accelerated to such a pace I could scarcely breathe. They were back. *He* was back. Alive. Although I wasn't sure at first if the man Guy carried from the vehicle was as well.

He was wrapped in blankets, cradled in Guy's arms as if he was a baby. I held the door open so he could pass through while Eliane ran ahead to summon help.

'How is he?' I murmured, catching a glimpse of Lionel's

face. It was deathly pale, his eyes closed, his lips cracked and blue.

Guy's eyes met mine. 'He's lost a lot of blood. A doctor there managed to stabilise him enough for the journey, but it's taken it out of him. We need to get another doctor here pronto.'

'I'll call Dr George,' said Eliane. 'Take him upstairs to your old room. I'll send Cook to light the fire and bring hot soup.'

'Are you sure that's wise – calling Dr George?' I asked as Albert and Guy moved towards the stairs.

'There's no one else we can trust.'

'Why don't I go and get him to make sure he's not followed? The pharmacist will help. I can use his van to pick up Dr George and then change vehicles there.'

Albert and Guy both looked so weary, their faces pinched with exhaustion and cold. They'd driven hundreds of kilometres on rough back roads, constantly on alert for German patrols. The least I could do was go and fetch Dr George.

Eliane shook her head. 'It's too dangerous for you, Elisabeth. They know what you look like.'

'Rubbish. I'm the Little Fox, remember? Besides, the Gestapo are far less likely to suspect a woman delivering medical supplies. I'll be in and out before they know it.'

I glanced up the stairs. Guy and Albert were busy with Lionel. Sefton was out with François, chopping down trees for firewood. I'd be gone before they knew it. Before they could stop me.

I shot into the kitchen, where Cook was busy kneading the bread she made twice a day. We didn't dare risk buying the vast quantities we needed to feed the amount of people who passed through the house.

'Madame, we have an injured man. They've taken him up to the green bedroom. We need to light the fire in there and give him and the two who brought him hot soup.'

She instantly shoved her dough to one side and moved to the sink. 'Leave it with me.'

'There's one more thing, madame. May I borrow your beret, coat and spectacles?'

She hesitated for no more than a split second before unhooking her coat and hat from the back door and handing them to me along with the glasses she removed from her nose. 'Of course. Take whatever you need.'

'Thank you. I'll bring them back, I promise. I should be a couple of hours. Maybe three.'

'Wherever you're going, my dear, may God go with you.'

Concern was written across her kindly face. I gave her what I hoped was a reassuring smile as I pulled on her beret and coat, tucking the spectacles in the pocket. 'Thank you. See you soon.'

With that, I was slipping out the back door and round to the garage. By the time they noticed I was gone, it would be too late to stop me.

Even so, I let the van coast down the drive before I turned the key in the ignition, hearing the engine roar as I pressed on the accelerator. I glanced in the mirror, tugging the beret down so that it concealed my hair, sitting low on my forehead. Along with the scarf wrapped around my throat and Cook's shapeless woollen coat, it served as an adequate disguise. On the surface.

A keen-eyed Gestapo officer would see through it in seconds, but that was all I needed. Along with a whole lot more luck to get past them and to get Dr George out unseen. The rest I would figure out as I went along. It was a tactic that hadn't failed me yet. And it wasn't going to fail me now. I'd make damn sure of that.

# THIRTY-SIX

I pulled up in the same spot Albert had used, remembering the pharmacy on the corner located not too far from the Vieux Port and Dr George's apartment. The pharmacist was serving someone as I entered, so I pretended to study the shelves of cosmetics until, at last, the woman departed, satisfied that she had every remedy under the sun for her dyspepsia.

'I'll take this,' I said as I placed a powder compact on the counter. 'I'm a friend of Albert's. He sends his regards and says to watch out for the girl in the blue beret.'

It was the standard command we gave all the evaders passing through the railway station here. Once or twice, I'd even been the girl in the blue beret, although more often it was one of the young *résistantes* who performed that task. The pharmacist peered at me more closely. I had to admit, I was quite a sight in the cook's beret and coat, her glasses perched on my nose.

'You'd better come through,' he said, opening the hatch in the counter so I could pass behind it and into the room behind while he scooted over to the door, locked it and pulled down the blind that said '*Fermé*'.

He gestured to one of the chairs that were set either side of a table on which his paperwork was spread, but I shook my head. 'No thank you. I'm afraid I don't have much time. I'm on my way to collect Dr George. One of our parcels is damaged, and we need his help.'

The pharmacist frowned. 'I see. That might prove rather difficult. Dr George—'

'Is under surveillance. Yes, I know. But I thought that if I could borrow your van, I might be able to get in to see him without arousing suspicion. There's a back exit from his apartment block. If I park at the front, my visit will appear legitimate, as if I'm making a delivery. When I go, I can cause a distraction so that gives him the opportunity to leave by the rear exit and meet me further along the road.'

He pressed his finger against his lips, thinking. 'It might just work. Although we need to do something about your disguise, if that's what it is. Wait here – I have some more cosmetics that should do the trick. I might also have something to cause that distraction.'

A few minutes later, I was gazing at myself in the tiny mirror the pharmacist was holding up, taking in the heavy foundation that made me look both older and pastier, the lines created by an eyebrow pencil adding to the effect. Instead of the beret, I now sported a proper white pharmacy hat with a wide brim and a white coat to match. My hair was scraped back in a tight bun, which, along with Cook's glasses, completed the look.

'Perfect,' I murmured.

'Here.' The pharmacist handed me a jar along with a small glass vial. 'This contains potassium chlorate and this one sugar. Add one drop of the potassium to the sugar and it will create a spectacular reaction.'

'What kind of reaction?'

'Instant white fire along with a lot of smoke.'

I tucked the jar and vial carefully into the pocket of the white coat. 'I add one drop and it works instantly?'

'Correct.' He then handed me a box full of paper packages. 'This is Dr George's regular order so everything appears entirely legitimate. You'll be doing me a service.'

'I hope I'll be doing us all a service.'

He inclined his head. 'Of course. Now, here are the keys. The van is parked around the corner. It's my wife who normally does the deliveries, so it won't look odd if a woman is seen driving the van, although it's best you try to get in and out as quickly as possible. I'll let you out the back door.'

He bustled me through a stock room piled high with boxes. I'd bet anything it wasn't just medications and the like they contained. I knew better, though, than to ask or say anything. An unshakeable rule of the Resistance as well as the escape lines was to keep a tight lip and an even tighter watch on those around you. Failing to do so cost lives, as we'd learned to our detriment.

'*Bonne chance,*' he muttered as he opened the back door and I slid through it, walking purposefully round the corner to his van without looking back.

I placed the box on the seat beside me and started the engine, easing off the brake as smoothly as I could and heading towards the port and Dr George's apartment. One thing you had to learn very quickly in my job was how to drive an unfamiliar vehicle without attracting attention. Luckily, most of these French vans were very similar, but it only took a false start or driving along jerkily for a German roadblock or patrol to pull you over and demand to see your papers as well as your permission to drive the vehicle.

I drove slowly along the street in front of George's apartment, straining my eyes for the slightest sign of anyone watching. The doorways were empty, as were the windows opposite as far as I could see. Still, I parked up carefully and busied myself getting the box out of the van, gruffly answering the concierge's greeting with a monosyllabic response before ascending to the apartment in the elevator, all the while wondering what exactly I would find.

Were they already in there, the Gestapo? It was one of their favourite entrapment methods after all. Make it seem as if everything was normal and then arrest anyone who came calling.

As I stood outside the door, ready to knock, I could feel my heart pounding; my knuckles rapping on the heavy wood sounded like an echo of it.

A moment. Then another. Should I knock again? Or run? Then, at last, the door opened, and Dr George stood there looking exactly as he always did, although a flicker of surprise crossed his face when he saw me.

'Your delivery, Doctor,' I said. 'Shall I bring it in?'

He must have heard the warning in my voice because he nodded at once. 'Yes, yes. Please, come in.'

He shut the door behind me and led me through into his consulting room, closing that door too.

I thrust the box at him. 'I'm sorry to burst in on you like this, but it's an emergency. We have a badly damaged parcel, and we urgently need your help.'

He didn't even flicker. 'Certainly. Where is this parcel?'

'At the chateau. I need to take you there. I have a van parked out front, but you need to leave by the back entrance to the building. Walk along to the next street but one, and I'll drive round and meet you there.'

He reached for his coat and his doctor's bag. 'Very wise. You know, of course, that they're watching me. Give me a few minutes to tell Fanny where I'm going, and I'll see you in the street. There's a bar there – the Bar du Port. I'll wait outside it.'

'Very good. I'll see you there.'

I passed the concierge on my way through the front hallway

and uttered the same grunt. Was she the one who'd sold Dr George out to the Gestapo? Maybe. Maybe not. There'd be time enough to deal with whoever it was later. For now, I needed to make sure all eyes were on me rather than on him.

I turned away from the concierge just by the front door and pulled the jar from my pocket, keeping my hands as steady as I could. I extracted the vial, unscrewed the lid of the sugar jar and added the one vital drop, pushing open the door with my elbow as I did so. Holding my breath, I let go of the jar, dropping it behind me so that it exploded in a white sheet of flame, sending smoke billowing into the air.

Almost at once, I heard a shout from across the street. So the Gestapo were there after all. And I'd flushed them out.

I clamped my hands over my mouth, screaming as I staggered towards the van. '*Au secours*! Help me!'

I was pointing towards the doorway now engulfed in flames, averting my face from the two men who pushed past me, the brief glimpse I caught of one sending an icy jolt through my heart. He had a narrow, ratlike face and the hard stare of a gangster. The kind of stare that brooked no mercy, seeking out its next target. I kept my head lowered as I babbled, 'In there. I saw him. A man. He must have had a bomb.'

The ratlike one kicked open the door, and they both burst through it into the building. I could hear the concierge shrieking for water as I leaped into the van and fired up the engine, roaring along the street and around the corner so I was out of sight. If they came looking, the pharmacist could claim ignorance. There was no insignia on the van to identify it – it was simply the van that visited two or three times a week. No doubt the pharmacist had plenty of sets of plates and a friend with a garage nearby who could give it a whole new look within hours.

I focused on finding Dr George, turning down the street he'd indicated, driving more slowly now, trying to act as normal as possible, my heart racing all the while.

There was no sign of him.

Oh God, had they got him? Where was he?

Then he stepped forward from under the awning where he'd been standing.

I slammed on the brakes and flung open the door. 'Hop in. We don't have much time.'

# THIRTY-SEVEN

Dr George emerged from Lionel's room, wiping his hands on the towel Eliane had given him. He looked tired but, as ever, raised a smile for all of us hovering outside. 'You can go in now.'

Guy hesitated, obviously bracing himself for bad news. I could see from the tender way he'd carried Lionel from the car how much he cared about his buddy. 'Will he make it, Doctor?'

Dr George regarded him with infinite compassion. He must have heard that question a thousand times and given the same answer a thousand times too. 'Time will tell. We'll know more in a few days.'

'A few days?' Guy's voice was harsh with anxiety. He checked himself. 'I'm sorry. I'm worried about him – that's all.'

'Of course you are. All I can say is that he needs to sleep and to heal. He has internal injuries consistent with sustaining a serious beating as well as the gunshot wound to his shoulder. Ironically, that's the most likely to heal well. It's the other injuries that could go either way.'

Such a fine line between life and death. One we all trod.

I took Dr George by the elbow. 'Come, Doctor. We have some coffee for you downstairs.'

As I led him away, I heard the bedroom door close behind us. Poor Guy. At least Hélène's death had happened far away. It was clear he and Lionel were as close in their way as Hélène and I had once been. Combat did that to you, forming unbreakable bonds in a matter of days, sometimes hours. No one was closer to you than the person who'd gone through hell at your side. I could only hope that this was a hell Lionel survived.

Downstairs in her study, Eliane had coffee waiting for Dr George, the real stuff and not the ghastly chicory substitute. God knows where she'd found it, but Eliane had her ways.

'Dr George, how good to see you!' she exclaimed, bestowing a kiss on each cheek. 'Here, sit down. Have some coffee. Albert, would you like some more?'

Albert was standing by the fire, a determined look on his face. He cleared his throat. 'George, we've all discussed this and you won't want to hear it, but it's foolhardy for you to return to your apartment.'

Dr George opened his mouth to protest, but Albert held up his hand. 'Please let me finish. We can get Fanny out, along with anything you might need, and inform your patients that you won't be available for a while. Today's events only prove that the Gestapo are keeping a close eye on you, and it's just a matter of time before they decide to descend.'

Before Dr George could say anything in response, the door flew open and Guy marched into the room, his face livid.

'Are you crazy?' he cried, rounding on me. 'Going there on your own and then pulling a stunt like that. You could have got everyone killed, along with yourself.'

I glanced at Albert, who shrugged.

'Thanks for nothing,' I snarled. I'd given him the briefest rundown when I'd returned with Dr George. He must have gone scurrying straight to Guy. So much for discretion.

'Don't blame Albert,' snapped Guy. 'He's as worried about you as I am.'

Eliane looked at us all, bewildered. 'Could someone please tell me what's going on here?'

'Elisabeth thought it would be a good idea to take the van and sneak off on her own to fetch Dr George. It seems she dropped in on our pharmacist friend, swapped vans with him and extracted a smoke bomb from him for good measure.'

'I didn't "extract" anything,' I snapped back. 'I needed to create a diversion so Dr George could get out of the building without anyone noticing. It was the pharmacist who suggested the smoke bomb, and believe me, it worked a treat.'

I realised Guy was staring at me and not in a good way.

'Was that your disguise?' he spluttered.

I raised a hand to my head, where the pharmacist's hat was still perched. I'd returned the van but, in my haste to get Dr George into mine, had completely forgotten about my outfit, never mind the make-up on my face. 'It was,' I replied. 'It certainly seemed to fool the Gestapo. They were far more interested in the smoke bomb than in me.'

'I repeat,' said Guy through gritted teeth, 'that you are certifiably nuts. If they'd recognised you, we wouldn't be having this conversation now. You'd be inside their fancy new building on Rue Paradis answering their questions. Trust me, it wouldn't be pleasant.'

A face flashed into my mind – one that was ratlike with cunning. 'But I'm not, am I? I got Dr George here to help your friend, and, what's more, I can describe the two men who ran into the building. One of them kicked the door down. They were Gestapo – I'm sure of it.'

Dr George took a gulp of his coffee then set down the cup, half-rising from his chair. 'Be that as it may, I would like to go home now. I must make sure that Fanny is alright and see to my patients.'

Albert flung his arms wide in exasperation. 'Didn't you hear a word we just said? The Gestapo are on to you, George. Elisabeth's little stunt may not have been the wisest, but it proved that they're watching the building and from not too far away. They don't need an excuse to arrest you both. They're already suspicious. They've probably only waited until now because they're hoping to catch some evaders along with you.'

Dr George drew himself up to his full height, eyeballing Albert. 'I repeat, I wish to go home now, and there's nothing you can do to stop me. I have work to do, just the same as you. I will return tomorrow to see to the patient.'

Guy sighed. 'And how are you going to do that without leading the Gestapo right here?'

'I can go and fetch him,' I said. 'From outside the bar, the same as we did today.'

'Absolutely not,' said Guy. 'Albert can go and get Dr George. You, Elisabeth, will remain here. It's bad enough that there are posters of you all over Marseille without you going into the city. Besides,' he added, his voice dropping ominously, 'I need you to come with me.'

# THIRTY-EIGHT

I folded my arms, wondering what the hell Guy was coming up with now. Whatever it was, I had a feeling I wasn't going to like it. 'What do you mean?'

'I have to go back up north,' he said. 'We still need to repair the line and get everyone moving along it again, as well as try to work out who's betraying us now, but I can't do that without my men. Right now, there's a bottleneck in a safe house south of Lyon. Albert and I had to leave them all stranded while we got Lionel out of there.'

'And you want me to come with you?'

'As you said, you're the best person for the job and, frankly, the only one who can do it. Albert will stay here, running the southern end, so we can pass our parcels on to him. You know the line and the towns and cities on it, although it's a shame we don't have Grant to guide us. In any case, you're safer away from here with all those damn posters everywhere.'

I had to admit he had a point. 'Alright. I'll do it. Grant gave me a couple of leads so we can start with those. There's a *comtesse* in Lyon who can apparently link us to the rest of the line, and the café owner at Avignon station is also part of it.'

Guy flashed me that triumphant grin I knew of old. He might have thought he'd won, but he'd soon learn that I wasn't a kid any longer. And I wasn't taking any crap from him.

'Excellent. We'll start with the *comtesse*, who I happen to know since we trained her in London. I also know that she's in Lyon right now with two parcels who need to be brought south. We leave first thing in the morning.'

I knew better than to ask him how he knew all that, let alone why he hadn't told me until now.

'What about Lionel?'

That shuttered look fell across Guy's face again. 'There's nothing I can do to help Lionel by staying. It's in the lap of the gods, as Dr George said. Our job is to save other lives, and that's what we're going to do.'

I could hear it, the rasp in his voice that spoke of immeasurable pain and loss. A loss even greater than mine. He was right. We had to focus on those we could try to save now and leave the rest to fate. Whatever that fate might be.

# THIRTY-NINE

## 4 JANUARY 1943, AIX-EN-PROVENCE, SOUTHERN FRANCE

The train for Lyon departed Aix-en-Provence at noon. We parked in a side street on the outskirts of the town and then walked to the station separately, each carrying a small suitcase, the outfit I'd cobbled together with Eliane's help respectable but by no means chic. My hair was newly dark blonde and set in curls so that it appeared shorter. High heels added a few extra inches to my height as well as once more altering my stride.

My story was that I was on my way to visit an ailing grandmother in Lyon, while Guy was to be a travelling salesman, his suitcase containing the agricultural samples that backed it up. As I stood on the platform, I made a conscious effort not to seek him out. We were two strangers, completely unconnected, as far as anyone else was concerned. And yet I could feel him there just as surely as if he was standing alongside me. It was comforting, in a way, to know that I wasn't alone.

The platform filled up as the train pulled into the station. There were entire squadrons of German troops as well as civilians like us, all crammed into carriages together. I found a seat in a compartment where a sweet-faced woman was knitting, a small child beside her.

'Is this taken?' I asked only to look up, aghast, when Guy entered the compartment and asked the very same question.

'No, my dear. Please sit.'

The woman smiled while I seethed, staring out the window so as to avoid looking at him. What the hell was he thinking? He could compromise both of us like this. Worse, two SS officers then entered and, without saying a word, took up the remaining seats opposite one another, stretching out their legs in a display of ownership that didn't pass unnoticed. The woman tutted under her breath but said nothing, while I continued to gaze out the window, hoping against hope that Guy would keep his mouth shut. A vain hope, as it turned out, but then I'd expect nothing less from a self-respecting Frenchman.

'Gentlemen, you appear to be squashing this young lady,' said Guy.

I turned from the window to see him indicating the little girl, who was now rammed up against her mother while the German officer spread himself out.

'She's fine,' muttered her mother. 'Come, *ma petite*, move up a little.'

The child shifted even closer into her mother's side, casting the German terrified looks, while he in turn sneered and pretended not to notice her discomfort.

'He's right, Franz,' said his companion. 'Give this young lady some room.'

I glanced at him, taking in his clean jawline and air of quiet authority. He was good-looking in a very Aryan way, big and blond with blue eyes. They'd probably promoted him for that alone. The SD diamond on his sleeve indicated he was Gestapo, as was the other smaller, darker one, who glared at him but pulled away from the child, tucking in his elbows and knees so that she had some space.

I flashed the blond one a smile then instantly regretted it. Now I'd drawn attention to myself in the stupidest way possible. Fortunately, he ignored me, staring instead at the book in his hand, but the damage was done. As we rose to leave the train, his companion blocked my path.

'What's your name?' he demanded.

I recited the name on my false papers. The one I'd practised a dozen times until it tripped off my tongue. 'Mireille. Mireille Mabillon.'

'What are you doing in Lyon, Madame Mabillon?'

He smirked as he gave me the once-over.

'She's having an assignation with me,' said Guy.

The German stared at him then burst out laughing. 'Bravo,' he said, patting Guy on the back. 'You're a lucky man.'

The woman with the little girl slid me a glance and moved along a fraction. I couldn't tell if she disapproved or was secretly envious, but at least the German's attention was diverted.

'I could kill you,' I muttered as we walked up the platform.

'I just saved your ass,' retorted Guy. 'That German was certainly interested in a piece of it.'

Only the presence of more Gestapo standing by the ticket collector stopped me from slapping his face. They were scrutinising everyone as we passed through, apparently looking for someone in particular. I clutched my suitcase all the tighter, hoping against hope it wasn't me as we shuffled closer, the line stretching back along the platform, although the German soldiers simply marched through. I could see the two from our carriage up ahead and immediately dropped back so I was walking alongside Guy.

'Pretend we're together,' I murmured as they clocked us, one nudging the other in the same shared joke. They might be laughing, but the Gestapo were no joke, and as we got closer, the hammering in my chest built to a crescendo, the echo of it in my ears drowning out everything save the one word I repeated over and over in my head: 'No, no, no, no.' No, not me. Not now. Not here. I sucked in a breath, trying to stay calm, to appear completely relaxed. These men were trained to look for signs of nervousness that might betray a *résistant* or an agent.

'Papers.'

I watched as the man two in front of us handed his over, noticing how his hand trembled. A tell. There was a muscle going in his cheek too. A pulse that the Gestapo officer in front of him must also have noticed because all at once there were more of them rushing forward, surrounding the man, marching him off in a matter of seconds. That was all it took. Seconds. Then the line moved up as if nothing had happened, and the woman directly in front of us passed over her papers before it was our turn.

Everything seemed to slow in that moment, the way the Gestapo officer's mouth moved, his eyes blinking just the once as he looked over first my papers and then Guy's, his mouth moving again, the words elongating.

'You are together?'

I tried a coy smile and nodded. He didn't look too convinced. Then came a burst of laughter from the other two German officers standing a few feet away, the smaller, darker one shouting out something vulgar, the Gestapo man nodding, unsmiling, flicking his hand to indicate we could pass. Moments later, we were out of the station, my heartbeat slowing to its normal rate as we crossed over and turned right, deliberately taking a circuitous route through the city streets until we were sure we weren't being followed.

'In here,' I muttered, entering the kind of backstreet café that was still a preserve of the locals rather than the occupying Germans. 'Order a coffee and drink it before you leave. I'm going out the back way. Wait five minutes and then you go too. I'll meet you at the address you gave me. It's safer if we split up. You have the map I drew for you? The traboules are marked on it. Destroy it if there's the slightest possibility the Germans will get hold of it.'

I knew the city like the back of my hand, including the traboules – or secret passages. Guy, though, would have to rely on that map tucked into his hatband. I knew he'd memorised it as far as he could, but Lyon was a labyrinth to anyone unfamiliar with its winding streets and hidden alleyways.

'I do. You have a kiss goodbye for me? Just in case anyone's watching?'

I leaned in to kiss first one cheek and then the other, murmuring in his ear, 'Be careful.'

'Of you or the Germans?'

'Both.'

He moved to the bar, and I made my way through the café to the door marked WC, banking on the fact it would be next to the kitchen. Sure enough, it was, and, as luck would have it, the service entrance was wide open. I slipped out and into an alleyway, emerging in a street I didn't know. A few feet further along, though, there was a junction I recognised. Beyond that was a door with a tiny lion symbol chalked on the wall beside it, the sign that indicated this was the entrance to a traboule, one of the secret passageways that the silk workers of Lyon had once used to keep their precious material dry as they moved around the city. Now we used them too, the Germans unaware of their existence.

I loitered a few feet from the door, pretending to adjust my shoe, until I was certain no one was around. Then I slipped through it, darkness descending as it shut behind me, a tunnel stretching ahead lit only by the daylight that played across the vaulted ceiling, filtering back from the archway that formed the exit. I emerged into a walled courtyard and passed through that into the street beyond, which was dominated by a church, its spires white against the leaden sky. From here, I knew I needed to head north-east into the suburbs where the safe house was located. There were no more traboules between here and there so I walked as briskly as I could, eyes down like every other citizen I passed.

Lyon was a Gestapo stronghold as well as being the seat of the Vichy government, not that it counted for anything, especially now the Germans had all but torn up the Armistice agreement and occupied the entire country. Still, the place was a hotbed of collaborators and *résistants* living cheek by jowl, the former toadying up to their Nazi masters while the latter did all they could to disrupt them, aided by our agents.

I wasn't here, though, to make contact with them. We ran the line, and they carried out their sabotage. Our paths only crossed when they needed to pass on an agent to us or to receive one who'd landed. The best way to stay alive in this war was to stay away from other factions as much as possible. The Resistance stuck to three connections at most. That was sensible. Any more than that and you risked what had happened to our escape line – a betrayal which all but destroyed everything we'd painstakingly built up because too many people were connected in a chain that had been smashed to smithereens.

I wasn't sure if we could even rebuild it, the fractures ran so deep. All I knew was that we had to try, starting here with this safe house and the *comtesse*. She was the first link in the new chain, one that we had to connect to the next and the next until we had an escape line once more that ran from Paris to the Pyrenees, the only way out from the south now that the waters were no longer safe.

As I scurried along the streets, I felt their footsteps following me, the padding of little feet, those tiny children who'd stood like silent angels on the sand only to be blown to the skies, consumed by a fire that would burn in my heart until the Nazis were no more.

# FORTY

The woman who greeted me at the door of the nondescript house looked more like a middle-aged English governess than a *comtesse*. She sounded like one too. Although she was slight, she made up for her lack of height with a manner so imperious I was left in no doubt as to her aristocratic credentials, pinning me down with her unwavering gaze. I glanced at her left arm, which was in a sling, her shoulder swathed in bandages, while another was wrapped around her left lower leg, visible beneath her tweed skirt.

'You're late,' she said by way of greeting, ushering me into the echoing hallway and, beyond that, a salon where the curtains were drawn and no fire burned in the grate. The place was cheerless and uninviting, but I could see why she'd picked it as a safe house, harmonising as it did with all the other houses in an anonymous street.

'How do you do,' I said, extending my hand. 'My name is Elisabeth.'

She ignored my hand and indicated a hard-looking sofa opposite the unlit fire. 'You're the first to arrive. Wait there.'

She might be a *comtesse*, but she was certainly no lady. I

had no choice but to sit and wait, silently seething, as she clomped out of the room in a pair of brogues that were far better suited to the English countryside than a French city. How the hell she'd managed to stay off the Gestapo's radar was a mystery to me.

I was beginning to reconsider the entire operation when I heard two knocks at the front door followed by four. Our prearranged signal. Moments later, she led Guy into the room and bade him sit beside me before sweeping out once more.

I gave him a sideways look. 'You made it then.'

'Thanks to your map. Bumped into a few Germans on the way, but yes, as you can see, I managed to get here. I see you've already met the *comtesse*.'

I rolled my eyes at the sound of her approaching footsteps. 'You could say that. I can only hope she knows what she's doing.'

'I can assure you I know exactly what I'm doing,' boomed the *comtesse*. She might look like a middle-aged governess, but she was as sharp as the jack knife I had concealed in my bag.

'Mary was trained by us after she used the line to escape in '41,' said Guy. 'Unfortunately, the Abwehr caught up with her first time around.'

'Rotten sods arrested me in Paris. I spent nine months in prison and was then spirited back to London. Best thing to happen to me. MI9 decided to teach me all kinds of tricks, and so here I am, back where I belong. On the front line.'

'And we're very glad to have you,' said Guy. 'I ran into Mary when Albert and I were here, collecting Lionel from another safe house. Mary will run another section of the line and provide a safe house in Ruffec. It's close to Limoges.'

'I see,' I said. 'So you're not based in Lyon?'

'Not normally, but I've been in hospital here. I was involved in a bicycle accident, you see.'

That explained the bandages. 'I'm sorry to hear that. Were you badly injured?'

'I'd been on a trip to Lyon with a companion from the Resistance. We were cycling back when a car full of collaborators recognised me and rammed us. The Gestapo heard about it and were searching the hospitals for me, but they hid me in the cellar. They tell me I nearly died, but I don't believe a word of it. I'm a trained nurse. Served with the VAD and the French Red Cross in the First War. Discharged myself when I heard about the two I have upstairs. It takes more than a carload of traitorous thugs to finish me off.'

Somehow, I could believe it.

'Come. I'll introduce you to my guests.'

We fell in behind her, following her meekly up the stairs.

Two men rose as she led us into a small room on the first floor at the back of the house. The room had evidently once been used as some kind of storeroom because there were no windows, merely shelves lining one wall and a couple of armchairs in which the men had been sitting. It was the perfect hidey-hole, invisible from the outside and with no need for the men to stay away from the window or keep the lights off. I studied the two as she introduced them.

'These gentlemen are a couple of your agents, I believe. They escaped from a safe house that was raided. Needless to say, they're high on the Gestapo's hit list too.'

'Name's Gilbert,' said the one with the beard. 'This is Maurice.'

'Good to meet you fellows,' said Guy, shaking their hands in turn.

I followed suit, my mind working as it always did when I met new parcels. Did they sound legit? Look it? Were they hiding something? Possible infiltrators? All of it ran through my head as I murmured greetings. No doubt Guy was thinking the same. Since the line had been compromised, we were more careful than ever, but it was impossible to plug every leak or crack in the chain. These two felt right. That was all I had to go on. Instinct. To be honest, it was the best barometer I knew. One that had worked for me so far, touch wood.

'We'll get you to the station,' I said. 'And onto the right train. Someone will meet you at the other end and take you to our safe house until we can get you over the border and into Spain.'

Gilbert clasped my hand once more. 'Very good of you. That all sounds splendid.'

They were pale, the pair of them, as a result of being cooped up in hiding all this time. It was what most of them found the hardest, doing nothing but waiting to be sent along an escape line when they were used to the adrenaline of action. Especially agents like these two. They must have been going stir crazy.

'It's just you?' asked Guy.

'Yes,' replied Gilbert. 'When our safe house was raided, we managed to get out of a back window and over the rooftops. The others in the house weren't so lucky. Gestapo got the lot of them, including the other parcels we'd helped get down the line and the family who owned the place. From what we heard later, there's an absolute madman called Drexler who led the raid. Vicious bastard. I don't give much for their chances.'

I could see the weight he carried for those people. It was the same weight I felt for all those souls who'd perished before my eyes, one that almost crushed me at times – as I'm sure it did him. War was cruel, men like Drexler even crueller. 'I'm so sorry,' I murmured. 'We'll do everything we can for you.'

Downstairs, the *comtesse* ushered us once more into the cold, bare salon. 'Do you have somewhere to stay tonight?'

I looked at Guy. 'Not yet. We're trying to repair the rest of the line. We were hoping to stay here tonight, get the men to the station first thing and be on our way.'

She tutted. 'I'm afraid there's precious little in this house. It was shut up, you see, when its owners fled south. I can offer you one bed and a couple of blankets, but that's it.'

'That's more than enough,' I said. 'We're grateful for a roof over our heads.'

'I'll send someone with food for you and the men. I'm staying elsewhere, in an apartment we also use. I'm heading back to Ruffec first thing in the morning to recommence operations there.'

'I see. So who's running this section of the line?'

'No one at present. They were all arrested. I wish I could, but it's too far from Ruffec, and I'm too well known here. You do need to get someone in place though. There are bottlenecks above and below Lyon, as you probably know. The agents you just met are blown. We need fresh blood.'

'I can send one of my men,' said Guy. 'Sefton. He's the only one I've got right now. The other one you met, Lionel, is still recovering, and we've yet to find Hammond. Can you let the other helpers here in Lyon know that Sefton's on his way and to hang tight until then?'

The *comtesse* inclined her head regally. 'Of course. Now to your arrangements. Someone will meet you at the station with the tickets. The password is "are you seeking the strawberries?" As for the rest of the line, you need to speak to Paul, the *patron* of the café at Avignon railway station. He can help you with the remaining safe houses on this section.'

The *patron*. I remembered Grant mentioning him too.

I looked at the *comtesse*, standing so erect in spite of her injuries. Redoubtable – that's what she was. One of a kind, except that there were others equally as special, scattered across France, risking their lives every day to help men like the two upstairs. Like all the people we tried so hard to save.

'I probably won't see you in the morning, so I'll wish you bonne voyage now,' added the *comtesse*. 'Your room is at the top of the stairs on the right. Please don't turn on any lights. Your food will be left outside the back door at eight o'clock precisely. There will be enough for you and the two men. Please take any leftovers with you.'

She was almost at the front door when she called over her shoulder, 'And don't send any more of your wretched agents my way. This is an escape route for airmen.'

In the silence that followed, I risked a glance at Guy.

He picked up both suitcases. 'Shall we?' he said.

# FORTY-ONE

The room upstairs was as dismal as the others, the horsehair mattress on the bed barely covered by a tired-looking sheet, two rough blankets the only other form of bedding apart from a bolster that looked as if it, too, had seen better days. Guy dumped our cases beside the bed. 'I can sleep on the floor.'

'Don't be silly. We have a long journey tomorrow, and you need your sleep. We both do. We can sleep top to toe like we used to when I stayed over at your house. Remember? Hélène would always tickle my feet in the middle of the night to make me giggle. Then your *maman* would come in and pretend to be annoyed when we begged her for one more story. She always gave in. She was wonderful at telling stories, your *maman*.'

Guy smiled. 'She was. Although I don't recall ever sharing a bed with you.'

'Well no, it was Hélène and me, but what's the difference really?' I was babbling now, feeling foolish. 'After all, it's just a bed, and we're two grown adults who've known each other since we were children. We have a job to do, and we need to make sure we get our rest, like any good soldier would. And that's exactly what I'm going to do.'

'Quite right. In that case, would you like to suggest a demarcation line?'

Guy's tone was grave, but there was a definite glint in his eye.

'I'm quite sure you can keep to your side while I keep to mine.'

'I'm not sure whether you're flattering me or insulting me.'

I glared at him. 'What on earth do you mean?'

He looked at me straight-faced. 'You're either suggesting that I have admirable self-control or that I'm completely cold-blooded, I'm not sure which.'

'You're laughing at me.'

'I'm not.'

He was seventeen again, hiding his grin beneath an ice-cool veneer, while I was a gauche fourteen-year-old who had no idea what to say next.

'Fine. Sleep where you like. I'm taking this side.'

With that, I kicked off my shoes and threw myself down on the bed, pulling the blankets over my head as I squirmed, trying to form some kind of hollow in the unyielding bolster. I felt the mattress sag beside me, and then Guy was settling on the other side, tugging a fragment of blanket over him. I flung the entire thing his way. 'Take it. I'll have this one.'

'Now you're being silly. It's freezing.'

It was extremely cold without any fires to warm the house's rooms, but I'd suffered worse. Many was the time we'd had to sleep out in the open, under the stars, which was far less romantic than it sounded, the cold seeping into our bones from the damp ground, sometimes without even a blanket to provide a tiny bit of warmth. Somehow, I drifted off, sleeping fitfully, dreaming of those nights, the stars melding with the faces that never left me, like Hélène's face, beseeching, her fingers reaching out to touch mine, almost meeting before the currents snatched them away.

'Shhh. It's alright.'

A voice whispering in my ear. Swimming up out of sleep. I was snuggled against something warm, cocooned in blankets. It felt so good I was tempted to sink back down again, safe now. Sinking like Hélène, like those children, the waters closing over me...

My eyes flew open. A soothing voice. A warm body pressed against mine. Then an arm tightening around me. 'Go back to sleep. It's OK. It's just me.'

Just me?

I wriggled round, throwing off the arm that had been holding me. 'What the hell are you doing?'

'Keeping you warm.'

I moved a good foot away from him, pulling the blankets around me. 'Thanks, but I can keep myself warm.'

'Come on, Elisabeth. We're agents in the field, and I've known you all your life. I'm fully dressed, and so are you. What exactly is the problem?'

He had a point. What was the problem? There really wasn't one except that I liked it, the weight of his arm around me, his body heat, the familiar smell of him. *No. Stop it, Elisabeth.* This was Guy. And I knew Guy of old, just as he said. Then there was that other thing, the one I hadn't even mentioned, although for the life of me I couldn't imagine why not. Or perhaps I could.

'Honestly, I'm fine,' I muttered, turning my back and curling my knees up in a foetal position to try and replace the human hot-water bottle that had been Guy.

'Well, I'm not. You've stolen all the blankets.'

'Oh God. I'm so sorry. I didn't mean to.'

I turned to face him again only to see that he was laughing.

'Here,' he said, snatching up the bolster and inserting it between us. 'There now. We can share the blankets with absolute propriety.'

'Great.'

I backed up to the bolster, tucking the blankets round me once more, careful to ensure there was enough left for Guy. I thought I heard him stifle a laugh, but I couldn't be sure. All I knew was that I missed the comforting feel of his arm as I lay there trying to get to sleep again; the warming presence of him. More fool me for making such a fuss. Or was I? It had felt so good. Too good. And therein lay the danger.

I'd seen it before – agents distracted by relationships, winding up in the arms of the Gestapo rather than one another's and I was absolutely determined that wasn't going to happen to me. Besides, this was Guy. Hélène's brother. My childhood friend. Or so I kept telling myself. But if he was just a friend, why was I already keeping a secret from him? Not a secret. A fact. One I was holding back.

In my heart of hearts, I knew exactly why.

# FORTY-TWO

## 5 JANUARY 1943, LYON, SOUTHERN FRANCE

The Gare de Lyon-Perrache was located in the centre of Lyon, in the second arrondissement. It took us around half an hour to walk there from the safe house, and I memorised every traboule and backstreet so we could relay the information to anyone we later used as a guide. I was leading, walking fifty yards in front of Gilbert while Maurice walked another fifty or so yards behind him and Guy brought up the rear. Both were under strict instructions not to communicate or even look at one another. If any of us were stopped, the rest were to carry on as if nothing had happened.

As I disappeared down the alleyway that led to the court-yard and then on through the archway to the tunnel, I could discern just one set of footsteps behind me. Good. They were sticking to the drill.

On through the tunnel and I could hear all of them now, their breathing audible as it echoed off the walls, along with the sound of their feet on the rough stone floor. Still, I kept my eyes front, moving at a steady pace. Almost there. Then we were emerging once more into daylight, past the door marked with the lion, heading down a wider boulevard towards the station and the perilous journey ahead.

They were two well-trained agents, but even so my heart started to race as we drew close, not least because of the building that loomed over the station. The Hotel Terminus had originally been built for rail travellers but was now the head-quarters of the Gestapo here in Lyon, the home of Klaus Barbie's notorious Section IV. I sent up a silent prayer as I passed through the shadow of the building and into the station concourse, looking out for the correct platform even as I headed to the ticket office, conscious of the soldiers guarding each exit and the Gestapo loitering by the platforms as well as dotted around, all visible to a trained eye.

I joined the queue, wondering where the hell the *comtesse*'s contact had got to. Without the correct paperwork, it was very difficult to buy tickets. If it came to it, I'd simply have to try and bluff my way through.

I'd almost reached the ticket-office window when a man stepped out from behind a pillar.

'Do you want strawberries?' he asked.

I halted mid-step. It was the correct password. Almost. I weighed up the odds. It was a risk I had to take. 'I am.'

'Let me show you where they are.'

As he drew me aside, I could feel the others watching, their eyes boring into the man, the same thoughts no doubt running through their heads as mine. Was he the real thing or a Gestapo agent in disguise?

He reached inside his jacket, and my heart stopped. Oh God. The password. It wasn't quite correct. I should have run. Then he was pulling out a couple of tickets and handing them to me with a nod and a smile before disappearing into the crowd that thronged the station once more. I gave him a minute then slipped into the crowd too, passing close enough to hand each man their ticket with my eyes averted, brushing fingertips with Gilbert as a final farewell.

I loitered by the platforms until the train for Aix pulled out, followed by the train for Paris, careful not to pay attention to either. I could see Guy out of the corner of my eye as I made my way back across the concourse, moving with the crowd as it surged towards the exit.

A poster attached to a pillar caught my eye. Dear God. It was me again. Or at least, the picture that was supposed to be me, my hair dark and straight, the nose and mouth still off. I hastily averted my eyes, cursing under my breath. *Act normal. Forget you saw that.*

A final few metres and I was out of there, in the fresh air, gulping in a lungful of it. I was just turning my face into the winter sun when a voice snapped, 'Papers.'

A shadow had stepped between me and the sun, a figure clad in the tell-tale grey-green SS uniform. Gestapo too, most likely. His companion was dressed in the same uniform, his countenance equally unsmiling.

I opened my handbag and withdrew my papers, handing them over in as relaxed a manner as I could manage, all the while feeling the clutch of alarm spiking my skull, digging in its claws as I remembered the poster and started to pray. *Please, please don't let them recognise me.*

'Madame Mireille Mabillon.'

'That is correct.'

'What are you doing in Lyon?'

'My grandmother is unwell.'

He gave me the once-over, his eyes affecting boredom, although I could detect a sharpened interest in them that sent a shudder through me. The glint of a predator that's spotted its prey. This was it. I was done for. He'd recognised me. Should I try to run? *No. Stupid idea. Stay calm. Bluff it out.*

'Stay here,' he snapped, disappearing through the door of the Hotel Terminus.

I eyed his companion, who stared coldly back at me.

All at once, I could hear shouts from across the concourse, where a kerfuffle was taking place. The Gestapo officer glanced over too, his hand reaching for his pistol as the unmistakable sound of a shot rang out.

When he started to run towards the disturbance, I seized my chance, racing instead towards the platforms, glancing back to make sure he wasn't coming after me, forcing myself to walk slowly now, moving with the people on the platforms, looking for a train that was about to pull out.

Platform two for Marseille. Leaving in one minute. I had no choice but to leap aboard.

Just as I did, I caught sight of someone jumping on as the train started to pull out.

I squinted through the train window. It couldn't be.

It was.

# FORTY-THREE

He strolled into the carriage a few moments later, looking as if he didn't have a care in the world. I shuffled up as he squeezed in beside me, nodding pleasantly at the woman opposite. The moment she got off at the next station, he moved to sit opposite, leaning forward to speak just loud enough that I could hear.

'The train's non-stop from here to Marseille. We're going to have to ride it all the way and then double back.'

I glanced up at the glass window in the carriage door. No sign of any Gestapo. 'Was that you back there in the station, firing?'

He grinned. 'You bet. I thought I'd cause a little distraction. Get that Gestapo asshole off your back. By the time he got near, the locals were running in circles, screaming. He had no idea what was going on, and neither did they. Don't worry – I only fired at the station roof, although it was tempting to aim at him instead.'

I couldn't help but laugh. He looked so gleeful. 'Well, thank you. You certainly saved my ass, as you would say.'

'It's worth saving.'

I looked at him, not entirely sure what he meant. He gazed back at me poker-faced. That was Guy all over.

The ticket collector appeared. I pulled my return ticket to Aix from my purse. He stared at it, then at me. 'This train does not stop at Aix, madame.'

I feigned horror. 'What? You're joking.'

'No, madame. I am not.'

I rounded on Guy, who was also clutching his ticket. 'You said this was the right train. You made me hurry for it. Now it turns out I was right all along. It *was* that other train. What are we supposed to do now, imbecile?'

Guy assumed his best beleaguered male expression. 'I'm sorry, my love. I thought this was the right train. Perhaps, monsieur, we can change somewhere?'

The ticket collector shook his head. 'It's straight through now to Marseille.'

'Marseille? Oh my God. What are we supposed to do now? Maman will have sent Papa to pick us up at Aix. This is all your fault.' I hugged my handbag to me as if I was about to hit Guy with it. The ticket collector gave him a comradely look of sympathy as only another Frenchman could, understanding the magnitude of his plight.

'When you get to Marseille, there should be a train within an hour that will get you back to Aix.'

'An hour?' I huffed. 'Lunch will be cold on the table by then.'

With that, the ticket collector slid backward through the door, shooting Guy a final glance.

I waited a beat. 'I think we got away with that.'

There were no more inspections until, finally, the train pulled into Marseille. I stood, reaching for my suitcase. 'I'll walk ahead once we're clear of the train.'

'OK.'

I tweaked my hat so it sat a little lower, strolling with as much ease as I could muster through the station. There were plenty of people milling about here too, doing their best to ignore the soldiers stationed at each exit. I did the same, trying not to catch anyone's eye, breathing slowly and evenly in spite of my racing heart. There was a tension here – I could feel it. As if everyone was waiting for something to happen. Not everyone. Just the soldiers, glancing at one another, then at me.

One stepped out to block my path, palm raised, another falling in behind me. It was a trap, and I'd walked right into it. This time there was no escape.

'Madame Mabillon?' said the one in front of me. 'Come with me.'

# FORTY-FOUR

The room was all brown, everywhere I looked. Even with the curtains open at the tall windows, the winter sun failed to penetrate. I was standing by those windows when a man entered from a door opposite the one they'd brought me through. I recognised him at once. It was the man who'd been watching George's apartment. The last time I'd seen his ratlike face, it had been through clouds of smoke.

'Madame Mabillon? I am Otto Drexler.'

He smiled – a smile that failed to reach those bestial eyes, which regarded me much as a predator might stare down its next victim, so dark they were almost black. Had he recognised me too? I had no idea.

All but one of his underlings immediately left the room, melting away at the sight of their superior. The one who remained was the same man who'd detained me at the station, still wearing the triumphant smirk of a hunter delivering his kill.

Drexler strolled towards me, his manner apparently mild, at odds with his reputation. When he drew close, he gestured towards the solitary chair in front of the desk which dominated the far corner of the room, alongside the door from which he had emerged.

'Sit.'

It wasn't an invitation.

I looked at him, weighing up my chances, everything I'd heard about this man running through my head. From what I knew, he was a vicious street fighter as well as a former gangster. He might appear calm and controlled, but all that could change in an instant.

I offered him a meek smile and moved to the chair. 'Thank you.'

Seconds later, I was on the floor, still trying to work out what had happened, pain exploding across my forehead where Drexler had punched me.

'Did I say you could move?' he screamed, spittle spraying from the corners of his mouth as he stood over me.

'I...'

'You do as I say. Get up.'

I staggered to my feet, reaching for the back of the chair to steady me, lurching forward once more as he knocked that, too, to the ground.

'Where are they?' he shrieked, his voice rising as he repeated it over and over.

I played dumb. 'Who?'

'The men you helped escape. Enemies of the Reich.'

'I don't know what you're talking about.'

This time it was a slap across my face that sent me reeling. As I tried to regain my balance, he grabbed me by the hair, yanking it so my face was inches from his. 'We know there were two men in Lyon. Enemy agents. What train did they take? Where are they now?'

I could feel the spittle raining down on my face now and his hot, fetid breath as he slapped me once more, smiling all the while. He liked it. He liked to inflict pain. A thought I stored up. If that was what he liked, I wouldn't give him the satis-faction.

Still, I feigned ignorance. 'I don't know anything about this.'

'Bitch! Liar!'

More blows to my head, my torso, my stomach. I doubled over, gasping, determined not to raise my head or cry out, to let him see how I was suffering. They kept coming until I thought I would pass out, which might be a blessing.

*No. Stay alert.* Otherwise, I was at this madman's mercy.

The room lurched, fading in and out.

*Focus. Fight. Focus.*

All of a sudden, he stopped with a snort of derision. 'Stupid woman. You will talk. They all do in the end.'

I heard the door open behind me and more voices. Two men. No, three. Were they all going to beat me up? Another voice. French this time.

Drexler grabbed me by the arm and wrenched me round. I couldn't hold back the cry that escaped my lips.

'Do you know this man?' he snapped as I stared into the eyes of the man who'd handed me the rail tickets back in Lyon.

What the hell was he doing here?

# FORTY-FIVE

I looked at the man from Lyon. Looked away again.

'No.'

'Take a good look. Are you sure?'

I took a deep breath and answered truthfully. 'I don't know this man.'

Better to stick as closely to the truth as possible – at least then I couldn't slip up under torture. But they seemed more interested in him than me. A tiny glimmer of hope began to form. Maybe they had no idea who I was and this poor bastard was their target. I could see the fear in his eyes, the muscle moving in his cheek. I assumed he was a *résistant*, but that could also be a mistake. Then again, if he was a plant, he was one hell of an actor. The fear, as far as I could tell, was genuine; I could practically smell it. It was a scent I knew well. My heart clenched for him.

Drexler turned on the man. 'Is this the woman you met at Lyon station?'

The man played dumb. 'What woman? I didn't meet any woman. I tell you, I'm a cleaner for the railways. It's my job to clean the ticket offices and the trains, not to deal with the passengers. I don't know what you're talking about.'

Too much. He was talking too much, gabbling under pressure, his eyes wide with fright. I could see the whites of them, speckled with pink, the sweat starting now on his forehead. A dead giveaway.

Without warning, Drexler grabbed him by the back of the neck and slammed his head down on the corner of his desk.

'Liar,' he screamed. 'Tell. Me. The. Truth.'

Each word brought with it another slam, the blood running down the man's face now, pouring from the gashes in his forehead, his eyes already beginning to swell. Still he played dumb, the only sound escaping his lips a low moaning.

Finally, Drexler flung him to the floor, where he curled into a ball as he kicked him again and again in the stomach. A final kick to his head rendered the man unconscious, his mouth slack, head lolling at a horrible angle.

Drexler gestured to his men. 'Get him out of here.'

He was speaking softly once more in that horribly calm way he had. His eyes drifted to me. He looked bored, as if kicking the life out of the man had extinguished any excitement. For now. Pain, that was his thing. And it looked as if I was next. Still, though, he stared at me without recognition. He really had no idea who I was.

There was a knock on the door, and another SS officer entered. I flicked him a glance. Then another. It was him – the blond captain we'd spoken to on the train from Aix. He was moving to Drexler's side, handing him a sheaf of papers. Then he saw me, his eyes taking in the situation while his face remained expressionless.

He leaned closer to Drexler and murmured something so low I couldn't make it out. Drexler nodded once and turned his back. Then the captain was at my side, taking me by the arm, marching me out of the office. They had recognised me after all.

I braced myself for what was to come. A bullet in the back of my neck maybe. That would be the merciful option.

'You're free to go,' said the captain, handing me over to the soldier guarding the top of the stairs.

'I... What?' I stared at him.

He gestured towards the stairs and walked off, but not before I caught the look he threw me. It told me everything I needed to know.

I practically ran down those stairs, keeping pace with the soldier, and emerged from the building still unable to believe what had happened. Outside, the sun was sinking beneath the horizon, gilding the tops of the buildings opposite as it went. I hesitated, unsure which way to go.

'Follow me,' hissed a voice.

I saw him walk past me and obeyed, staying the requisite fifty yards behind as he headed away from the station, weaving his way through the streets as if he'd known them all his life. Which he had.

Finally, he stopped by a doorway, one I recognised. It was my father's old office building, now standing empty. After darting a look up and down the street, I slipped inside.

He was there, in the lobby, waiting for me.

As soon as I got close enough, he pulled me to him, his voice rough with emotion. 'I thought I'd lost you.'

'It takes more than that to get rid of me,' I quipped, almost collapsing into his embrace from relief.

He leaned away from me, staring at my forehead, my cheek. 'What did that bastard do to you?'

'He punched me. That's all.'

Now that he mentioned it, my head was still pounding. But I was alive. And free. Unlike the other poor sod.

'He punched you?' Fury gravelled his words.

'He might have battered my flesh, Guy, but he certainly

didn't break my spirit. A few cuts and bruises are nothing compared to that.'

He brushed my forehead with the tips of his fingers as if he was trying to erase Drexler's handiwork. 'I don't think anyone could break your spirit, for what it's worth. You've always been like this, Elisabeth. Principled. Brave. It's one of the reasons I love you. That I think I've always loved you. The thing is, I'm not sure you could ever love me.'

I gazed at him, not knowing what to say.

All at once, his face was flooded with light – someone had opened the street door.

I whirled round, my hand reaching for the pistol I still had strapped to my thigh, saw who it was and gasped.

# FORTY-SIX

'I've been following you since you left Rue Paradis,' said Albert. The Gestapo headquarters in Marseille were housed inappropriately on that street. 'I had to make sure there was no one tailing you.'

We were sitting in his favourite bar near the Vieux Port. I knocked back the cognac Guy had ordered, his declaration still echoing in my head, although we had more pressing matters to deal with first. 'What I don't understand is why the Gestapo just let me go like that. There was this SS officer, you see, on the train to Lyon. We told him and his companion we were meeting for an assignation. The same officer walked into Drexler's office. He was the one who persuaded him to let me go.'

Albert frowned. 'What did he look like? This officer?'

'Good-looking. Fair-haired. Quite tall. He carried himself like an officer, if you know what I mean.'

'Ernst Bauer. Drexler's right-hand man. You're right to worry. He may not have recognised you, but he'll certainly have had a good reason for letting you go. Unlike Drexler, he prefers intelligence to violence. Which makes him perhaps even more dangerous.'

I let that sink in, my mind churning. 'I honestly think it's because he recognised me from the train, but there's also the fact they knew two men had escaped. How did they know that? They must have seen us with them at the station.'

Guy shook his head. 'I doubt it. We were spread out, and even when we were in the station, we kept apart. Everything points to another leak.'

I stared at him helplessly. 'Maybe. Maybe not. It could just be bad luck. The Gestapo were all over the place in Lyon. They might just have spotted them.'

'If they'd spotted them, they'd have stopped them. Seems to me someone informed on us just a few minutes too late, which is great for our evaders but not so good for you.'

Also true. 'Who then? The *comtesse*? One of her helpers?'

'The *comtesse* is one of us. She would never betray anyone. She proved that time and again when the Germans got hold of her before. I doubt it's anyone who works with her either. She's too careful.'

'So who then?'

'I wish I knew.'

We looked at one another, the stark reality laid bare before us. As we suspected, there could be yet another traitor in our midst. Just when we were trying to rebuild the line along with our evaders' trust in it.

Guy reached out and gently touched my face again. 'That looks like it hurts.'

I shrugged it off, still confused by his words. Or, more accurately, by how I felt. 'It's not so bad. Bruises, that's all.'

'Even so, you need to see a doctor to make sure it's nothing more serious.'

'I agree,' said Albert, 'but first we need to get you away from Marseille. Now.'

'No, we need to get you out of France.' Guy's voice was quiet but implacable. 'Face it, Elisabeth. You're burned. You may have got away with it until now, but someone is sure to spot you sooner or later. That was too close a call with Drexler. I'm ordering you to leave.'

I gaped at him, feeling the sick lurch of betrayal. How dare he after what he'd just said? 'You're ordering me? As far as I'm concerned, it was Captain Grant who issued the orders, and now I suppose it's me. Drexler didn't know who I was, and I don't believe that anyone else will recognise me from that poster. It was just bad luck they picked me up. The picture doesn't even look like me, for God's sake.'

Guy threw up his hands. 'Don't be so damn stupid. For five million francs, an awful lot of people will try and recognise someone, even if it isn't you. Except that one day, it will be. The only option is to get you out of the country and let the Germans know that the Little Fox has evaded them. For good. I should have insisted you get out when the first posters appeared. To stay any longer is lunacy. MI9 is in charge of the line now, not Grant and not you. I'll be in touch with Lisbon to arrange your evacuation back to London. That's an order, like it or not.'

Order my arse. I was the one who'd come face to face with the Germans time and again without being apprehended. Until today. And yet they'd let me go. Why I didn't know, but I was going to make damn sure the line was fully restored before I would even consider leaving France, no matter what the Gestapo might have planned for me.

'Alright,' I said, 'I'll use the line to escape once we've put it back together properly. Is that a deal?'

'Fine,' Guy sighed. 'Have it your way. But the minute the line is complete once more, you're over the Pyrenees.'

'Suits me,' I said.

'So we have a deal?'

'We do.'

He didn't shake my hand; he didn't need to. My word was as good as his, and we both knew what that meant. Even so, I whispered, '*Croix de bois, croix de fer, si je mens, je vais en enfer.*' Cross my heart and hope to die... It was what we'd always said as kids.

He blinked once, twice, as if trying to unsee something. Or perhaps forget. 'I'm already in hell,' he muttered. 'I have been since Hélène died.'

I stared at him, stricken, hearing her voice chanting that same phrase, '*Croix de bois...*'

'Why stay in hell,' I murmured, 'when you know Hélène's not there?'

# FORTY-SEVEN

## 6 JANUARY 1943, AVIGNON, SOUTHERN FRANCE

We holed up in Albert's apartment that night until we could be absolutely sure the Gestapo weren't tailing us again, Guy taking the couch while I had the spare bedroom. The next morning, Albert drove us to Avignon. We parked up in a quiet street outside a café where he muttered, 'Wait here one moment.'

We were huddled in the back of his van, the silence between us hanging heavily until Albert returned. I'd tossed and turned half the night, running Guy's declaration through my mind. In the heat of the moment, emotions were running high. He hadn't meant it. In fact, the best thing was to pretend it had never happened.

Annoyingly, he appeared to have slept like a log. And yet, he couldn't meet my eye, never mind exchange a word. Instead, he gazed into the distance as if lost in thought. Typical. Proclaim that he loves me and then go cold on me because I wouldn't leave until the line was restored. Well, two could play at that game. I'd simply act as if he'd never said a word.

Albert threw open the van door. 'Follow me.'

I automatically glanced up and down the street before

hopping out. Clear. But then I would expect nothing else from Albert.

Inside the café, he took us through into a back room where coffee was already waiting.

'This is Paul, the patron,' said Albert, introducing the portly man who beamed as he placed a large basket of brioches in front of us. 'He's our contact in Avignon.'

'It's good to meet you,' I said. 'Captain Grant mentioned you. I understand you might be able to connect us to the other helpers who are in hiding right now.'

Paul's eyes swept over me, assessing. The avuncular front evidently hid an astute mind. 'I can do that, yes,' he said at length.

'Good. Then we can piece the line back together on this section and get it working again. We already spoke to the *comtesse* in Lyon. We'll be putting a man in there.'

I avoided Guy's gaze as I said this. Let him think what he wanted. This was a joint op, and he could like it or lump it.

Albert looked from me to Paul, an unspoken assent passing between them. 'Once the line is running properly again, Paul will send word to me when parcels arrive, and I will meet them here. If for any reason I cannot come or am late, Paul and his wife will look after them.'

'Excellent,' said Guy. 'We're happy to reimburse any expenses.'

Paul looked offended. 'I don't want your money. It's an honour and a privilege to help in any small way we can.'

Except that it wasn't small. Far from it. If they were caught harbouring escapers and evaders, they would pay with their lives.

'You're very kind, *monsieur*,' I said. 'Please don't be insulted by this offer, but there are so many parcels now that we can't possibly expect you to carry the financial burden. It's already asking a lot to use your café as a rendezvous as well as a safe house.'

He gave us a little bow of his head. 'Very well then. Please let me get you some more coffee. I understand you have already had quite a journey.'

I could feel him trying not to look at the bruises I hadn't managed to completely cover with make-up. 'Thank you, but we still have plenty of ground to cover. We need to get to the next safe house as quickly as possible now that the Gestapo are breathing down our necks. Perhaps you could point us in the right direction.'

'Of course. You must get the next train to Montélimar and get off there. I will send word to the conductor. He's one of us. He'll make sure someone is there to meet you and take you to the safe house.'

'That sounds perfect. Thank you. What time is the next train?'

Paul glanced at his watch. 'In thirty-five minutes.'

'Even better. That gives us plenty of time for breakfast.'

'So we're agreed?' said Albert. 'In that case, I'll return to the chateau and inform Sefton of the plan, although I'll await your instructions before doing anything else.'

'Very good,' muttered Guy. 'I'm sure Elisabeth will let you know what those instructions are in good time.'

'I certainly will. Thanks, Albert.'

I smiled sweetly at Guy, who dropped his eyes, tearing a chunk off his brioche before concentrating fiercely on smothering it with the jam on the table. Great. So it was going to be like that. The Guy I'd known wasn't given to sulking, but he'd evidently changed in the intervening years. Too bad that I'd grown tougher as well. I was no longer the girl who'd hero-worshipped him from afar. And I wouldn't just jump when he snapped his fingers, no matter what.

I'd sworn to restore this line, and that's what I would do, not just for me but for the hundreds who needed to escape. For all those downed airmen and agents who were hiding from people like Drexler right now. For the little boy we'd yet to find. Most of all, for those we couldn't save. We owed it to them to get this done. *I* owed it to them. If he really loved me, Guy would understand that.

He had no other choice.

# FORTY-EIGHT

I looked straight at Guy across the table, daring him to meet my gaze, to break the silence that had dragged on for far too long. 'We should head for the ticket office in fifteen minutes or so to give us just enough time to buy our tickets and catch the train. I'll go first. Leave it a couple of minutes and then follow me.'

'I'll go first.' His eyes still wouldn't meet mine.

I wanted to shake him. Instead, I smiled. 'Very well.'

It was a short walk to the ticket office from the café. I gave him a couple of minutes' head start then followed at a decent distance, my headscarf tied tight so that it covered my hair and forehead. I could see Guy ahead as he reached the ticket-office queue and fell back, pretending to adjust my stocking, surreptitiously looking to and right, checking for soldiers – or worse Gestapo.

The station here wasn't half as busy as at Lyon, and the queue was moving fast. Guy was three people ahead of me, pocketing his ticket, ignoring me as he strode off in the direction of the train, just as he should. Then it was my turn. The ticket clerk didn't even bother to look up when I requested a ticket to

Montélimar, my heart beating faster as it always did at these moments.

So far, so good.

Something clattered on the ground beside my feet.

'*Pardon.*'

The man behind me reached down to pick up some coins, glancing at me as he smiled an apology and moved back into his place.

The clerk passed my ticket through the window. I was already turning away too when he suddenly whispered, 'Madame.'

'*Oui?*'

I stared at him through the window, at the way he was staring too, not at me but at something behind me. Or someone. Then he quickly put a finger to his lips before flicking it to indicate I should move. Fast.

As I turned, I saw what he meant. That damn poster again, stuck to the wall next to the entrance to the platforms. I hurried past it, searching for the platform, striding down it as confidently as I could before darting into the first open door and making my way through the carriages, all the while keeping a lookout.

There was Guy, sitting by the window in a carriage opposite an old man who appeared to be asleep. I carried on, slipping into the next but one along, settling into a seat between a buxom woman dressed in black and another old man who kept sniffing. Opposite me sat a younger woman who stared at the box she was holding in her lap as if her life depended on it.

'Tickets.'

The same man from the office. This must be Paul's friend. I gaped at him then quickly out of the window. The train was already pulling out. Was this a trap?

'Thank you, madame.' He punched mine and handed it back to me. 'I believe you want the next station, madame.'

'I do?'

'Yes.'

His inference was clear. I cast my fellow passengers a surreptitious look, but they appeared to be entirely oblivious to my presence. Of course, that meant nothing. It was the silent listeners who did the most damage, scuttling off to pass on the information they'd gleaned straight into the ears of the police or Gestapo.

The ticket collector reappeared just before we started to slow for what I assumed was the next station and nodded through the open carriage door. I stood as unhurriedly as I could and stepped through into the corridor, walking slowly past Guy's carriage so he would see me and hopefully get the message. But when I glanced in, he wasn't there.

Instead, three men were sitting where he and the old man had been. I hesitated for a fraction of a second, trying to work out what was going on. Maybe I'd got the wrong carriage. No, it was this one, two away from mine. I took a deep breath and carried on towards the door.

We were still slowing, the platform not yet in sight, when I heard someone hiss, 'Jump.'

A hand reached over me, wrenching open the door, and then I felt a push in the small of my back. Instinctively, I jumped, aiming for the grassy bank in front of me, tumbling over as I hit it. Guy hauled me to my feet. At the same moment, bullets started to ricochet off the ground all around us.

'Come on,' shouted Guy, pulling me down the bank after him as more shouts came from the train.

I could see the three men who'd been sitting in his carriage standing in the open doorway, preparing to jump too as they carried on shooting at us. Then, with a lurch, the train speeded up again, accelerating instead of stopping for the station. I wanted to cheer. The *cheminots* – the railway workers who'd aided the Resistance since the beginning – had done it again. I thought I caught a glimpse of the ticket collector waving at us and then the train was rounding the bend, out of sight, hurtling along as it headed for Montélimar.

'Are you OK?' Guy asked as he dusted himself down.

'I'm fine. What the hell happened?'

'Those three were Gestapo. Came into my carriage and kicked me and the old guy out. I hung around in the corridor, listening in. It was obvious they knew you were on the train. Someone had spotted you. It was the ticket collector who confirmed it. Told me the man after you in the queue started asking awkward questions so he swapped jobs with his buddy and got aboard our train.'

'There was this man behind me who dropped some coins by my feet. Took a good look at me as he picked them up. Of course. It was all a ploy. What the hell do we do now?'

I looked around. We were standing in a dip, concealed from the line by the bank we'd tumbled down. Ahead of us stretched a field and beyond that what looked like a lane.

Guy grabbed both suitcases from the ditch where they'd landed. 'We start walking. The Gestapo will send some of their bully boys to look for us the moment they reach the next station. Thank God for that driver and ticket collector. We'd be dead meat without them.'

I barely heard him. I was too busy staring over his shoulder at the posse of armed men approaching across the field, rifles raised. 'Don't speak too soon. We might still be dead meat.'

# FORTY-NINE

'I'm sorry we scared you.'

I accepted the flask the farmer was offering and took a grateful gulp. Firewater. Rough country cognac that was exactly what I needed. I handed it back with a smile. 'You didn't.'

'We thought the Boches might be coming after you, so we were ready to fire first.'

'How did you know we weren't the Boches?' asked Guy, wiping his upper lip after he, too, had taken a gulp from the flask.

We were crouched in a barn on the far edge of the field we'd entered. Two of the men who'd marched towards us with guns raised were keeping lookout while we sheltered in here with the farmer and what appeared to be his three sons.

'You jumped from the train. No one does that unless they're running from those sons of whores. If you pardon me, madame.'

I waved away his apology. 'Does that happen often here? People jumping from the train?'

'Now and then, usually from the opposite direction. It's the ones who take the train from Lyon we look out for, especially the ones headed south, to Toulouse and Marseille. We know that's where they send the ones who are trying to escape. The trouble is, the Nazis know that too, especially now after the trouble.'

Guy's gaze sharpened. 'Trouble?'

'From what I hear, some evil son of a bitch – pardon, madame – betrayed the guides and the helpers to the Gestapo. They arrested nearly three hundred people, all told, from here to Lyon and further north. That's why we ran out so fast when we saw you. We haven't seen anyone trying to escape for weeks now. Maybe even months.'

His grizzled face, like that of most French farmers I'd ever met, fell naturally into weatherworn folds, but right now it was taut with fury. He spat on the ground in front of him when he uttered the word, 'Nazis,' his sons grunting in assent.

It was clear where their loyalties lay so I risked another question. 'Do you know who's in charge of the Resistance around here? We have to make a rendezvous.'

His gaze now was calculating, his eyes assessing me as he rightly should. Only a fool would trust a stranger on sight these days, and this farmer looked to be as canny as they come.

'I will make some enquiries,' he said. 'In the meantime, we can take you to our farmhouse. You'll be safer there. If it was the Gestapo you were running from, they'll have patrols out looking as soon as they make their report. They can do that from the next station.'

'How far is that from here?' I asked.

'Twenty-one kilometres.'

Guy whistled through his teeth. 'They'll have already got there. I guess you're right. Time to move.'

The farmer grinned, revealing a row of broken teeth. 'We have a special way of doing that.'

He stuck his fingers between his teeth and let out a piercing whistle. A distant barking drew closer and closer until a huge shaggy dog burst into the barn, smothering its master with licks.

'Down,' commanded the farmer. He then pointed at the two of us. The dog looked at him as if he understood. 'Follow him,' said the farmer. 'We'll take the road so we can spot any of those Germans bastards coming this way. The dog will lead you over the fields to the back of the farmhouse.'

I gaped at him. They'd obviously done this before. 'What's his name?' I asked.

'Jean Moulin. He was born in 1940, you see. Just after Moulin was arrested.'

Jean Moulin, the hero of the French Resistance. If I had any remaining doubts about the farmer's allegiance, they were swept away at that moment.

'In that case,' I said, getting to my feet, 'I'm sure we're in very safe hands.'

Guy offered his hand to the farmer. 'Thank you, *monsieur*. We're so grateful you found us.'

Shaking it, the farmer broke out another gap-toothed grin. 'Anything to fight the Boches. *Allons-y*, Jean. Off you go.'

The dog trotted towards a gap in the hedge while the farmer and his gang set off down the lane, guns slung over their shoulders as if they were returning from rabbit hunting. I could hear their cheerful chatter as we crossed the lane, keeping up with our faithful friend while he led us along a stream that wound round through the trees, snaking back so that it flowed close to the farmhouse we could see on the other side of a hedgerow. The dog ran to a makeshift stile and looked back, making sure we were still following. He then jumped over and hovered on the other side until we caught up, treating us just as he would the sheep he was likely more used to herding.

The back door of the farmhouse opened at our approach and Jean ran up to greet his mistress. She shooed him away with one hand while she shooed us in with the other, exclaiming how cold and hungry we must be as she insisted we sit at the rough-hewn farmhouse table.

Moments later, the men arrived, minus the couple who'd kept watch.

'Don't worry. They've gone to fetch some people who can help you,' said the farmer, setting his gun down as he settled himself at the table and poured us another large tot of brandy all round. Firewater it might be, but it brought the life back to my limbs along with tears to my eyes. The farmer laughed as I blinked them away. 'You like it?'

'I do. It's very good.'

'Will your men be long?' asked Guy, glancing at the clock on the mantelpiece. I could see he was getting twitchy and tried to quell my own growing unease. The farmer said all the right things, and yet that could be just a bluff. Then again, the dog was called Jean Moulin. He even answered to it. I'd tested him out as we tramped along the stream, calling his name softly, and he'd instantly turned and gazed at me with soft, wise eyes as if to ask how he might please me. Still, time was ticking on.

Just as I thought Guy might explode, I heard noises outside the back door. I glanced at the farmer, but he appeared unconcerned. Then the door opened, and the two missing men entered along with another, the dog sloping in after them. My jaw dropped, and a chair clattered to the floor as Guy shot to his feet.

'Hammond. What the devil are you doing here?'

# FIFTY

I gaped at the British agent I'd last seen in Marie's courtyard at Canet-Plage. He was thinner, certainly, his corn-coloured hair longer, but it was him.

'You have no idea how glad I am to see you, sir.'

I could have sworn I detected tears in Guy's eyes as he embraced him, patting him between the shoulder blades in that way men do before stepping back so he could take a good look at him.

'How did you wind up here? Take a seat, man, for goodness' sake. No need to stand on ceremony.'

Hammond did as he was told, accepting his share of brandy.

'He jumped, just like you did,' said the farmer, looking round at the other men. 'We came to find him the same way we came for you. He's been here ever since, hiding in the next farm to ours. Our friend there is a patriot too.'

This was said with the kind of quiet pride I so often heard from men and women like this. Ordinary folk who took the most extraordinary risks, doing everything they could to save the people who were trying to free them from their hated occupiers.

Hammond looked bewildered, evidently still shocked to see us both here. 'You had to jump from the train as well? How did that come about?'

'Long story,' said Guy.

'Sefton told me you'd jumped,' I said, still trying to take in the fact it was really Hammond. 'But I had no idea it was around here.'

Hammond's eyes lit up. 'Sefton? Did he manage to get away too?'

'After a fashion. We extricated him from a prison camp. Sabourin is also free, although he was badly injured.'

'Will he be alright?'

Guy smiled. 'He'll be fine.'

Hammond knocked back the rest of his brandy, smacking his lips in delight. 'Best news I've had in a long time.'

The farmer held up the bottle. 'Some more? To celebrate?'

'Thank you,' I said, 'but we need to be on our way. We were due to meet someone at Montélimar station who was going to take us to the next safe house. I fear we've missed that rendezvous so it might be best to head back to Avignon and start again.'

'No need,' said the farmer, pouring another generous measure. 'I can take you there directly.'

I ignored the amber liquid in my glass. 'You know where the safe house is near Montélimar?'

He tapped his nose. 'Of course.'

First rule of the Resistance. Say as little as possible, at least if you wanted to stay alive. 'Can you take us there now?'

He slugged back his brandy then slammed his glass down. Taking this as a cue, we all did the same.

'Hammond, you stay here until we return,' said Guy.

I put my hand on his arm. 'We need to get a message to Paul in Avignon. Ask him to send word to Albert as well. We have no idea how many, if any, are at this safe house, but we must be prepared to move them as quickly as we can.'

'I can go,' said Hammond. 'Avignon isn't far from here.'

I looked at him dressed in his French farm worker's outfit. He could blend in well enough. 'It's not a bad idea,' I said.

Guy gave him the once-over. 'Very well. Paul is the proprietor of the café at Avignon station. We were with him just a few hours ago. He can contact Albert and tell him to expect the parcels from this safe house, although we have no idea how many as yet.'

Hammond snapped to attention. 'Yes, sir.'

'My son here can take you to Avignon in our other truck,' said the farmer. 'Safer than the train.'

He gestured to Guy and me to follow him out, but I lingered to give the dog a final pat.

'You be a good boy, Jean Moulin.'

He thumped his tail and leaped up to lick me on the cheek.

'Do you have that effect on all the boys?' Guy deadpanned.

'Only the big hairy ones.'

The farmer chortled. 'You remind me of her, you know. The lady you're about to meet. She might be a servant of God, but she's one strong woman, and she makes excellent wine.'

'Not the abbess?' I gasped. 'The last I heard, they'd taken her and some of her sisters.'

'Apparently, she threatened them with all kinds of punishment from God. Given the choice between Him and the Gestapo, the Vichy police decided to take their chances here on earth and let her and the sisters go.'

I threw back my head and laughed. 'I can believe it. The abbess taught me the cancan.'

Guy blinked. 'She did what?'

'She danced at the Folies Bergère before she became a nun. Rumour has it she was also a courtesan and a princess.'

'How exactly do you know this woman?'

'I recruited her in Lyon. She was based at the abbey there.'

'Did you now?' The spark was back in Guy's eye when he looked at me. 'You're full of surprises, Elisabeth.'

I met his smile with one of mine. 'Oh, you haven't seen anything yet.'

# FIFTY-ONE

The abbess was just as I remembered her, deceptively slender under her habit but with a will of steel, her wimple framing the astute eyes that ran over us both, lingering as she sized up Guy, warming as they turned to me. I kissed the cheek she offered, as cool as her courage.

'My dear, it is so good to see you again,' she murmured. 'But what on earth happened to your face?'

I touched the bruise on my cheek, still just about visible in spite of my efforts. 'An encounter with one of our German friends. Name of Drexler. He's with the Gestapo in Marseille.'

Her eyebrows shot up to the edge of her wimple. 'The Gestapo? Oh, my dear.'

'Not to worry. I'm here safe and sound, aren't I?'

She studied my face, those eyes missing nothing. 'I've thought of you often, especially after that awful business with King. I hear he started working for the Gestapo almost as soon as they picked him up.'

'It would appear so, but we carry on. I understand you're now helping out from here.'

She smiled impishly. 'But of course. Those Nazi thugs

aren't going to stop me. I'm so glad you found me. It's been far too long. But how on earth did you get here? We're a long way off the beaten track.'

The abbey was tucked away on a remote hillside overlooking its vines. The perfect place to hide people on the run.

'We bumped, or rather jumped, into a farmer who brought us here. He's another helper, and he knew about you. We're trying to put the line back together, you see. Captain Larose here was sent to help us along with his men.'

'I see. And what about Captain Grant? Is he here too?'

'Captain Grant is no longer with us.'

She looked startled. 'He's dead?'

'Mercifully not. He should be on his way back to London as we speak. We personally took him down the line and over the Pyrenees, so I can assure you that he's safe.'

'That is a relief. I'm hoping you can do the same for our guests.'

'I understand you have quite a few at the moment.'

She rose from her chair in the visitor's salon, and we did the same. 'I do. Would you like to meet them? The poor souls have been in there far too long, packed like sardines. We haven't been able to move them on, you understand. Not since all those arrests. I'd been hoping we'd hear from someone to tell us what to do. The fact that you, my dear, are actually here, in person, is more than we could have expected. Now follow me.'

We obeyed, walking behind her as she swept along echoing corridors and down a long flight of stone steps to the wine cellars below. There, she produced a key from the large bunch at her waist, unlocking the solid oak door that opened onto a vast, vaulted space lined with wine barrels. The place smelled of must and ripe fruit, of fermenting grapes and aged cedarwood. Further along, I caught the aroma of vanilla and oak. These must be the older barrels, ready to drink.

As we reached them, the abbess suddenly veered to the

right, squeezing behind the barrels to what seemed to be just another part of the cellar, pulling aside a wooden rack to reveal a hidden door. She produced another key and unlocked that one too, holding it open so that we could enter.

I went first, bending low so as not to hit my head, wondering how on earth Guy was going to manage, straightening once I was through to stare at the scene in front of me.

Never in all my days had I seen anything like this.

# FIFTY-TWO

The dimly lit cavern was crammed with people, some sitting on camp beds, others on the floor or at the table formed out of old wine barrels. I had to hold my breath so as not to gag on the stench that arose from so many human beings forced to live in close proximity with only a grille at one end to let in some air.

The abbess didn't appear to notice, concentrating instead on a little boy who looked to be five or six years old, sitting on the floor, colouring in a picture of an aeroplane. I looked over his shoulder, recognising the Lancaster bomber on the page. He'd coloured it a deep purple, drawing in orange flames shooting from it.

The abbess kneeled beside him and held out her hand. 'That's very good, Robert. May I see?'

I stared at him, transfixed. So this was him – this was Robert. I heard Guy make a tiny sound in his throat as he, too, gazed at the child. The miracle boy.

Robert was peering at the abbess shyly from under a conker-brown fringe, holding out his book for her to see. His eyes were huge, I noticed – his lashes almost as long as Guy's. A woman was sitting behind him, her haggard face creased with concern as she eyed us both.

'Robert and his guardian, Andrée, have been here for some time, along with these brave men,' said the abbess, indicating the airmen who were dressed in the odd assortment of clothes we'd come to expect from evaders and escapers. Most were taller than the local men and so their hosts found it hard to find anything to fit their guests. Shoes were the hardest, and I could see some of the men were standing in stockinged feet rather than try to squeeze them into tight, ill-fitting shoes.

'We need to get you men some better clothes,' I said to them in English, 'or you'll stand out like sore thumbs when we move you. We're going to get you out of here – all of you.'

'Does that include us?' whispered Robert.

I looked down at him. 'You speak English?'

'I learned it at school.'

'My goodness. How old are you?'

'Six.'

'He speaks three languages,' said Andrée, twisting her hands. She had deep hollows under eyes that bore that shell-shocked look of someone who'd seen things no one should ever see. I could only imagine what.

I smiled. 'Well then, Robert, I can tell you're going to be a great help to us.'

He dipped his head shyly. 'I will try my best.'

'That's all any of us can ever do, and I know your best will be excellent.'

One of the airmen stepped forward. 'Any idea when you can start moving us out, ma'am?'

I looked at him, taking in the freckles across his nose and his perfect teeth. He was so fresh-faced he looked as if he'd joined up straight from school. 'You're American?'

'Sergeant Arthur Bridge, ma'am. Royal Canadian Air Force.'

'Good to meet you, Sergeant,' said Guy. 'How many more Canadians do we have here?'

A half-dozen men raised their hands.

'Americans?'

Another ten raised their hands.

'Welcome. I guess the rest of you are Brits?'

'Don't forget us Aussies, mate,' shouted someone at the back.

Guy smiled. 'My apologies. How could we ever forget you guys?'

A ripple of laughter ran around the cellar room, slackening the tension. My heart went out to them all. They'd been shunted from place to place for weeks after crash landing or bailing out into enemy territory then cooped up here for yet more time in increasingly cramped conditions. And that was our biggest problem now. There were so many of them. Too many. Which only made it much more dangerous to move them now. Except we had no choice but to do so. The Nazis were here too, now, hunting down people just like this. If we left them here any longer, they would all die, including little Robert. So much rested on those tiny shoulders, but he was, after all, just a child. A child we had to save, no matter what.

# FIFTY-THREE

## 7 JANUARY 1943, MONTÉLIMAR STATION

The cargo car was packed to the brim with neatly stacked crates, most of them containing food supplies destined for the German troops in the south. It made it easy for us to hide among them, knowing that no one would be opening the car until the train reached Marseille. We'd be getting off before that, at Aix, where Paul's conductor friend had promised to unlock the car and where Albert and Hammond would be waiting.

'You'll only have a few minutes to get out,' the conductor hissed before he locked us in. 'The Germans don't normally have a checkpoint there, but you never know.'

'What about the other checkpoints? Will they insist you open the car?'

'Not if I tell them it's full of their own food supplies. They won't risk anyone trying to steal it.'

The Resistance had carried out quite a few successful raids on German food supplies. It was no wonder they were wary. Then again, this was French food that was literally being taken from the mouths of people who barely had enough to eat. I peered into the crates, itching to liberate a few items myself but knowing it would be folly when so much was at stake.

Beside me, Robert sat silent, his knees drawn up to his chest. Andrée had her head tilted back and her eyes closed as she slumped against the crate, but he was watching everyone and everything, taking it all in. A few feet away, Guy was squeezed between two groups of men, as vigilant as Robert, constantly scanning the door as well as the rest of the car to make sure no one was doing anything that would give us away.

'Put that out,' he snarled as an airman pulled out a cigarette and lit it. 'The Germans see smoke and they'll be on to us before you know it.'

Sheepishly, the airman did as he was told, muttering an apology. We had the bulk of them with us, fifteen in total, while the abbess was sending the rest with local helpers the next day.

'Don't worry,' the abbess had said as she'd bidden us farewell, 'we'll make sure everything runs smoothly for you from here.'

Now, as we hurtled along the tracks heading south once more, the train rocking us all with its rhythm, I could almost believe everything was going to be fine. Almost. In my experience, things never worked out like that, especially not when you were operating an escape line. Still, it had gone smoothly so far, with our team pulling together to make this happen. We'd accomplished what we'd set out to do, and now we were on our way back to Chateau Bleu aboard the train that was a vital cog in the machine of our new escape line.

For a while, I let myself sink into that rhythm, listening to the rumbling as we drew closer to a station, then the hiss and squeal of the brakes. Holding my breath as we stopped, hearing distant shouts and the slamming of doors before we chugged off once more, picking up speed, rocking from side to side, the slats that let in air allowing enough light through that I could make

out the faces around me, their eyes gleaming like night crea-
tures', although most tried to get some sleep.

'Andrée,' Robert whispered. And then louder: 'Andrée.'

Her eyes flickered open. 'What is it?'

'I need to pee.'

She looked frantically around. 'There's nowhere to go,
Robert.'

I placed a hand on his shoulder. 'Do you think you can hold
on? Just for a little while longer? We're almost there.'

He nodded, his face contorted with discomfort.

It was true though. Barely half an hour later, the conductor
banged on the connecting door twice to signal we were
approaching Aix. Another squeal of brakes and we were slowing, daylight flooding in as the conductor flung open the far side
of the cargo car before we came to a halt.

'Everyone out.'

I jumped first, holding my hands up to help Andrée while
Guy lifted Robert down. 'This way.'

I began to move as fast as I could across the tracks, keeping
low as we wove our way through the stationary trains, towards
the maintenance platform where the conductor had assured me
there was a workman's entrance.

There it was. There, too, was Albert with Hammond
standing by, pretending to share a smoke. All we had to do was
reach them.

At that moment, the train began to pull out.

'Hurry,' I said, gesturing to the men straggling behind. In a
few more seconds, we'd be visible to anyone standing on the
main platform, including the railway police or even their
Gestapo friends.

Albert was so close now I could make out the stubble on his
chin as well as the look on his face as he took in the situation.
Both he and Hammond ditched their cigarettes and pulled their
weapons as I finally reached the steps that led up to the mainte-

nance platform, reaching back to grab Andrée by the hand and haul her behind me.

I was at the top of the steps, Guy with Robert right behind us, when I heard someone shout, 'Stop!'

I looked the way we'd come to see that our train had left, and we were totally exposed, the police on the far platform blowing their whistles furiously at the sight of the party of men who were surging after me up the steps.

'Keep down!' shouted Albert.

The bullets were flying now, he and Hammond giving us covering fire.

I shoved Robert and Andrée through the entrance to where I could see the trucks were parked, urging the men forward and through the gap too.

'Come on. Faster,' I cried as they kept coming, one stumbling as a bullet nicked him, Guy running back to help him up, then staggering as he, too, was hit, this time full in the chest, blood spreading, scarlet, as he slumped to the ground. I tried to push my way back through the men who were still coming, all the while shouting, 'Let me through!'

'It's OK, ma'am. We've got him.'

I could see the young Canadian, Sergeant Bridge, with one arm around Guy, while another man had him on the other side, dragging him up the steps, his legs apparently lifeless.

'Into the trucks,' yelled Albert, signalling to his men, then reaching to grab me. 'You too.'

'No.' I ran back to the men who were hauling Guy through the gap now, heading towards the trucks, lifting him into one. I jumped in beside him, and we were off, weaving our way through the backstreets, trying to throw off the police, my hands pressing down on his wound, feeling the blood seeping through my fingers, warm and sticky – Guy's lifeblood – chanting over and over in my head, 'Please, please let him live.'

# FIFTY-FOUR

'He's lucky,' said Dr George. 'The bullet missed the aorta by millimetres. I've extracted it and cleaned the wound. I'll be back tomorrow to change the dressing and make sure there's no infection.'

'Thank you, Doctor,' murmured Eliane. 'Please, come and have something to eat.'

The doctor reached for his hat and coat. 'That's very kind, but Fanny has already prepared something. Another time.'

His face was grey with exhaustion. He'd been in with Guy for over three hours, two of which I would never forget as long as I lived. With precious little anaesthetic to be found, he'd had to use the bare minimum, Guy drifting in and out of consciousness as the doctor dug around in the wound, extracting the bullet and then carefully cleaning it before sewing him up while we did our best to soothe him. A hopeless task as the sweat poured from his brow and he grimaced in agony. At times, he couldn't help crying out in pain despite the piece of leather we'd stuck between his teeth.

I handed the doctor his scarf. 'Is he asleep now?'

'He was. You might want to go and sit with him.'

The doctor's kindly eyes were trying to tell me something. I felt a clutch of fear. 'He will be alright, won't he?'

'He should be. In time. Thanks to you putting pressure on it, the wound stopped bleeding, allowing the blood to coagulate. The main danger now is from infection. He must rest, and we need to keep that wound scrupulously clean.'

'You can count on me. I'll make sure he rests, and if you show me how to clean it, I can take care of the wound so you don't have to come out here every day.'

He smiled. 'I can show you. By the way, he said something after you left the room. I wasn't sure if it was the anaesthetic talking or him.'

'So what did he say?'

'That he will always love you. At least, I assumed it was you. I'm fairly certain he's not in love with me.'

With that, Dr George doffed his hat and followed Eliane down the stairs, both of them smiling.

I stared at the door in front of me, unaccountably nervous. Telling me that he loved me was one thing, telling the entire world quite another. Alright, Dr George and Eliane hardly constituted the entire world. Still, I hesitated, until I forced myself to push the door open and tiptoe into the room.

His eyes were closed, the covers pulled up to his chin. At least his breathing sounded regular. Thank goodness the bullet had also missed his lungs.

I crept around the bed and sank into the chair beside it, gazing at his face, so white his skin appeared almost translucent, those lashes sweeping down, his eyelids flickering now and then as he slept. A lock of hair had fallen over his forehead. I reached out and brushed it aside with my fingertips. He stirred, and I held my breath until he settled into sleep once more.

With his face relaxed like this, he looked more like Hélène than ever, the cheekbones they shared sculpted so he resembled a statue, his mouth softly curved just like hers. They had a

similar nose too, fine and straight, although Guy's was more
masculine. It was the expression, though, that reminded me of
her the most. For once, he appeared vulnerable, the sweetness
in his character revealed. It struck me then how similar we were
too, how much we both hid our real selves.

'Hey, you,' he rasped, his eyes fluttering open. He winced as
he spoke, and I reached for the water set on the table beside me.

'Here, drink this. I'll help you.'

I slid my hand under the back of his neck, raising his head
as I held the cup to his chapped lips. He took a few sips and
then lay back on his pillows, attempting a grateful smile even as
he winced in pain.

'Easy now,' I murmured. 'You've been through a lot.'

'Thank you for being there,' he mumbled.

I picked up the compress Eliane had left and gently pressed
it against his lips as he watched me, his eyes never leaving my
face. 'There now – that should feel a bit better.'

'Seeing you makes me feel better. You were here, weren't
you, with the doctor? Or was that a dream?'

He looked confused, the anaesthetic still fogging his brain.
'I was here. You were very brave.'

His hand reached for mine, clasping it, his grip weak. 'You
gave me strength. You always do.'

It was there, naked on his face, tenderness mixed with longing. He was defenceless, unguarded. My heart lurched as I
gazed at him. 'You should sleep now. You need to rest so that
you can recover.'

A squeeze of my hand, so light I scarcely felt any pressure.
He was drifting off again when his eyes flew open once more.
'Lionel – how is he?'

'He's fine,' I answered, tucking him in. 'Already up and
about, sitting in an armchair downstairs.'

Another smile and he was gone, his breathing slowing and
deepening as sleep overtook him. I stayed for a few moments,

watching to make sure he was alright, then I tiptoed from the room as silently as I'd come in, my heart now in knots.

Downstairs in the salon, I found Lionel just as I'd described, a blanket draped over his legs as he sat by the fire.

Eliane was just lifting a tray from his side table as I entered. 'How's he doing?' she asked.

'He's sleeping now. I gave him a little water, but he's still pretty woozy from the anaesthetic.'

Lionel looked up at me. 'He'll be OK?'

'He will.'

'Thank God. I've been sitting here, thinking about him, about us training together. He's something special is Guy, but then, you already know that.'

I smiled at him. 'I do.'

'Come.' He indicated the chair on the other side of the fireplace. 'Sit with me for a while.'

I sank into the armchair, all at once feeling immensely tired. It had been a long day. A very long day. 'How are you feeling now?'

'Me? I'm OK. Us Quebecois, we're made of tough stuff.'

'Is that where you're from? Quebec?'

He nodded. 'Montreal. I'd just left university there when I joined up. First day at training camp, I met Guy. We clicked, you know? Like two peas in a pod. He likes to work hard and play hard, same as me. The only difference is, he takes life more seriously. Me, I live for today, but Guy... he can be so deep sometimes. He's a thinker.'

This was a whole new perspective on Guy – one I was beginning to think was the real him. 'You seem to be great friends. He was worried about you. Asked me just now how you're doing.'

Lionel's eyes misted over. 'That's the kind of man he is. Never thinks of himself, always his men. And maybe one woman.' He dropped me a wink.

I feigned indifference. 'Oh really? Who?'

'You, of course. He never stops talking about you.'

'Me?' I stuttered.

'All through training I tell you. Blah, blah, blah about this girl he'd left behind in France. You could tell he never got over her.'

'Some of us are just unforgettable,' said a voice, its silvered tone sending a spear through my guts. We both looked round to see Charlotte slink into the room, a triumphant smirk on her face as she looked at me. 'Isn't that right, darling?'

# FIFTY-FIVE

## 8 JANUARY 1943, CHATEAU BLEU, SOUTHERN FRANCE

The telephone rang so rarely at the chateau that I jumped when it did as I was passing. It sat in the hallway, by the front door, largely forgotten until we needed it. I looked at it for a second, wondering if it would stop, but whoever was calling clearly needed to speak to someone. I picked it up, listening hard, waiting for them to speak first. I thought I heard a tell-tale click on the line, but I couldn't be sure.

'*Allo?*'

'Albert, is that you?'

'*Allo,* can you hear me?'

There was so much noise in the background I barely could. It sounded as if he was somewhere crowded, the voices all around him almost drowning him out.

'I can hear you. What is it?'

'It's our friend. He has some unwelcome guests. I'm in my favourite bar, waiting to see if they leave.'

'Oh God, no.' My knees gave way, and I slumped to the floor, leaning against the wall for support.

'What is it? What's happened?' Eliane was hurrying down the stairs.

I looked up at them both sightlessly. 'It's Albert. He just more or less told me they've raided Dr George's apartment. He was here just last night. I can't believe it.'

She looked at me helplessly. 'There's nothing we can do, Elisabeth. Except wait until we find out what's happened to them.'

Alice and Robert came racing towards us along the corridor at that moment. I hastily rearranged my face, smiling brightly at both of them.

'Come and see, come and see,' they cried, dragging Eliane and I by the hand to the ballroom, their faces alight with a happiness that warmed my heart.

François was sitting, sketching the men, as we entered. He looked up from his work as he saw us. 'Everything alright?'

Eliane kissed the top of his head. 'We'll tell you later.'

'Those are so good,' I breathed. 'You've captured them exactly as they are. You're very talented.'

François beamed. 'Thank you, but you're the one who should be proud. You saved them all.'

'They're not saved yet. We still have to get them over the Pyrenees,' I muttered. Given the news I'd just received, that felt like a more daunting task than ever.

'I'll just go and have a word with Cook about dinner,' murmured Eliane.

I glanced at her. 'When Albert gets here, we can talk. Make a plan.'

She patted my shoulder. 'Don't worry too much. We'll find a way to help them.'

I nodded absently, my gaze drifting over the men, wondering how the hell we were going to get them all out of here and safely over that border.

I noticed a couple huddled together away from the rest and recognised them from the American contingent. They looked like your average Midwesterners – hair neatly combed, faces almost too clean. The one thing they were missing were those eager expressions most of them wore, but then, these two had seen combat. That tended to tarnish the eagerness in any man. It was interesting how they divided up into their groups, countrymen sticking close to one another, although there was a general camaraderie. We were all in this together, for better or for worse.

'How are the patients doing?' called out Sergeant Bridge.

'They're doing well, I'm pleased to say. They'll be back on their feet in no time. Now, does anyone else want to be sketched?'

'Hell, yes,' shouted a strapping aviator, striking a pose. 'This here is my best side.'

The others clustered round as François settled down once more and began to sketch him, his lightning-quick pencil strokes drawing whistles of admiration.

'Draw me next!'

'No, me...'

I laughed at their enthusiasm. It broke up the boredom of the day for them as well as helping them to bond. They would need that bond in the days ahead as they tackled the Pyrenees. The mountains were unforgiving at the best of times, but in winter, with patrols everywhere, they were lethal.

I noticed the two who'd been huddled in the corner sidling towards the door, looking furtive. It pricked my curiosity. Walking over to them, I smiled. 'Don't you want François to draw you too? He's very good.'

One gave me a dull-eyed stare. 'No. Thank you.'

The other seemed twitchy. Whatever it was they were discussing, they clearly didn't want me listening in.

'Right, then.' I beat a retreat, a faint alarm bell ringing in my head. Silly. I was on edge because of what had happened yesterday. The men were entitled to their privacy. What they probably wanted was a drink on their own and a quiet smoke.

Even so, I wandered over to Sergeant Bridge as casually as I could. He struck me as someone with eyes and ears on the pulse, not to mention a swift intelligence. 'Those two over there,' I murmured. 'Don't look. The ones by the door.'

'You mean the hillbillies?' he whispered back.

'That's what you call them?'

'On account of their accents. The other boys said they'd never heard anything like it.'

Interesting. So much for Midwesterners. 'You mean the other American boys?'

'Yes, ma'am. Most of them are East or West Coast, university boys. They reckon those two came straight out of the Appalachians with straw still sticking to their hair.'

'I see.'

I also saw the way they were looking at little Robert as he clung to Alice's hand, watching François work. They were staring at him with an intensity that bordered on hatred. For a second, I couldn't breathe. How could you hate a little boy? Perhaps I was mistaken – the next moment, they were conferring once more, ignoring everyone else. Maybe they weren't looking at Robert at all. He was just standing in their sightline.

I was still pondering that one as I wandered back out into the hallway and walked straight into Charlotte.

'Well, well, well,' she purred. 'If it isn't Guy's little girlfriend.'

'I'm not his girlfriend,' I snapped.

'Oh, that's right. You were friends with his little sister. What was her name? Hélène? Shame about that. Still, it happens. This is wartime after all.'

I glared at her. 'Are you always this hateful?'

She threw back her head, emitting a tinkling laugh. 'The kitten has claws after all.'

My fingers itched to wrap themselves around her throat, but I restrained myself. The Charlottes of this world were never worth it. 'Don't you have something better to do? Maybe spend some time with your husband instead of leaving him to find company in a bottle?'

Two spots of colour stained her cheeks. 'You know nothing about us,' she snapped.

'I know what I see.'

'Oh? And what's that?'

'Two people who can't stand one another but have to stay together because of their child. A child you certainly don't deserve. She's a wonderful girl. Kind-hearted, talented. Always prepared to see the good in people. I assume she takes after her father, although, as I've never seen him sober, I can't be too sure.'

She sucked in her breath, looking for a second as if she might implode. Her words floated out on her exhale, each landing like a poison dart. 'She certainly does take after her father, except you can't see it, can you? You're blinded by rose-coloured glasses, you silly little fool.'

# FIFTY-SIX

Eliane reappeared at my shoulder some time later as I stood, still watching François sketch. 'Sefton and Hammond have returned, along with Albert. Captain Larose has asked that we all meet in his room. He wondered if you'd be kind enough to give him a hand first.'

My stomach plunged. 'Of course.'

'We need to talk,' he said, the moment I entered the room.

'We do?'

'Yes, and I think you know why, but first things first. Here – help me sit up.'

I ignored his tone, slipping an arm around his back to help him. 'I'm not sure this is a good idea. What if your stitches burst?'

He grimaced. 'Then you can sew me back up.'

'I can't sew. We'll do this on three. One, two...'

A moan as he hauled himself up without waiting for me.

'I told you this was a bad idea.'

He ignored me, putting on a brave face as Albert and the other two men entered the room. 'Glad you could make it.

Although I'm sorry to hear what happened to Dr George and his wife, Albert.'

Albert glowered. 'Fuck the Gestapo. Fuck that concierge even more. I swear it was that woman that sold them out.'

'Could have been, but it might also have been Harry King,' said Guy. 'He stayed there after all.'

Harry King. That man had so much to answer for. 'He's been gone a while though. Why now? Why wait this long to raid the apartment?'

Albert shrugged. 'We know Drexler has been watching the place. My guess is they were hoping more evaders and escapers would show up.'

'Or perhaps even you, Elisabeth.' Guy's voice was dry.

My stomach plunged once more. I could feel what was coming.

'I think, given what's happened, it's imperative we get these men and the little boy out as soon as possible. We need to wait and see what happens with Dr George and the others though, whether they break under interrogation. In the meantime, we have to be ready to move at a moment's notice. As you've learned, Drexler is capable of anything.'

I could see the effort Guy was making. His words might be strong, but his breathing was laboured, his face pinched and wan. 'We need to find a new route across the Pyrenees as well. It's too dangerous now in the west. That's why Sefton and Hammond were in Toulouse today. The Germans have troops at all the western border crossing points, so we're looking to the east. It's longer and more dangerous, but there's nothing we can do about that either.'

Sefton spoke up. 'We've already made contact with a Basque guide, sir, thanks to a woman who runs one of the safe houses which are still in operation.'

The eastern Pyrenees. Not as high as the central route but tougher than the west where we'd crossed with Grant. It would still be crawling with German patrols, although the more treacherous terrain kept the numbers down. 'When do we take the first party across?'

'In the next day or two, weather permitting,' said Guy. 'Elisabeth, you'll be going with them, but it's a one-way trip for you.'

His voice was husky, although his eyes burned with something I recognised of old.

'I'm not going anywhere,' I said.

He stared back at me, implacable. 'You promised, Elisabeth. You said you'd use the line once we'd restored it, and we have. Or are you going to break your word?'

He had me, and he knew it. 'I... I did say that, yes.'

'So you'll be going with the men? We'll send them over first to make absolutely sure of the route before we risk taking little Robert and Andrée that way. You can lead one group while Sefton and Hammond take another.'

I stared at him, feeling the sting of betrayal. He knew how much my work here meant to me. Then again, he was right. I was burned. Completely compromised with those damn posters everywhere and the Gestapo desperate to get their hands on me. Thank God Drexler hadn't realised who he had in his clutches. Or maybe he did. Maybe it was all part of some hideous plan they'd cooked up. Either way, it was time to leave. I knew that. We all knew that. Even though it would break my heart to go, for more reasons than I cared to admit.

'Very well then,' I muttered. 'I'll go.'

I turned away, pretending to stare out the window, not wanting them to see the tears that were threatening to spill.

'It really is for the best,' murmured Guy, but I was no longer listening. I was staring out into the night, wondering if I would ever return, if I would be able to carry on the fight here or spend the rest of the war stuck in some office in London. Most of all, I wondered if I would ever see Guy again.

# FIFTY-SEVEN

## 9 JANUARY 1943

Barely twenty-four hours later, I was standing in Guy's bedroom once more, only this time it was to say goodbye.

'We're leaving at dawn,' I said. 'We're heading first to Toulouse and the safe house. The guide will meet us there. I'm taking the first group on the train, Sefton and Hammond the second. Lionel is coming with us.'

I was pleased to see there was a little more colour in Guy's face as he gazed at me from his pillows. 'You look better,' I added. 'How's the pain?'

'Physical or emotional?'

I hesitated, unsure what he meant.

'Come here,' he said, patting the bed.

I moved to the chair beside it.

'No. Here.'

Not sure where this was leading, I perched on the bed where he'd patted. 'Happy?' I asked.

'That you're here with me now? Yes. That you're leaving? No. But you can't stay, Elisabeth. I would never forgive myself if anything happened to you. I don't want you to go, but I'm terrified about what might happen if you remain in France. Drexler will never give up until he finds you again.'

He was pleading with me to understand – I could see it in his eyes, hear it and feel it as he reached for my hand, but some obstinate streak made me snatch it away.

'You would never forgive yourself? What about me? I'll never forgive myself if anything happens to you or to the other people in this house. Let me at least come back and get Robert and Andrée over the border too. I know the mountains. Your men don't, and you're not fit enough to get them over safely. You saw with Pedro that you can't completely trust those guides. What are you going to do if you get stuck out there with that child?'

Guy sighed. 'We'll work it out. I'm getting stronger by the day. I'll soon be fit again. Come now, Elisabeth. Don't be mad. We can't part like this.'

I folded my arms. 'Why not? You're so keen to see me gone, what do you care if I even say goodbye?'

He threw back his head and burst out laughing. I stared at him for a moment in mounting fury and then, unaccountably, felt a bubble of laughter rising in me too. I was being ridiculous, I knew that, and yet deep down I wanted him to say it, to beg me to stay no matter what.

'You know what you look like?' he gasped, wiping his eyes. 'You look like you did when you were twelve and your mother said you had to go to bed rather than stay up with the grown-ups.'

I looked at him, trying to hide the fact my lips were twitching. 'I do, do I?'

'Yes. Totally. You had that same look on your face then, the one that said you weren't going to miss out on anything if you could help it.'

'Well,' I said, sitting up taller, 'if you remember, Hélène and I went off to bed every time. What you don't know is that we then sneaked down the back stairs and listened from the hallway while we drank chocolate and had a little party of our own.'

'I know you did. I saw you.'

'You did? And you never said anything?'

His grin was as mischievous as it had ever been. 'How could I? I'd also sneaked out for a cigarette and a little encounter with someone or other.'

'Ah yes. Your encounters. There were a lot, as far as I remember.'

Except it wasn't as funny as it had been at the time. Back then, Hélène and I had giggled over his parade of admirers. Now, all that memory brought back was a piercing pain somewhere near my heart. Actually, right through it. 'Hélène and I, we used to spy on you sometimes.'

He raised an eyebrow. 'You did?'

'Yes. We used to mimic you kissing them.' I kissed the back of my hand as I had then, making smooching noises.

Guy groaned. 'Oh my God. You two.'

Us two. Me and Hélène. 'We were so good together.'

My words seemed to echo around the room, although I'd barely raised my voice above a whisper.

Guy reached for my hand again, and this time I let him hold it. 'We're good together,' he murmured. 'You and I.'

'Then why are you making me go?'

'You know why.'

I could feel it, that pull between us, the one anchoring me to this place, to him, making it impossible to leave. I wanted to hear him say it one more time, in case I never heard it again. In the same way I wished I could talk to Hélène one more time, except that she was gone, forever. At least we had this place and this time, even though tomorrow I'd be gone. Back to my old life. My responsibilities.

'I love you,' he whispered, his eyes tracing every curve and angle of my face, his fingers reaching out to do the same. 'I love you so much, Elisabeth. I wish you could understand quite how much. I know you think I'm trifling with you like I did with all the others, but that was never me. I was just a boy trying to appear confident. Those other girls you talk about, they meant nothing. It was always you.'

I watched his mouth, mesmerised, as he spoke, staring at those lips, wanting to kiss them so much. Still, something else held me back. Or made me speak up, the words tumbling out before I could stop them. 'What about Charlotte?'

'What about her?'

His voice was guarded, harsh even, the face that had shone naked with emotion only seconds before closing down, his eyes hardening as he stared back at me. It took me a moment to realise he wasn't staring at me like that but rather a memory. For some reason, he hated her, and I had to know why.

'What happened between you?' I murmured.

'It's ancient history.'

'It doesn't look like it to me. I can hear it when she talks about you or to you. You have unfinished business. Or at least, she does. If you ask me, she's still in love with you.'

Another bark of laughter from Guy, this one very different. 'The only person Charlotte has ever loved is herself.'

He was hiding something – I could feel it. 'If that's true, then tell me what happened. Why does she act the way she does about you?'

'Alright,' he said, pulling himself up higher on his pillows so he could look me straight in the eye. 'I'll tell you. Charlotte and I had a brief affair in Paris when I was eighteen. You remember I was there for a year, studying, before my family emigrated. We met through friends of my parents at a party, and I admit I was dazzled by her. She seemed so sophisticated and glamorous. She was twenty at the time. It was only later I realised that what I thought was sophistication was a brittle layer that covered a cold heart. All Charlotte has ever wanted is money and a title. She got both with that man she's married. Too bad he's a drunk.'

I got the sense there was more to the story, but I didn't press him. 'I see. Well, thank you for telling me.'

'Elisabeth.' That pleading note once more, his fingers twining around mine. 'Don't go. Stay the night. Here, with me.'

'I can't do that.'

'Why not? You don't trust me? I promise, I won't lay a finger on you. I just want to hold you.'

'It's not that. I don't trust myself.'

Our eyes locked. Deep in my gut, I knew this was one of those moments that could change everything. Yet still I hesitated, knowing I might never see him again, fearing that more than anything.

'Alright,' I whispered. 'I'll stay.'

# FIFTY-EIGHT

It's funny how, even in the dark, you can feel someone's eyes on you.

'Why are you looking at me?' I muttered, lying a careful distance from him on my back, arms folded across my chest. I was watching shadows on the ceiling once more, cast by the moonlight streaming through the window. When I turned my head to look at him, I could see it reflected in his eyes.

'So I don't forget.'

I rolled over on my side, careful not to touch him. I told myself it was because I was afraid of hurting him, but in reality I was more afraid of what I might feel. 'You'd forget how I look that easily?'

'No, silly. I don't want to forget this night.'

Our faces were so close on the pillows. Too close. I stayed where I was, absorbing the smell of him, the scent of his skin only inches from mine, feeling his breath tickle my face as he spoke, watching his lips move, wishing they were touching mine. 'Why? What's so special about tonight?'

His mouth curved in the way I loved, one corner higher than the other. *Loved*. A big word.

'You're here. That's special enough for me. We don't always need champagne and roses, although both are nice. But just being here, with you, that's what I want to remember, to hold close to me when things get tough the way I want to hold you.'

I could see his lashes; count every single one of them. Those damned lashes, framing eyes I could drown in. 'Why don't you hold me then?'

A sharp intake of breath. 'I didn't think you wanted me to.'

'You have no idea how much I want you to. But I'm scared.'

'Of hurting me?'

'Of hurting both of us. There are things you don't know about me too. Things that happened in the years we've been apart.'

I barely felt his fingers as they reached for a tendril of my hair, twining it before letting go. 'Elisabeth, I don't care what you've done. It's your life and your business. All I care about is you. Period. The rest is history, as far as I'm concerned.'

'Actually, it's not.'

I could hear his heart beating; sense the blood pulsing through his veins – the lifeforce that was Guy, calling out to me, just as it had always done. The minute I opened my mouth, all that would be over. He would shut down and turn away from me, just as I feared. But I had to do it. I had to tell him before it really was too late.

'What do you mean?' he murmured.

I covered my face with my hands, my heart breaking. 'I'm engaged. To someone else. I know I should have told you before, but it never seemed the right moment.'

He flinched as if I'd struck him, rolling away from me to lie on his back and stare at the ceiling just as I had done.

'Guy, say something. Anything. Please.'

When he at last spoke, his voice was flat, emotionless. 'Who is he?'

'He's the son of a friend of my father's. They do business

together. We met over lunch at their house, and we hit it off. He's deployed overseas now. I have no idea where.'

He was still gazing at the same spot on the ceiling, although I got the sense he was seeing something else entirely. 'Do you love him?'

'I— Yes. No. I thought I did.'

'You thought you did? How come you didn't write Hélène about this? I thought you girls shared everything?'

He couldn't hide the bitter note, and I didn't blame him. To be fair, he sounded more betrayed than bitter. 'I did. She must have got the letter after she...'

'Oh. I see. So this was a recent engagement?'

'Yes. On my last leave before I was sent back out here. I wrote to ask Hélène if she would be my bridesmaid too, but here's the thing... even as I was writing it, I knew I was pretending.'

I caught the gleam of his eyes in my peripheral vision as he turned to look at me. 'Pretending? How?'

'Guy, listen to me. I knew I was settling – that Peter wasn't the love of my life but that he would do. I know that sounds cruel and selfish, but my parents were so happy, as were his. Even as I said yes, I knew it was a mistake, but I promised myself I would make him happy. You were gone, remember? I hadn't seen you in years. I knew that at some point I had to give up on my dreams and accept it was never going to happen. I was never going to be with you.'

My words fell into the void between us, the crevasse of disappointment and heartbreak I knew would open up the moment I spoke. Across the silence, I could feel his mind working.

'Are you telling me you were waiting for me all this time?'

'I suppose I am,' I whispered.

'I guess I showed up just a little too late.'

'I guess you did.'

# FIFTY-NINE

## 10 JANUARY 1943

'It really is goodbye then.' I hugged Eliane one final time, reluctant to let go.

'Not goodbye. *Au revoir*. I know you, Elisabeth. You're not the sort to disappear forever.'

I smiled into her wise eyes. 'You're right. I'm like a bad penny, always showing up. Very well. *Au revoir*, my friend. I'll miss you all.'

She and François tugged their robes around them as I opened the door, letting in the cold dawn air. The men were already in the vans, divided into two groups, Lionel among them now that he was fit enough to walk.

One final hug. 'Thank you both for everything.'

I could feel my heart crumble as I climbed into the passenger seat, Albert at the wheel, forcing myself not to look up at Guy's window but to focus on the road ahead until we were well down the track.

'Are you OK?'

I glanced at Albert. 'I'm fine.'

He snorted. 'You're a bad liar, Elisabeth.'

'I hope not. I'd hate to think I'd been getting past the Gestapo purely on luck.'

At that, he laughed. 'Point taken. I hope you at least said goodbye to him.'

I wasn't going to insult his intelligence by pretending I had no idea who he was talking about. 'I did.'

A goodbye that still sat like a lead weight in my gut.

After my revelation, there had been little more to say. Even so, he'd insisted I stay, and I'd finally fallen asleep just before dawn broke only to awaken and scramble for my things. He'd still been asleep, worn out no doubt for the same reason I was. I'd looked down at him breathing, seeing his chest rise and fall, the shadows under his eyes matching mine, the face I would love until the end of time.

'Goodbye,' I'd whispered. 'I love you.'

Then I'd crept from his room, every bone and sinew screaming at me to stay.

I blinked, trying to erase the image from my mind, that last look at him lying there, a look that might have to sustain me for a lifetime, however long that might be.

As we drew closer to the station, my instincts kept telling me to turn back, that something was off. No. Those weren't instincts. That was my own selfish nature trying to override what was right.

The van came to a halt, and I ignored the voice in my head shouting at me, talking over my shoulder instead to the men crammed into the van.

'When I get out, I want you to count to ten and then follow me in ones and twos. The station is busy at this time so you can move along with the crowd. You all have your tickets and papers. Please keep them safe. Try to sit in separate compartments to one another and remember to go to the station café when we arrive at Toulouse. The owners of the café run an operation to help people avoid the ticket collectors and awkward questions. You enter the gentleman's toilet and exit through another unlocked door into the street, crossing it to go into the bar opposite, where we'll all rendezvous in the back room. If there's any problem, the phrase to use is, "There doesn't seem to be any paper in the WC." Oh, and don't forget you're either a deaf mute or asleep on the train. Keep your ticket somewhere obvious so the collector can simply stamp it without disturbing you. Any questions?'

A chorus of, 'No, ma'ams.'

'Excellent. Let's do it.'

As I hopped out of the van, I muttered to Albert, 'Good luck, my friend.'

The train was already quite full as I boarded, making my way down the carriages until I found a spare seat. Not ideal but it meant the men would have to scatter around the train too instead of instinctively sticking together. I caught sight of several uniforms as I passed, deliberately ignoring them. There were German soldiers on most trains these days in the south, along with SS and, sometimes, Gestapo. The trick was to blend in as much as possible and to rely on the fact that most of the *cheminots* were on our side.

I spied a seat ahead and made for it, arriving at the same time as a German officer, resplendent in his Wehrmacht uniform. I made to carry on past, but he gave me a little bow. 'Please. There is room for two people.'

I wavered, knowing that if I refused, it would only look insulting or suspicious. 'Thank you.'

I took the window seat, closing my eyes as I leaned my head against the glass to ward off any attempts at conversation, although, in truth, it was a struggle to keep my eyes open.

Unfortunately, the officer was the chatty sort. 'Are you travelling far?'

'Not too far.'

'To visit family?'

'Yes. I have an aunt there who's on her own with the children. I've offered to go and help,' I improvised, expanding on
the cover story I'd already dreamed up. My travel permit stated
that my purpose of travel was to visit relatives, so it wasn't too
much of a stretch.

'That's very kind of you,' he said, drawing his wallet from
his jacket and opening it to reveal a photograph. 'This is my
wife, Hilde, and my children, Rolf and Ilse.'

I peered at the woman, her hair swept up in a severe style
although she had a gentle smile, as did her daughter. 'She's very
pretty; your wife and your children are charming. You must be
very proud of them.'

'I am.,' He smiled, stuffing the wallet back in his pocket.
'What about you? Do you have any children?'

'Not yet. I'm engaged to be married, but...'

I trailed off. I'd been about to blurt out that he'd been called
up, but then I remembered where I was and who I was
supposed to be. 'But he's away, you know. Working.'

'Ah yes.'

The officer pursed his lips and said no more at the sugges-
tion my fiancé was one of those forced to labour in Germany,
one of the many prices France paid for the privilege of being
occupied by men such as he.

The train chugged on, lulling me into a doze. I heard the
distant sounds of whistles and brakes as we stopped at stations,
keeping one ear open for Toulouse. As soon as the conductor
announced it was the next station, I gathered my things and
began to walk back through the train, making sure the men saw
me before we disembarked, clocking Sefton and Hammond as I
passed.

This was the most dangerous part of the journey. At any
moment, a German soldier might challenge me to produce my
papers or a plain-clothes Gestapo officer could rise from his seat
and arrest me.

Neither happened. With a deep inward sigh of relief, I stepped down onto the platform and made my way along it to the café, where I glanced around before slipping into the toilet and straight out the other door, across the street and into the bar opposite.

There, I walked straight up to the counter.

'A café noir please, with extra sugar.'

'Right this way, madame,' murmured the proprietor, leading me to a corner table next to a heavy curtain which he twitched aside, giving me just enough room to dart behind it.

I looked around. I was in a large storeroom stacked with all manner of supplies on one side. On the other, there were bicycles. Dozens of them. As the room filled up with the men, they glanced at them too.

'Say, ma'am, are those for us?' ventured one of the Americans.

'They certainly are, so I hope you can all ride a bicycle, because that's how you're getting to the safe house.'

A chorus of assent.

Out the corner of my eye, I saw Sefton march in with four of the Americans, shoving the two country boys ahead of them, their arms held to each side.

'What's going on?' I demanded.

Sefton drew to a halt, signalling to the others to do the same. 'According to these men here, these two are imposters.'

'Is that right?'

'Certainly is, ma'am,' said one. 'We've been watching them ever since we saw them eat last night.'

The men had dined together the previous evening instead of in shifts in the kitchen, a parting treat from Eliane, who insisted on laying the enormous dining-room table complete with silver and fine linen. 'What do you mean?'

'They eat with a knife and fork, ma'am. No self-respecting American does that. We eat with just our forks. The knife is for cutting, then we lay it aside. It's you Europeans who use both. No disrespect, ma'am.'

I had to admit he had a point, and I kicked myself for not spotting it.

'We decided to ask them a few questions on the train,' said another of the airmen. 'Turned out these two couldn't answer them. Any damn red-blooded American would know the answers, if you'll pardon my language.'

I stared hard at the two accused men, their faces sullen as ever.

'What did you ask them?'

'The usual stuff. Who won the World Series. Things like that. But it was when we got them talking about lorries that we knew. The Brits call them lorries; we call them trucks. Thing is, the Germans teach them British English. Which means these two are German infiltrators. I'd bet my life on it.'

I stared at the suspects. They kept their eyes averted, refusing to look at me. 'Did you let these two out of your sight on the train?'

'They went for a smoke, ma'am,' piped up one of the airmen.

I glanced at Sefton, who nodded.

'There were SS and Gestapo on that train. We have no idea if they passed on any information to them.'

I thought fast, scrutinising the two of them, seeing now the anomalies I'd excused as hillbilly habits. Even the way they stood didn't quite fit. It all made perfect sense. But how had I missed it? We'd double-checked all their identities, radioing back to London. Or we had done, until the radio operator was arrested along with Dr George. Shit and double shit. That was how they'd slipped through. Pure, dumb luck.

'Well done, men,' I said. 'Alright, you two. I think it's time we had a little chat.'

# SIXTY

The first blow knocked him sideways; the second sent the chair crashing to the ground. His hands were tied behind him, the rope wound tight through the chairback, but still I kept my gun trained on him and his mate, who was tied to another chair, forced to watch.

'Who are you? What is your name?' grunted Sefton as he systematically kicked and punched him.

The men stood around silent, hands on hips or arms folded. There were murderous looks on each and every face, but they were too well disciplined to break ranks and beat the hell out of him. I was itching to do it myself.

'Name. Rank. Serial number,' snapped Sefton, taking a moment's respite.

The man tied to the chair squinted at him through swollen eyes, spat out a tooth and laughed.

'You think this is funny?' I snarled, aiming for his kneecaps. 'Wait until I blow those off and then we'll see how funny you think it is.'

He peered up at me, unsure if I was serious.

I smiled. 'Oh, I'm serious alright. Want to try me?'

Blood was running from his mouth, dripping down his chin. He licked his lips, tasting it. 'Go fuck yourself,' he mumbled.

I raised my pistol once more and took aim. The blast ricocheted around the room, bringing the bar owner running back. He stared at the man now moaning and rocking on the ground, more blood spurting where my bullet had nicked him.

'They're German infiltrators,' I said.

'Dirty Krauts,' he spat. 'Finish them off.'

'Is there anyone out there?' I asked, waving my gun in the direction of the bar.

'No, I put up the "closed" sign after you arrived. I'll put the shutters across too. No one nearby will give us away. We're all involved with the station operation.'

'Oh dear,' I said to the man on the ground. 'It seems no one will hear you scream. So what do you say? How about you tell us who you are, or my next bullet will hit you square in the kneecap, I can promise you that.'

He'd stopped moaning and was staring straight ahead, his gaze fixed. I hoped that meant he was weighing up his options and deciding on the better one, but it could just as easily mean he'd resigned himself to a slow death.

I looked at Sefton then the other German suspect sitting mute in his chair. 'We can't wait for them to talk – their Gestapo friends could be here any minute. I say we finish them both off and get out of here. They can do what they want with their bodies.'

That worked.

'My name is Rolf Schafer,' the first one muttered. 'I am an agent of the Gestapo. I do not have a serial number. We are a civilian organisation.'

'I am Horst Gruber,' said the other. 'I am also an agent of the Gestapo.'

'That's better,' I said. 'Although, as civilians, you were

posing as members of the United States Army Air Force. I believe that's a war crime.'

'You bet it is, ma'am,' snapped one of the Americans, a flight lieutenant if I remembered right. 'This guy here and his buddy claimed to be from the Eighth.'

'Doesn't surprise me,' I said. 'They steal the uniforms from men they've captured and use them to disguise themselves so they can infiltrate lines like ours. We would have rumbled them sooner if we'd been able to carry out our usual checks, but our radio operator was arrested.'

'So what do we do with them now?' asked Sergeant Bridge.

'That depends on how much he tells us.' I looked at Sefton. 'I have to call the chateau and warn them.'

The bar was dark now the shutters were drawn. I heard the metallic rasp as the bar owner shot the bolts across the door. 'That should delay them a little longer,' he said with satisfaction as he came back through the curtain. 'Wouldn't want to make things easier for our Gestapo friends if they decide to come calling.'

'How far is their headquarters?' I asked.

'In Biarritz, around eight kilometres away. I reckon we have around forty minutes to get you out of here.'

'What about you and your bar?'

'Don't worry about me.' He squared his shoulders. 'By the time the Gestapo get here, if they get here, there will be no evidence for them to find. I've already called a friend to come and collect you and the bicycles. I'll claim I wasn't even here. I have a standard alibi. They can prove nothing.'

'I hope so, for your sake,' I said. 'May I use your telephone? I need to let our people know what's happened.'

He shrugged. 'Help yourself, but if I were you, I'd make sure those Krauts never spoke again and get the hell out of here.'

'Thank you.' I smiled as I dialled the chateau. 'That's good advice.'

There was a faint buzz on the line, and then it started ringing. 'Come on, come on, answer,' I muttered under my breath.

I let it ring twenty times before I disconnected and tried again. Still no answer. There was only one thing for it. I slipped back behind the curtain and to Sefton's side. He had his pistol pointed at the nearest German's heart, while Hammond had his aimed squarely at the one in the chair.

'I've just tried to call the chateau. No answer. One of us has to go back and warn them. We don't know if these two jokers have already told their bosses where it is or not, but we can't take that risk.'

'I'll go,' said Sefton.

'I can go with you,' added Lionel.

'You can't. I need you to get these men to safety, Sefton, and you, Lionel, are only just fit enough to make it over the Pyrenees. I made it this far. I even spoke with a Wehrmacht officer on the train without anyone recognising me. I can get back there the same way.'

Rolf spat out another gobbet of blood. 'You think so? We know who you are. The Little Fox, isn't that right? We overheard you talking about those posters. You think you can evade Obersturmführer Drexler? Think again. He's been on your tail ever since he realised the mistake they made letting you go. And this time, he's going to find you and kill you, wherever you run.'

# SIXTY-ONE

---

I rammed my pistol under his chin, pressing just hard enough that he could still talk. 'What do you mean Drexler let me go? Was this part of a plan?'

He stared at me mutely. I pressed harder, hearing the blood gurgling in his throat. Good. I hoped it choked him.

'I-I don't know.'

'Yes you do. Try again, or I'll blow your head off.'

The men were gawping at me in silent respect, or so I assumed. But I was beyond caring what anyone thought. All I knew was that some of the people I held dearest were in terrible danger and I had to help them.

'Tell me,' I ground out through my teeth, pressing the gun in so hard he almost choked. 'I'm going to count to ten. And then I'm going to blow your head off. One, two, three, four...'

'Alright. I will tell you. They knew you had something to do with the escape line because they'd seen you take those tickets. They decided to let you go and follow you so that you would lead them to the others and, in particular, they hoped to find the Little Fox. They had no idea that was actually you. An agent was tailing you, but you lost him. We'd already infiltrated the line and found out where your safe houses were. We couldn't believe our luck when we arrived at the chateau and found out who you were too.'

I didn't blink at the Little Fox part; I wouldn't give him the satisfaction. As for the rest – it was clear now these two were responsible for all the recent arrests. Three hundred people taken thanks to them. It took all my willpower to stop myself pulling the trigger there and then. 'How did you get in? Who helped you infiltrate the line?'

'We had information from a man called Harry King.'

King. That bastard again. 'What information?'

'He told us about this farmer and how we should jump from the train at a certain point as it slowed, pretending we were Eighth Army Air Force. Said the farmer would take us to the Maquis, who would feed us into the line thinking we were evaders. It worked.'

'I don't believe you.'

He sniggered. 'It's true. Ask your friend King when you see him next. He hates you, by the way. Called you a little bitch.'

'I'll take that as a compliment.'

I eased my gun away from under his chin, careful to keep it trained on him. 'Sefton, can you and the other two get these men to the safe house?'

'Of course.'

'Then I'll take the next train back. The chateau is hard to find unless you know the way, which may buy me some time. They've only been up and down the track once, and the turning is unmarked. With any luck, they won't have been able to describe where it is.'

Rolf gazed up at me, that stupid smile once more on his face. 'You won't even get there. They'll stop you wherever you go. Drexler will have his men at every station and border crossing.'

'Is that so?'
I pulled the trigger.

# SIXTY-TWO

Three minutes after the truck departed loaded with the men and the bicycles, I was heading back to the station, making my way through the toilet door and back onto the platform. There was no train for Aix but one due in twenty minutes that stopped at Marseille. I'd have to take my chances. In the meantime, I returned to the station café and ordered a coffee, smiling my thanks at the woman who brought it as I murmured, 'Lock the toilet door. The Gestapo may be on their way.'

She hesitated, evidently wondering if this was a trap. 'There doesn't seem to be any paper in the WC,' I added.

At this, her face clouded. She bustled off, disappearing behind the counter then emerging with a key, before vanishing once more into the toilet. I checked the time. Another fourteen minutes until the train was due.

I sipped at my coffee, head down, reading the newspaper someone had abandoned on the next table, savouring the anti-German sentiment as the article laid out how the young in France were rebelling against forced conscription, or what they called 'becoming slaves for Hitler', by joining the Maquis.

My mind drifted back to the farmer and his band of men,

Maquis to the hilt, wondering what he would do if he knew the two Germans had managed to infiltrate the line by jumping from the train as Harry King had told them and pretending to need his help.

Both their bodies were even now on their way to the safe house, where I had no doubt they would dispose of them in a fitting manner. I could see the look on the face of the other one now when I'd spun on my heel and shot him too. A flicker of fear and then his head dropping forward. Another clean kill, through the heart. They were never going to tell us anything significant – I knew that. And from what little they *had* said, I had to assume they'd already told their Gestapo buddies where to find the chateau.

I had to beat them to it. There was no way I'd let them take Eliane and François. Little Robert. Alice. Even Charlotte and Matthieu. Most especially Guy. If only someone had answered the phone. But they hadn't. I would just have to go back and to try and make contact with Albert before he delivered another convoy of men to the villa. Dear Lord. They could even be arriving tonight. Then they'd all be sitting ducks at the mercy of Drexler and his men – at least according to that sneering bastard, Rolf.

Did I believe him? I wasn't sure. He certainly knew who I was, but that could have been a bluff.

No, that was no bluff. I'd seen the certainty in his eyes.

Nine minutes until the train.

I heard someone else come into the café and kept my head down. Even if the Gestapo turned up here now, the bar opposite was shuttered and closed and the exterior door in the toilet here locked. The café operation had been running for a long time through, no doubt, many close shaves. With any luck, they'd survive this one as well.

Luck. Something I desperately needed right now too.

Six minutes. Another train arrived at the platform, this one bound for Bordeaux. People disembarked, making their way along the platform. Out the corner of my eye, I thought I saw a couple of familiar grey-green uniforms. But they passed me by, on their way somewhere else.

A shadow moved between me and the window. 'Is this seat taken?'

I barely glanced up. 'No. Please sit down.'

A pause. 'Don't take the train to Marseille. It's a trap. They're expecting you.'

I froze, staring down at the newspaper, my mind racing. Then I slowly lifted my gaze to see an ordinary little man sitting opposite, his bland features at odds with the ferocity of his gaze.

'There doesn't seem to be any paper in the WC,' he added, 'or I would use it. Instead, what I might do is cross the platform and go out the other exit. There's a man waiting there with a motorcycle. You will pretend to be his girlfriend, arriving from the train bound for Marseille. He has a spare helmet for you and some goggles that will provide an adequate disguise.'

I blinked. Gathered myself. 'Thank you.'

I could hear the sound of a train approaching and then the shriek and squeal of the brakes.

'Wait until it starts to pull out and then cross over. You'll find a workman's entrance at the far end of the other platform. Go through that,' he said, taking a sip of the coffee that had appeared in front of him. Evidently, he was a regular.

'Who are you?' I whispered.

'A friend. Good luck to you, madame. France owes you a great debt.'

People disembarked, and then the train started to pull out. I stood, stuffing the newspaper into my bag. It might come in handy down the road as something to hide behind or even a weapon.

I joined the throng heading along the platform, crossing over to the opposite one and weaving through the people standing on it, walking towards the far end and scanning the walls for a workman's entrance. There it was, just beyond the waiting room.

I paused, pretending I was about to enter it, fiddling with my purse as I surreptitiously scanned the platform. All civilians, although they could be agents in plain clothes. There was a man sitting on a bench on his own, holding a book he wasn't even reading. I watched as he glanced up and then looked down again at the same page, not even bothering to turn it. Watching and waiting.

The workman's entrance was around five metres to my right. I could make it in a few strides.

I shot another quick glance down the platform, but the man on the bench was no longer there. The back of my neck started to prickle, red-hot darts of foreboding shooting up and down my spine. I darted through the workman's entrance, exiting onto a backstreet.

No sign of a motorcycle. Shit. Was the man in the café one of them after all?

A sweet roaring reached my ears – a motorcycle racing up the street towards me, its driver shouting, 'Jump on,' as he held out a jacket, helmet and goggles. I threw on the jacket and crammed the helmet onto my head, thrusting my bag between us as I laced my arms around him. Then we were off, threading our way through the side streets of Toulouse, heading for the open road, back to Chateau Bleu.

# SIXTY-THREE

We ran out of luck around twenty kilometres from the chateau, screeching around a long bend to see a roadblock up ahead. It looked as if that Gestapo bastard Rolf had been right. There was no getting past them. At least ten soldiers. Three jeeps and a truck. Probably more soldiers in the truck.

'*Reste calme*,' the driver shouted back.

Stay cool.

One hundred metres. Fifty. We'd be on them any second.

All of a sudden, the driver shot off the road and up a narrow track I hadn't even noticed between the trees. My teeth rattled in my head, bones juddering as we hit rut after rut then skidded down another track, parallel to the road below, the pines masking us, although I could hear the distant crack of gunfire as they aimed at where they thought we were, their jeeps too wide to follow.

He seemed to know exactly where we were going, so I left him to it. Besides, the wind was whipping away my breath, the constant jolting leaving me battered and bruised.

Finally, I began to recognise where we were, on the mountain track high above the chateau, winding our way past the shepherd's bothy hidden among the trees. The place where Alice had first spotted Grant.

As we descended, I could see the chateau below, its red roof glowing in the setting sun. Was I too late? I had no idea. The roadblock might just have been a coincidence. Might.

'There's no such thing as a coincidence.' My father's words ringing in my ears. He'd have made a fine agent. He'd already been a fine soldier in the Great War.

Another thing he'd tried to teach me was to always proceed with caution. On that score, he'd failed, although I put that down to my inheriting Mama's hot Spanish blood. Not that she was fiery. Far from it. No, that was all me, and it was something I tried hard to temper. Too bad for Rolf and his buddy I hadn't been able to hold back. And if there were any more of his kind here, I'd be doing the same to them.

We skidded to a halt outside the front door. Everything seemed as normal, especially when Eliane flung it open and came running down the steps.

'Elisabeth! What on earth are you doing back here?' she gasped as I pulled off my helmet and goggles.

My driver did the same, revealing a face that rang a few bells.

'My name is Nicolas,' he said. 'I'm Albert's cousin. You go inside. I'm going to hide my bike.'

'Don't do that,' I said. 'Go and warn Albert. He's meeting a group off the train in Aix. He might even be on his way back with them, driving a truck. You have to stop him before he gets here, or he could walk right into the arms of the Gestapo.'

Nicolas slung his leg back over his bike. 'I'll find him,' he said. 'Then I'll make sure we find you.'

I took Eliane by the arm, walking her back up the steps. There was no time for hugs. 'The Gestapo could be on their

way here right now. Two of the airmen were German infiltrators. Don't worry – I shot them but not before they had the
opportunity to pass on intel about this place. We ran into a roadblock around twenty kilometres from here. Drexler knows
everything.'

She was staring at me in confusion as I hustled her back
inside.

I took a breath, trying to slow my racing heart. 'Otto
Drexler, who works for the Gestapo in Marseille. He knows I'm
the Little Fox and that I'm working with the escape line based
here. We're hoping that he can't find the place but, to be honest,
there's not much chance of that. I need to get you all out before
he turns up.'

'Oh, it's you,' said Charlotte, her voice dripping with scorn
as she emerged from the salon. 'I came to see what all the noise
was about. What's going on?'

'What's going on is that you're leaving. Now. This minute.
Everyone is going before the Gestapo get here. Pack your things
as fast as you can. You can bring one bag and that's it.'

François appeared behind her. 'Eliane? Elisabeth? Is there a
problem?'

'Not at all,' Eliane replied, smiling as she spotted the children. 'Elisabeth popped back to tell us that we're all going on a
trip. Isn't that exciting?'

Robert gazed at her from under lowered lids, his lower lip
trembling. He'd seen all this before. 'Where's Andrée, Robert?' I
asked.

'Upstairs. She's asleep.'

'Go and wake her. Tell her to pack a bag for each of you. I'll
go and tell Guy.'

I was already taking the stairs two at a time, my heart
pounding faster with each one. They could be here any minute.
How the hell was I supposed to get all these people to safety?

Stay cool, Nicolas had said. It was good advice.

I took a breath and pushed Guy's door open. He was lying on his bed fully dressed, as if he'd been expecting me, although the look on his face was a picture as I burst into the room.

'Elisabeth! What the hell?'

'There's no time to explain. We have to leave. We're blown, and the Gestapo are on their way. I have no idea when, but it could be any moment now.'

He was off the bed in an instant, grimacing as he swung his legs down.

'Here,' I said, holding out an arm, 'Let me help you.'

'Don't worry about me. I'm fine. Can you pass me my gun? It's there, on the dressing table.'

I snatched up his pistol, checking to make sure it was loaded. He tucked it into his belt. 'What about your bag?'

'I'll travel light.'

I looked at him, taking in the purple shadows under his eyes and the way he moved – stiff with pain and the exhaustion it brought. 'I'll carry a few things for you.'

Before he could protest, I snatched up a change of clothes and stuffed it into his knapsack before slinging that over my shoulder too and hustling him down the stairs. In the front hall, Eliane and François were waiting along with Charlotte and Matthieu. 'Where are the children?' I asked.

'In the kitchen with Cook. Andrée is in a bad way,' said Eliane.

'How do you mean?'

Eliane gestured towards the salon. I could hear a noise that sounded like someone keening – that was the only way I could describe the unearthly wailing that emanated from the woman I found rocking backward and forward in a chair, her eyes vacant.

I kneeled in front of her. 'Andrée, you have to come with me now. We all need to leave. Immediately. The Gestapo are coming.'

At that, she stopped her rocking and stared at me, wild-eyed. I held out my hand, but she backed away in her chair, shaking violently.

'Please,' I begged, grabbing her hand and pulling her to her feet while she twisted and writhed. 'We have to go, or they'll catch us. Do you want them to take you? To take Robert?'

She went limp, her mouth hanging open, all the life apparently draining out of her. I wanted to hold her and tell her it would be alright, but we had no time to lose.

'Come on.' I pulled her after me into the hall, where the children had now joined our little group. They were wearing their coats, as was Guy, and each had a small bag.

I looked at the others. 'Why aren't you ready?' I asked.

'We're not coming,' said Eliane as François slipped his arm around her. 'We're going to stay here and delay them as much as we can. There's no way François could get across the Pyrenees anyway. He's suffering from cancer, you see.'

I stared at them both, realisation dawning. That would explain the long absences in his studio, apparently to paint and draw when in reality he was probably resting.

'We'd like you to take this with you,' added François, handing me a book. 'Please make sure it gets into the right hands.'

I choked back a sob. 'Of course. What about you two?'

Charlotte had lost her customary sneer, and even Matthieu looked more sober than I'd ever seen him. 'We're not coming either. Matthieu will never leave France, and my place is with him, but we would like you to take Alice with you and make sure she's safe. She has a grandmother in England who can take care of her. Her passport is in her bag.'

My mind was spinning. So much to think about and yet we had no time. 'Very well,' I said, stuffing the book into my knapsack. 'Everyone ready?'

Andrée was struggling into her coat, Eliane lending her a hand. I could feel the minutes ticking past and wanted to scream with impatience. But that would solve nothing, especially as the woman was clearly fragile.

She was finally buttoning it up when someone hammered on the door. We all jumped.

'Open up. Gestapo.'

# SIXTY-FOUR

'Quick – out the back.' Eliane shooed us towards the kitchen and the back door. 'We'll keep them talking. Go up through the woods and bear left until you come to the bothy.'

'I know it,' I hissed. 'Follow me.'

The cook had tears in her eyes as we passed through, reaching out to fling her arms around Alice and Robert, pressing little packages into their hands as I hurried them out the door.

'Alice.'

I turned to see Charlotte running after us, tears streaming down her face too. The woman had a heart after all, one that was evidently cracking as she embraced her daughter.

'Be good, darling. I'll come and fetch you once this horrible business is over.'

She straightened, her eyes locking on mine as she leaned to whisper in my ear. 'She's his. Guy's. I know you love him. Please look after her.'

Then she was running back inside, Cook locking the door behind her.

I stared after her, open-mouthed, trying to collect myself, looking round for Robert and Andrée and realising she wasn't there. That was when we heard a distant screaming followed by the sound of a single gunshot.

I grabbed Robert's hand. 'Come on, darling. Alice, you too. We must be very, very quiet.'

Guy was already ahead of us, leading the way. We followed him up through the trees, the children clutching their bags, faces tight with apprehension. I could hear the sound of our breathing and twigs snapping underfoot. Aside from that, there was a resounding silence. What the hell had happened?

'Give me that,' I whispered to Robert, who was labouring to hold on to his bag. I slung it over my shoulder with the rest, our breath coming harder now as the slope grew steeper, heading up the hillside. It had seemed barely a few moments on the motorbike. On foot, it felt so much further.

Finally, we emerged in the clearing where the shepherd's hut stood, a welcome sight.

Robert stared at it, eyes growing larger by the minute. 'I don't want to go in there. Where's Andrée?'

'She's coming soon,' I said. 'Don't worry about this place. It's a little cottage. We're going to rest here for a while and wait for our friends. I'll hold your hand all the time.'

Guy was standing in the open door. 'Come on,' he whispered. 'It's fine.'

I took Alice by the hand too and led both children in, my eyes gradually becoming accustomed to the gloom. We didn't dare use a torch, but I struck a match so we could orient ourselves – taking in the bare wooden platform that was once used as a bed, the solitary chair by the hearth – before I blew it out again. 'You sit here,' I whispered, settling the children on the wooden platform.

'Why are we whispering?' asked Robert.

'Hush. We're playing hide-and-seek. If you're too loud, then they'll find us.'

I heard Alice sniffle beside me. 'It's the Germans, isn't it?' she murmured.

I placed my finger on my lips and shook my head. She got my meaning.

We sat, Guy on sentry duty by the door, me with an arm around each child, for what felt like many hours. In reality, it was probably only a couple. Robert's head turned heavy against my shoulder as he fell asleep, sliding down so he was curled in my lap while Alice sat rigid, staring at the door, waiting for our promised friends to arrive. At last, we heard a faint throbbing sound that grew louder.

'What's that?' I hissed.

'Sounds like some kind of engine,' muttered Guy, pulling his pistol from his belt.

Alice's hand grasped mine, her fingers digging into my palms. I extricated myself as gently as I could, lifting Robert off my lap so I could pull my own weapon.

Alice gasped at the sight of my gun, and I pressed my finger against my lips once more. 'It's alright. Just a precaution.'

Guy and I stood either side of the door, listening as the throbbing sound drew closer and closer. It was definitely an engine but what kind we had no idea. All I knew was that the track up here was so narrow that only a motorbike had been able to get through.

The throbbing was so loud now it must be right outside. Then it cut out.

More silence. One that extended for what felt like forever before we heard something else. A tiny knock at the door, then a hushed voice calling to us.

'It's me, Albert. I've come to get you.'

# SIXTY-FIVE

We stared at the truck outside the shepherd's hut, a hulk of a thing in the moonlight, its canvas top and tank-like wheels signalling its provenance. It looked like a German military half-track, capable of going over any terrain.

'Where the hell did you get that?' asked Guy.

'We liberated it from a panzer division,' Albert replied, grinning, as a head popped up from inside the vehicle.

It was Nicolas, holding out his arms for Robert as Albert hoisted him up. Alice climbed up unassisted while I clambered after her, offering a hand to Guy.

'Thanks, but I think I can make it on my own.'

I looked at his wan face, the smile he was using to mask his suffering. 'Are you sure about that?'

'When it comes to you, no.'

He spoke so softly that I barely caught his words. I wasn't even sure if I was meant to hear them, but they brought a warm glow nevertheless. Then I remembered what Charlotte had said. How on earth was I going to tell him about Alice? If it was even true.

Later. We'd deal with that later. For the moment, surviving was enough.

As the truck rumbled off, I held Robert against me, wondering what had happened to Andrée, fearing the worst. The poor woman had been quite unhinged before the Gestapo even showed up, traumatised by everything they'd been through and the ghastly events at the orphanage. If there was one thing I could do for her now, it was to make sure Robert was safe. I could feel the bulk of the book in my knapsack resting against my legs. Another sacred duty.

I hadn't had a moment to ask Albert if he knew what had happened to any of them as we scrambled into the truck. There would be time enough for that when we stopped. Wherever we stopped. The truck was going downhill now, towards the road. Surely we had to swap vehicles there? Driving along in this thing was tantamount to suicide.

Alice tugged on my arm. 'Are we there yet?' she mouthed, her eyes glistening, enormous, in the moonlight filtering through the filmy windows in the canvas. We were driving without lights, slicing through the forest in darkness so as not to give away our position. I was silently grateful that Albert and Nicolas knew this terrain so well.

I put my arm around her, pulling her closer so that she could nestle against me. She was such a good child, so stoic, that I'd almost forgotten how very young she was and how frightened she must be, especially as she was without her mother too. 'Nearly.'

'That's good.'

I could smell the top of her head, like cinnamon, her hair silky under my chin. Hair the same colour as Hélène's, although Alice's was already darkening, streaks of caramel running through the white-blonde strands, setting off her eyes. Eyes that were as dark as Guy's, a striking combination. Hélène and I had joked that our blue eyes made us sisters, although mine were paired with dark locks. At least, when they were natural. I couldn't count the number of times I'd dyed them as a disguise. I reached up and rubbed a strand of my hair through my fingers. It felt coarse, no doubt thanks to the chemicals I'd used.

Guy leaned across from his seat and stroked the strand back into place. I smiled into his eyes, and that was when I knew for certain that what Charlotte had said was true. His eyes, Alice's... They were the same shape, the same colour. That time in the chateau when I'd thought I was staring at Hélène when in fact it was Alice... How could I have been so blind? It was obvious.

She was his daughter.

# SIXTY-SIX

We changed vehicles at the edge of a quarry where Albert had parked his van. Once we were safely down from the German truck, Albert put it into gear and jammed the accelerator pedal in position with a lump of wood before releasing the brake. We all watched as it ploughed over the edge and tumbled down into the quarry, turning over and over until it landed on its roof at the bottom.

Albert let out a little whoop of triumph. 'Let them find that.'

Robert clapped his hands in glee. 'Take that, *les Boches!*'

I glanced at him, amazed by his strength. He'd lost everything he ever had twice over – first his parents, along with his former life, and then his sanctuary at the children's home with all the friends he'd made there. Yet this little boy was somehow able to keep smiling, as was Alice. Children could be remarkably resilient, but even so, it must have been so hard for them, all alone in the world now.

Perhaps not so hard for Alice though. I tried to stop myself looking from her to Guy, comparing them, but it was almost impossible not to. As we sat tightly packed in the van with its crates of vegetables ready to hide behind in case of a roadblock,

I could feel him on one side of me and Alice on the other, their body heat passing through me, melding and meshing. Or so I imagined. Half of me wanted to protect her even more as a part of him, while the other half wrestled with an irrational jealousy that cut deep. He'd had a child with Charlotte. Not me but her. The pity of it was, he didn't even realise it, but then, men weren't as attuned to these things as women, in my experience.

At first glance, you would simply say she took after her mother. Charlotte was fair too, with fine features that accompanied that aristocratic air. But it was there that they differed. Alice was all life and joy, while her mother was glacial. Charlotte seemed to have sold her soul long ago to the notion of a good marriage and a title, although there could be nothing good about being married to a drunk like Matthieu when she could have had Guy.

Could have had. Past tense. But what had happened? How did he not know he had a child? Because, of course, she hadn't told him. Which begged another question. Guy was from a good family too. Perhaps not as aristocratic as Matthieu's but well bred and, more importantly, well brought up. He was a gentleman, much more so than Matthieu. The gentleman I loved. I knew that now to my very core, deep in the place that some might call my soul, my essence. A soul that only half existed without Guy, as I now realised. I couldn't bear to lose him again. Except that was exactly what might happen once he discovered the truth about Alice. A truth I had to tell him, come what may.

# SIXTY-SEVEN

Her hair was black streaked with grey, wound in two plaits around her head, the cigarette dangling from her mouth more ash than anything. She looked us up and down through her spectacles, ignoring the cat weaving in and out of her legs, purring loudly. When the cat rubbed its head against my leg, she grunted. 'You'll do.'

I took that as a sign we could stay, although to be honest we had little choice. Albert had deposited us at the villa outside Toulouse, announcing that he would return in a short while. Meanwhile, Madame Béatrice would look after us. Madame didn't look too thrilled at the prospect.

'I know Captain Grant,' she announced as she put the coffee pot on the stove. 'A good man.'

'He is,' I said. 'We set up and ran the line together. Now he's gone down it. Things got too hot for him here.'

She looked at me for a second then glanced at the children, still hovering by the door, unsure what to do. 'Do you like cats?' she asked.

Alice's face lit up. 'I love them.'

'Then come along. Michou here has had kittens. Three of them. Would you like to see them?'

They both nodded eagerly, following Béatrice into the next room.

'Another strange one,' Guy murmured.

'She's legendary,' I muttered back. 'Runs her own line. Grant adores her, although I thought she was in Bergerac.'

There was so much more I could say, but I could hear her footsteps returning.

'There now,' she said as she closed the door behind her. 'That will keep them occupied. I assume you don't wish the children to hear what we have to say?'

'They've already seen and heard more than I would ever wish,' I said. 'Thank you for your discretion.'

'Discretion is how we survive, my dear. I've only just managed to return here from Bergerac thanks to the indiscretion of Harry King. My apartment in Toulouse became much too dangerous, so I've rented this place. I always thought that one was trouble, and now I've been proved right. Michou hated him.'

There was no fooling Béatrice – I could see that. Her instincts were sharper than those of any cat. I was only pleased that we passed muster.

'What has Albert told you?' I asked.

'Only that you needed sanctuary and that you will be leaving in the morning for Anglet, where you will meet one of my guides. Not that the morning is too far away.'

I glanced at my watch. It was well after midnight. 'Oh my goodness. We need to get the children to bed. Otherwise, there's no way they'll make it even as far as Anglet.'

'Don't worry,' said Béatrice, lighting up another cigarette. 'I bet they're already asleep. Come and see.'

There was no point tiptoeing in her footsteps. She made no effort to walk quietly as she led us along the corridor to the next room and threw open the door. The children were curled up on the floor, their heads resting on cushions, each clutching a kitten while the rest of the litter snuggled into their warm little bodies.

'There, you see. Sound asleep.'

Béatrice covered them in blankets and closed the door on them.

'Maybe I should sleep in there too,' I said. 'In case they awaken and are scared.'

'Don't be stupid. You need your sleep too, and there's a room prepared for you upstairs. One for you as well.' She pursed her lips as she gave Guy the once-over, noting the bandages poking from his collar and the way he unsuccessfully tried to disguise the pain he was in. 'Just a moment.'

She rummaged in a drawer, producing a packet of pills and a jar of salve. 'Take two of these now. They will help you sleep. Apply this around the wounded area and again when you need it. It will dull the pain.'

Guy looked dubiously at the items she was holding out, then took a couple of the pills and swallowed them. 'Perhaps, Elisabeth, you could help me apply the salve.'

I was torn between slapping him and hugging him. Even now, he could rustle up some cheek and charm. 'Of course I will.'

Béatrice sucked at her cigarette. I had no doubt she was taking all of this in. 'Don't worry about the children. I'll be here, in this room. I rarely sleep anyway. Haven't since this damn war began. I doze by the stove and wake if I hear anything. They'll be perfectly safe, so you can both get some rest.'

If I hadn't known better, I would have sworn there was a nod and a wink behind her words. Béatrice was a French-woman, after all, and there was nothing the French loved more than a little romance.

'Thank you,' I said, picking up our bags. 'Where are our rooms?'

'At the top of the stairs and turn right. They're next to one another. The doors are open so you can't miss them. Goodnight.'

'Don't even try to take your bag,' I muttered to Guy as we mounted the stairs.

'I wouldn't dare,' he murmured. 'She's almost as terrifying as you.'

I stopped outside the first door. 'This can be your room.'

'Aren't you going to apply my salve?'

I swiped at him playfully. 'Do try and behave for once.'

'How can I,' he whispered, grabbing hold of my hand and pulling me into the room, 'when it's you?'

## SIXTY-EIGHT

His kiss was sweeter than I could ever have imagined, infused with so much of him that I wanted to weep. I felt myself dissolving into him, the touch of his lips on mine slowly igniting something in me as they grew more demanding, my body on fire now, wanting only to be consumed by him, my breath coming in short gasps until all of a sudden he drew back.

'Go to bed, Elisabeth.'

My heart plummeted, shame and disappointment washing over me. He didn't want me after all. Of course he didn't. Stupid of me. 'You don't want me.'

There, I'd said it. Blurted it out loud so it could never be unsaid.

He took my face between his hands. 'Oh my God, no, darling. It's not that. Of course I want you. That's the problem. If you don't go to bed right now, I swear I can't be responsible for my actions.'

'Then don't be.'

I'd thrown the gauntlet down between us.

He groaned, shaking his head, half-laughing. 'You're impossible, you know that? Absolutely impossible. But then you always have been. It's one of the reasons I love you so much.'

The heart that had plummeted now juddered to a halt. No matter how many times he said it, I could never quite believe him. 'Do you love me as much as you loved Charlotte?'

I'd done it again. Gone and ruined things. His face took on that look I'd seen before – the expression he wore at the sight of her or the mention of her name.

'Why in hell's name would you say that? I've already told you how I feel about Charlotte.'

I'd have done anything to take back my words, to swallow them whole. But they were out there, between us, and the chasm they'd created was growing wider by the minute. And still, I dug myself in deeper, driven by some demon inside of me. The same demon that drove me to think Guy didn't really mean it, that he could never love me, that he was just saying it because we were here, right now, running for our lives with every sense heightened by danger.

'Would you feel different about Charlotte if you knew you had a child with her?'

He stared at me, bewildered, confusion turning to anger. 'Why would you say such a thing? How could you even suggest it?'

I felt the first tear well and trickle down my cheek as I whispered, 'Because it's true.'

The colour left his face. 'What do you mean?'

'Charlotte told me before we left the chateau. She said that Alice is yours. As soon as she did, I started to look more closely, and you can see it, Guy, in every feature. She's a mixture of you and Charlotte and even Hélène.'

He sank onto the bed and buried his face in his hands. For a long moment, I thought he was crying, but when he looked up again, his cheeks were dry. His eyes, though, were awash with something I didn't recognise at first.

'It's possible,' he sighed. 'Charlotte and I were together for maybe six months. Then I came back home to join my parents and Hélène before we emigrated, if you remember. I'd broken up with Charlotte by then. A nasty break-up. I certainly never expected to hear from her again, although she could have written or called. I would have stood by her and done the honourable thing. She knew that.'

That look in his eyes – it was shock mixed with wonder. I gulped back the lump in my throat. Of course he would be thrilled to know he had a child. Guy was like that. It was just that it wasn't my child but hers. Theirs. And there was nothing that would ever change that.

'Of course she did,' I said. 'That's why she didn't contact you. You said it yourself – Charlotte had other aspirations. She probably conned Matthieu into marrying her when she was only a little way gone. It wouldn't surprise me if that's why he drinks so much. She played him as much as she played you.'

I hadn't meant to sound so harsh. It just came spilling out, fuelled by jealousy. I hated myself at that moment as much as I hated Charlotte, perhaps more.

Guy looked as if I'd hit him. 'If you don't mind,' he muttered, 'I'm going to try and sleep now.'

I hesitated, not wanting to leave it like this. 'Guy, I'm sorry. I spoke out of turn. I have no idea what happened, not really. All I know is that I love you too, and I can see that I've hurt you. Please, please forgive me.'

If I'd thought my declaration would sway him, I had another think coming. He barely seemed to have heard what I said, never mind digested it. I might as well have saved my breath, if not my heart. He so obviously wanted me to leave, and the more I lingered, the worse it was getting. 'Alright then – I'll leave you to it. Goodnight, Guy.'

'Goodnight.'

I'd barely closed the door when I heard it – a single, heart-wracking sob.

# SIXTY-NINE

## 11 JANUARY 1943, TOULOUSE, SOUTHERN FRANCE

It felt as if I'd barely closed my eyes before someone was banging on my door, calling to me to get up. I stumbled out of bed, splashed water on my face and was downstairs, fully dressed, within ten minutes. The children were happily playing with their kittens in the kitchen, feeding them from the bowls of warm milk that were supposed to be their breakfast. I threw back the coffee Béatrice handed me.

'Albert will be here to fetch you shortly. He's bringing the next convoy of men after he's taken you to Anglet.'

He'd probably had about as much sleep as we'd had. 'I see. Does that mean you're taking on this part of our line?'

She poured me more coffee. 'I'll be merging it with mine. Don't worry – I know what I'm doing. I've moved maybe three hundred men through already. I can certainly cope with a few more.'

'I have no doubt about that,' I murmured, averting my gaze as Guy entered the room.

He looked as if he hadn't slept a wink, his face ashen and the shadows under his eyes more pronounced than ever. I could see he was trying not to stare at Alice, but his gaze kept wandering to her. God only knew what he was thinking.

She must have felt his eyes on her because she looked up and smiled. 'Would you like to hold my kitten?' she said. 'His name is Bisou.'

Bisou, for the kisses with which she was smothering him.

Guy attempted a smile. 'Thank you. but I think he's happier with you.'

I was dreading the children asking if they could take the kittens with them but, in the event, they were happy to leave them with their mother when Albert appeared bearing a beignet for each of them.

'Where on earth did you manage to get these?' I asked as they fell on the sugary pastries with delight.

Albert winked. 'I have my sources. Are you all ready?'

'As we'll ever be.'

My voice was artificially bright to make up for Guy's aloofness. Not that Albert noticed. He was far too busy making arrangements with Béatrice.

'I'll be back tonight with the first convoy,' he said. 'We managed to find them another safe house for last night, but we really need to move them as soon as we can.'

Béatrice took another drag of her ever-present cigarette. 'I will have everything ready. Now you'd better be on your way if you want to get to Anglet and back before then.'

'What about Eliane and the others?' I murmured. 'Any news?'

Albert glanced at the children and shook his head. 'I'll tell you later.'

I sat twisting my hands in the back of the van all the way to Anglet, wondering what exactly Albert had meant with that shake of his head. Had they all been arrested? We'd only heard one gunshot. What on earth had happened? I'd assumed it was Andrée who'd been shot, God help little Robert. He was happily playing with Alice, squashed behind the crates once more, their hands clapping in some counting game.

Guy was watching them too, his gaze only shifting when Alice looked his way. Otherwise, I could see him taking in every curve of her face, the way she bent her head, her hair falling forward in a sleek curtain as Hélène's had once done. His fingers twitched then as if he longed to smooth it back just as he'd smoothed mine. I closed my eyes, shutting everything out for a second, wishing with all my heart that I'd kept my mouth shut, wondering if I would ever feel the touch of his fingers again.

At last, we reached Anglet, after one rest stop so that Robert could relieve himself, his small face screwed up with anxiety, desperate not to cause offence. He was so young and yet he'd already endured so much. I could see that he thought if he kept as quiet as possible, perhaps nothing more could happen to him.

As I helped him back into the van, he clung tighter to my hand. 'Is Andrée coming soon?' he whispered.

'I don't know, darling,' I answered, unable to lie to him. 'But we're here, and we'll look after you.'

That seemed to satisfy him, at least for the moment.

The safe house turned out to be a farmhouse which at first looked abandoned, although once we were inside, it was homely, the woman who scooped Robert up and onto her hip instructing him, 'Call me Tata.'

*Tata.* Auntie. It suited her, although I doubted the Germans would have thought of her in such kindly terms had they known she was a key player in one of the escape lines.

A man came through from the yard outside, wiping his hands on a rag. He smiled and nodded at us but said nothing.

'Bernard is our handyman,' said Tata.

Handyman and a lot more besides, I suspected.

'It's good to meet you,' I said.

I glanced at Albert then at the children. 'Is there some-where they could play? They've been cooped up for so long.'

She smiled. 'Of course. I'll ask my own two to play with them. They're a little older, but they'll be very happy to have some new company.'

'Is it just you and Bernard running things here?'

'My husband is at work, but you'll meet him later, along with your guide. He has a job translating and interpreting for the French with the German army, which comes in handy. We have just one rule which is that you don't leave the house without one of us. The German military commander lives less than a kilometre from here, and we don't want you inadver-tently bumping into him or any of his men. There's also his Gestapo friend, Otto Drexler, who likes to visit from time to time, no doubt to snoop around. He knows the escape lines run close to here. I'm sure he'd love to catch us in the act, but so far, he's failed.'

Drexler. The man was everywhere.

Robert's mouth was working, his eyes out on stalks. 'Will he come and get us?' he whispered. 'He's the bad man who came before, isn't he? Does he know that we're here? Does Andrée know where we are? She might get lost.'

I kneeled in front of him. 'Don't worry, Robert. Remember, we're here to look after you. Now why don't you go with Alice to find Tata's children? You can all play together.'

Tata held out her hand. 'I'll take them. Give you a chance to talk.'

As soon as they were out of earshot, I rounded on Albert. 'Well?'

He shook his head. 'It's not good. From what I understand, Eliane was doing her best to delay the Gestapo when Andrée came flying at them, screaming as if she'd lost her mind. Drexler shot her dead on the spot. Then he arrested all of them.'

'My God. She's dead? That poor woman. That poor child too.'

I clutched at my throat, feeling the bile rise. She'd given so much, looking after those orphans, saving little Robert, only to be cut down by that beast. The same beast who now had our friends in his clutches. I swallowed hard, fighting back the tears. Robert truly was on his own now, and I had absolutely no idea what to tell him. All I knew was that I had to save him. *We* had to save him. That vile madman wasn't getting hold of this little boy.

'So it was Drexler who came to the chateau?'

'Yes.' Albert's eyes were sombre. 'He was looking for you.'

# SEVENTY

'If it wasn't for me, he wouldn't have taken them all,' I muttered.

'You don't know that,' said Guy. 'Drexler knew they'd been harbouring people there because his own spy told him. And Eliane and François knew the risks, Elisabeth. You can't blame yourself.'

'They chose to help the escapers and evaders. They took me in under sufferance.'

'That's not true and you know it. Eliane loves you, and so does François.'

I loved them too. Albert was already on his way to collect the convoy and take them to Béatrice's house, promising to send any news that he could. Not that there would be any. The Gestapo made sure of that. 'And there's no way we can rescue them?'

A forlorn hope.

Guy shook his head. 'None at all. The best thing we can do now is get those children over the mountains and get you back to London. You've done everything you can, Elisabeth. Time to let someone else take the reins.'

Through the window, I could see snow beginning to fall.

Those flakes whirling in the breeze could prove deadly in the Pyrenees. He was right. We needed to get over those mountains and take the children to safety. As for London, that was another fight. One I intended to win.

'Elisabeth, it's snowing!' Alice came running in, her face flushed with excitement. 'Come and see.'

'Let's all go,' I said. 'Come on, Guy. Is there enough to make snowballs?'

The snow was falling faster now, beginning to settle on the ground as we emerged into the yard where the children were playing, Robert kicking a football to an older boy while Tata and a teenage girl were busy in the barn that adjoined the house, scattering corn for the chickens who were scratching around among the straw.

Alice scraped up enough snow to form a snowball and hurled it towards us. It hit Guy full in the face, exploding into white powder as she roared with laughter. He chased after her, scooping up snow in turn and getting her on the back of her head. I could have been watching him chase Hélène, although fifteen-year-old Guy wouldn't have moved quite so stiffly. His injuries were obviously still bothering him even though he put a brave face on it. Would he even make it across the mountains? I wasn't so sure. What I could see was him falling in love with his daughter even as he grew used to her existence.

Splat – a cold burst of snow in my own face as Guy got me too. I wiped it away from my mouth, sputtering with mock rage, hearing the children's giggles as I grabbed my own lump of snow. Let them enjoy this. Tomorrow, things would be very different. The snow that was a plaything now might become their worst enemy, making the crossing so much harder as they had to trudge across it for hour after hour, leaving a trail that anyone could easily follow. And not just anyone – the patrols that combed the mountains, looking for people like us, escapers and evaders desperate to get over the border into Spain and freedom.

It was odd to think that I was now one of them, a fugitive running for my life while trying to protect the lives of those with me. Two innocent children who had no real idea of the danger we were in. A badly wounded man I loved very much. The whole thing was madness. No sane person would attempt half the things we did. The one thing I knew with absolute clarity was that I would do whatever was necessary to make sure they all came through this alive. Even if it meant paying the ultimate price.

## SEVENTY-ONE

Our guide was a wiry Basque with a weathered face and a gap-toothed grin. I could only hope he turned out to be more reliable than Pedro.

'Franco,' he introduced himself. 'Like the general.'

A code name for sure and one that bore a devilish nod to the fascist dictator the Basques loathed. He'd arrived with Tata's husband who insisted we call him Uncle and who looked more like an accountant than a *résistant* running an escape line.

Uncle had spread a map in front of us on the dining-room table. We'd eaten royally, the children gobbling up the pot-au-feu Tata had placed in front of us and then falling on the tarte tatin she produced afterwards. She'd encouraged them, knowing that they would need fuel for the journey ahead. A journey that, judging by the map, would be hazardous to say the least.

'We will ascend the mountain here and spend the first rest here, in this shepherd's hut on the hill. It's so remote I've never seen a patrol anywhere near it,' said Franco. 'The slopes are steep, but the mountains are not so high here, which is why we use this route.'

I stared at the route he was tracing with his finger. 'Where are we most likely to see patrols?'

He pointed to the slope that led down from the ridge we had to walk along after the shepherd's hut. 'They're every-where, but this is where they're most likely to see us. There is no tree cover until we get to this point, on our descent to the river. We cross it here, just past this farmhouse where there are natural stepping stones the Nazis know nothing about. At this time of year, it's flowing fast, but there's no way round it. The nearest bridge is four kilometres away, heavily guarded now by the Germans. There was a bridge here, upstream, but it was blown before the war, although this building is a power plant that's still in use, also guarded.'

I could hear the children chattering in the next room and wondered if they could even swim. 'Which means there's nothing for it but to cross the river?'

Franco nodded. 'Yes. This is the safest route now with all the extra patrols. It should take us forty-eight hours to the safe house at Sarobe, another farm, and then the rendezvous point if we keep a steady pace. More if anything happens to hold us up.'

'What happens at the rendezvous point?'

'Someone from the British consulate will be there with a car.'

I stared at the topography of the terrain, seeing the tight curves that denoted steep slopes. 'You know we're taking two children with us?'

Franco sucked his teeth. 'How old are they?'

'Six and eight.'

He squinted at Guy. 'Can you carry them if they get too tired to walk?'

'He's injured,' I blurted out. 'He can't carry anything heavy, or he might burst his stitches.'

Guy shot me a look. 'Don't worry about me,' he said quietly. 'I can carry them on my back if necessary.'

I opened my mouth to protest but thought better of it.

Franco was already shaking his head. 'I don't know...'

'We can do it,' Guy cut him off. 'We have to do it before Drexler catches up with us.'

Franco scratched his head. 'Drexler?'

'Otto Drexler,' I said. 'He works for the Gestapo in Marseille. The man is an absolute animal, and he'll do anything he can to stop us.'

Uncle adjusted his spectacles. 'This is the man who's trying to catch you? The one who comes to sniff around here from time to time?'

'Yes.'

'Then we'll make sure he fails,' Franco said, grinning.

I wished I could share his bravado. For a moment there, I'd thought he might even refuse to take us, but he seemed to relish the challenge. Like every Basque I'd ever met, he hated authority and loved the underdog. You couldn't get much more authoritative than someone like Drexler.

'Tomorrow at dawn I'll take you to this village here, on the border,' said Uncle. 'Franco will meet us and walk you across this bridge and on to the house of another helper, where you can rest and prepare for your crossing tomorrow night. Is that clear?'

'I'm friendly with the guard on that bridge,' added Franco. 'He's German but he never suspects the people he thinks are my friends are, in fact, airmen. With you, it's a little different. If he asks, I will tell him that you are family. You have a Spanish look about you, so it shouldn't be hard to convince him.'

He was looking keenly at me.

It was true – I'd inherited my mother's dark hair and olive skin, although my blue eyes came from my father. 'I'm half Spanish,' I said. 'If necessary, I can speak the language.'

'That's useful to know,' said Franco. 'Although all of us guides are Basque.'

They were a proud people, the Basques, and fiercely protective of their own language and heritage. After Guernica had been destroyed in 1937 by Nazi and Italian bombs, they'd come to hate the Germans with a passion, even more so once Franco and his fascists won the civil war. I didn't need to ask why our Franco was doing this or how he'd come by his code name. I knew I could trust this man with my life and, more importantly, with the lives of my companions.

'It will be an honour to walk with you,' I said.

'The honour is all mine.' Franco bestowed another toothless smile on us all. 'Now I must bid you goodnight. I will see you tomorrow, at the bridge.'

The bridge that marked the beginning of our journey into Spain. A trail that would either lead us to freedom or into the clutches of Drexler. So much depended on luck. And I had no idea when, or if, ours would run out.

# SEVENTY-TWO

## 12 JANUARY 1943, ANGLET, SOUTHERN FRANCE

The bridge was a busy road bridge that spanned the river flowing beneath us. Uncle parked his car at one end of it. 'I have a Ministry badge,' he explained, 'so they never ask what I'm doing here. They assume I'm here on military business. Ah, here's Franco.'

I could see him approaching from the other side of the road, his beret tilted at a jaunty angle on his head. As he drew near, Uncle embraced us all one by one. 'Good luck,' he murmured. 'We will be thinking of you.'

Franco held out his hand to Robert. 'Come – you can help me lead everyone across this bridge.'

Robert solemnly kept pace, taking this duty seriously, as we proceeded towards the guard standing at the checkpoint.

'Good morning,' said Franco cheerily. The guard smiled and gave him a friendly nod. Then we were through, still strolling, looking for all the world like the family on an outing we were supposed to be.

Once across the bridge, we kept walking, pausing now and again for the children to have a short rest before we set off once more, Franco occasionally pointing out a landmark here or there.

'That was the safe house the Nazis raided two months ago,' he muttered as we passed a shuttered farmhouse. 'Terrible business. The poor woman who ran it was arrested. Her children live with her sister now.'

'Do you know what happened to her?'

'From what I heard, they sent her to one of their camps in Germany. Such a brave soul. She was a widow and ran the safe house on her own. Now her sister runs another one not too far away. It's a matter of pride, you see, especially around here. These are Basque lands and Basque people just as much as they are over the border. We will do anything we can to fight the fascists, and that includes the Nazis.'

I looked back at the farmhouse he'd indicated. It must have taken such guts to run a safe house here, knowing that the Germans were breathing down your neck.

'Look,' Alice cried, 'the sea.' She nudged Guy as she said it, pointing towards the coastline to our right, where we could make out colourful boats bobbing in a harbour. 'Are we getting on one of those?' she asked, the gaiety draining from her voice to be replaced with fear.

Poor Alice had said goodbye to the children she'd played with at Christmas only to hear what had happened to them when the Germans blew up their boat. She'd never said anything, but it must have stayed with her. She was an observer as well as a deep thinker. Just like her father.

'No, sweetheart, we're not,' replied Guy. 'We're hiking over the mountains. It'll be fun – you'll see.'

He had his face tilted town to hers, their profiles so similar that I couldn't understand why I hadn't spotted the resemblance before.

She smiled up at him, reassured. 'That's good.'

We were ascending a hill now that overlooked the bay. The snow that had fallen further north had bypassed this place. The sky was cerulean, almost the same colour as the sea where the two met. From here I could see back the way we'd come and ahead to the distant Pyrenees. It felt as if we were standing between two lives, the one we were leaving and the one we were trying to reach.

Franco led us round the back of a house perched halfway up the hill where a woman opened the door to us. Yet another ordinary person doing something extraordinary. She welcomed us as warmly as Tata had done, fetching hot chocolate for the children while Franco went to find espadrilles for us all.

'They're not the sturdiest mountain footwear, but they muffle your footsteps,' he explained as he handed them to us to try on.

Mine fitted fine, but the children's were too large and Guy's a tight squeeze.

'It's the best we can do, I'm afraid,' said Franco. 'We don't get them back, you see, so we have to keep making new pairs.'

I looked at Guy across the hearth where we were sitting, the children at our feet, trying to make it all feel like a game. Crossing the Pyrenees wearing espadrilles seemed like insanity, and yet it was the only option. Far more terrifying than the mountains with their deadly crevasses and almost impassable tracks were the patrols that were increasing as more and more escapers and evaders made it out. The Nazis knew only too well the value of airmen who succeeded in reaching Spain and freedom so that they could fight again. Just as we knew the value of these brave people who put their own lives on the line to help.

People like this slender woman, not that much older than me, who was sharing all she had with us while men like Franco trod the routes they'd learned as smugglers to take us to safety. It warmed my heart even as it sent a chill trickling down my spine. All it took was one person to denounce them, and these people would be arrested and most likely killed. It was a sobering thought.

'Try and rest now,' said Franco. 'I will return for you just after midnight. You need to conserve as much energy as you can for the crossing. Especially the children.'

The children. One a boy who represented hope; the other Guy's daughter. I could see him beginning to shrink from the idea of leading her into danger even though he knew we were at the point of no return. There was only one way to go, and that was forward. Anything else and we were all dead. The dogs snapping at our heels were savage and the stakes impossibly high. Drexler couldn't care less about some reward, not even one of five million francs. It wouldn't go to him anyway. What he longed for was the glory. He worshipped gods like Himmler and his beloved Führer. Men who wielded terror as yet another weapon and would stop at nothing to get what they wanted. And what Drexler wanted was me. Not even me but the Little Fox, the myth the Nazis had partly created when all I'd done was rely on a few disguises and dumb luck.

It was still nagging at me, that feeling my luck had run out. Our luck. I could put myself on the line, but putting innocent children there too was another matter. Especially when Drexler also wanted to get his hands on one of them. It was obvious from Guy's expression that it troubled him too. And yet, we had no choice. Stay here and die or cross the mountains and live. Or die. It was in the lap of the gods. Our gods.

All I could do was pray they were looking down on us once more.

# SEVENTY-THREE

Franco arrived just before midnight, as promised. I'd listened to the chimes of the grandfather clock in the hallway on the hour, every hour until he came. The children blinked at me like baby owls when I went to rouse them, getting out of their beds still fully dressed and trooping downstairs, where we bundled them up as best we could against the cold, lacing up their espadrilles and handing them the walking sticks Franco had brought for each of us.

'You will see,' he said, catching my dubious look, 'how you can walk faster and silently in them.'

I hoped so, for the children's sake if not ours. The skies might be clear here, but once we hit the snowline, our feet would quickly become wet and cold through the thin canvas. At least the sticks would help give us some purchase as well as something to lean on when the going got rough.

As it turned out, the espadrilles proved far more comfortable than our heavier shoes as we trudged behind Franco, walking in his footsteps as he led us towards the foothills of the Pyrenees, carefully avoiding the patrols who criss-crossed the area.

'Is it much further?' whispered Robert as we began to weave our way through the thick forest that covered the lower slopes.

'Not much,' I lied, knowing we had around a ten-hour hike ahead of us before we rested for the night. Mercifully, Robert had no idea of time, although his little legs would soon start to tell him. Behind us, Alice marched in resolute silence with Guy bringing up the rear. Every now and then, I glanced back, barely able to make out his face in the moonlight, although the set of his shoulders told me that his injuries were playing on him.

Franco picked his way along the path with the absolute confidence born of many years spent smuggling at night, backward and forward over the border. They called it *gaulan*, or nightwork, in Basque, and these paths were known only to *mugalari* like Franco and a few shepherds. Even so, I kept my eyes peeled and my ears open for the slightest sound that might indicate a patrol was near. Spain was just over these mountains. We were so close to safety. Which was precisely why someone like Drexler would have doubled down on men in this area.

Drexler. I had to stop worrying about him. The man was miles away, in Marseille, probably even now interrogating Eliane and François with his own special methods. It didn't bear thinking about. I could feel the guilt dragging me down like a lead weight I was carrying. If it wasn't for me, they might still be free.

No, that was sheer arrogance. Drexler went after anyone and everyone connected with the Resistance, especially those who helped others escape. I might be the one with the largest price on my head, but that didn't make me special. I was just another body to him. A lump of meat to beat to a pulp until I gave up my secrets.

'We rest here for a few minutes,' murmured Franco, pulling a bottle of cognac out from under a large rock he then patted to indicate the children should sit. Guy and I stretched our legs, easing out the muscle ache that was already setting in. Three o'clock in the morning. At least seven more hours to go until we could have a real rest.

'How are you doing?' I whispered to Guy.

'I'm fine.'

He didn't look it. He was favouring the arm on the side where he'd been shot, hunching slightly to protect the wound and leaning heavily on his stick. It had been several days since the wound was properly cleaned. I thought I could see the sheen of sweat on his forehead that indicated fever. The wound was probably infected.

Without asking, I reached up and touched his forehead. It felt hot and clammy. 'You're burning up,' I said. 'We need to get you some more antibiotics.'

'Out here?' He managed a semblance of a smile, his teeth flashing white. 'I'll be OK.'

Somehow, I didn't think so. I glanced up at the sky; the moon was full and fat. I wondered how many planes were dropping agents into France right now, some of whom would end up treading this very path. It was the perfect night for drops, but not so good for us. It made us all the more visible to patrols, especially higher up where the treeline thinned or petered out altogether.

Franco offered us both one last swig then tucked his bottle back under the stone. We were off once more, thighs and calves screaming as we headed up the slope, the path growing steeper as we ascended, the children's breath growing shorter along with Guy's. I listened as he tried to muffle the rasp and wheeze, painfully aware that every sound mattered.

At last, we emerged onto a plateau which, although flatter, offered scarcely no cover. I lifted my face, my skin tingling at the icy flakes falling onto it, stinging my eyes, frosting my lashes so they glued together. It was snowing again.

Not just snowing but whipping up into a howling blizzard.

The speed of it was frightening. One moment we'd been marching through the trees; the next we were out here, barely able to see a foot ahead as the snowstorm whirled around us.

Franco turned and made a gesture with his hand, pointing off the path to our right where the mountain rose once more. I followed blindly, holding tight to Robert's hand, feeling Alice clutching my coat as we stumbled after him.

All of a sudden, Franco disappeared. I blinked, swiping my hand across my eyes, then spotted the fissure in the mountain-side where he'd vanished. It was a cave entrance.

'Follow me,' I urged Robert as I picked my way in, brushing past a tangle of ferns and squeezing through into an inner cave that opened out, wide enough for all of us. Franco was there, holding up a lantern, beckoning to us to keep coming.

As soon as we were all safely gathered in the circle of light in the recesses of the inner cave, he made his way back to the entrance, carefully smoothing over our footprints before tugging the ferns back across, although the snow was falling so fast, they would soon be covered anyway.

'I found this place many years ago,' he murmured, hunkering down on his haunches. 'Saw a goat come out of here. Wouldn't have spotted it otherwise.'

I hugged Robert to me as he whimpered. 'When's Andrée coming?'

'Soon, sweetheart, soon.'

In the lamplight, I could see beads of sweat on Guy's brow. He had his eyes half-closed, and his lips were moving. I strained to hear what he was saying, but it was no use. He was on the edge of delirium, if not there already. I handed Robert to Alice and pulled my water canteen from my bag before crawling over to Guy and holding it to his lips.

'Drink,' I murmured. 'That's it. Drink up.'

He managed a few sips although his eyes were still unfocused.

Franco pulled a hip flask from behind another rock. 'Here, try this. I keep it here for emergencies.'

This certainly counted as one, but I couldn't get Guy to take more than another sip before he coughed and spluttered it out.

'How long do you think the storm will last?' I asked.

Franco shrugged. 'Impossible to say. As you see, they start so fast, and they can end just as quickly. I will go out in a minute and take a look. Check if there are any patrols around too.'

'They patrol this high?'

'Oh yes. They requisitioned a farmhouse not too far from here and use that as a base. They're very determined, the Germans, but then so are we.' He cracked his gappy smile. 'I fought with the Republicans, you know. We consider it our duty to keep fighting.'

The lantern flickered, and Franco instantly sat straighter, holding a finger to his lips. We all waited, ears and eyes straining, until he relaxed once more. 'The wind,' he muttered. 'I will go and check.'

His shadow loomed over us as he stood, elongated in the lamplight. He looked like some demon that had arisen from the depths of the earth. 'I won't be long,' he murmured. 'Keep the lantern back here.'

For half a second, I was reminded of Pedro and his promise to return with a rope. Would we ever see Franco again? I knew in my heart we would. Pedro smuggled people across the mountains for money. Franco did it out of a burning sense of justice and desire for revenge. In my experience, you could trust a man like him.

'Good luck,' I whispered, but he'd already disappeared into the darkness that shrouded the mouth of the cave, passing through it like a wraith before being swallowed up by the snowstorm. I saw the ferns part and an inferno of whiteness before he pulled them back in place. The storm wasn't abating. If anything, it was getting worse. I wanted to call after him and tell him to come back, but Franco knew these mountains far better than I did. Or so I told myself.

I kept telling myself the same thing as the minutes ticked past and turned into hours. There was a sliver of light now where the entrance was. Dawn was breaking. I thought I heard the wind dying down a little and then another sound. Voices. Shouts echoing off the mountainsides.

I turned to Guy. 'Did you hear that?'

He was sitting upright, his eyes open and lucid. 'Yes.'

We waited.

More shouts, closer now. The baying of a pack following a scent.

'They're on to us,' I muttered. 'Where the hell is Franco?'

At that moment, the lantern guttered and died.

# SEVENTY-FOUR

Alice sniffled, and I reached out to pull her to me. 'Hush now – it will be alright.'

My whisper echoed off the stone, a sigh that engulfed us just as the darkness did. I could smell the flowery scent of Alice nestling against me. Heard a stifled cough from Robert. Caught the gleam of Guy's eyes as they met mine.

'Here.'

He passed me his coat, and I wrapped it around the three of us, peering through the gloom. Guy's profile was turned towards the cave entrance, keeping watch. I saw him wince as he massaged his chest and shoulder, and my heart went out to him. How he'd made it this far I would never know. Or perhaps I did. His hand reached out to touch mine, and somehow, I felt everything was going to be alright.

And then we heard it. A gunshot.

'Is it them?' whispered Alice.

I shook my head. 'Probably just a hunter.'

Another shot, echoing off the hillside. I drew my pistol; saw Guy's in his hand. More shots, moving closer. And shouts. In German.

'Not a word,' I murmured to the children.

I stared at the cave entrance, seeing shadows now passing in front of it. Shadows shaped like soldiers, wearing a uniform I knew only too well. I held my breath, praying that they would keep looking forward, the way they were marching. A single turn of a head – that's all it would take. Noticing something beyond the ferns that covered the entrance or getting curious.

They kept on marching, eyes front, weapons at the ready, a whole troop of them. I counted the seconds in my head. Three hundred. Four hundred. Staring at the sliver of light where there were no more shadows, listening out for them coming back, finally realising that they weren't, that those were just snowflakes, dancing like falling stars. I let out a long, slow breath and looked down at the children.

Robert's mouth was agape. Then he shrieked, pointing towards the entrance, at the shadow that filled it. It was one of them. They were back.

He pushed the ferns aside and stepped into the cave, raising his weapon. At the exact same moment, I pulled my trigger. Maybe Guy did too. There were bursts of fire and blasts bouncing off the cave walls, the children's faces briefly illuminated as they screamed, the sound of it drowned out by gunfire. The soldier's face briefly lit up too. Oh my God. It was him. Drexler. We stared at one another for a second, his mouth twisted in a ghastly grin. Then he was gone, staggering back out of the cave, clutching his arm.

My hand was shaking, the noise of the gunfire still resounding in my head. I put my hand up to my forehead. It was wet. I looked down at my fingertips, but it was just water.

I could make out the children crouched on the floor of the cave next to me. I touched each one in turn, feeling their breath coming in short pants, their hands pressed against their ears. Slowly, I turned, hardly daring to look. Guy's eyes glinted back at me. We were alive. All of us. For now. But where the hell was Drexler?

I sat stock-still, staring at the cave entrance, counting once more. One hundred. Two hundred. Three hundred. No one came. My heart thudded in time as I carried on counting. Four hundred. Five hundred. There was nothing else for it.

'We have to go,' I said. 'Before they come back.'

Robert shrank into Guy, the tears starting to roll down his face. 'Come on, little man,' he murmured. 'You have to be big and brave.'

'I'll go first,' I said. 'Wait for my signal.'

I edged towards the cave entrance, cautiously peering out, expecting at any moment to see Drexler staring back at me or hear the shouts of the Gestapo ordering me to give myself up.

There was no one out there. Just scuffed snow where they'd marched. No sign of Drexler.

Then I saw them – footprints in the snow, one set traversing the mountain, heading down, and then a whole muddle of footprints following, deeper and with a more regular tread than the lighter pattern made by the first. Espadrilles, at an educated guess, with boots in pursuit. A smudge far below of what was obviously blood, crimson against the white. 'Franco,' I murmured. 'He led them off.'

The gunshots, the shouts... Franco had sacrificed himself to save us. The bravest of all soldiers; the best of men.

I turned in the other direction, upwards towards the pass that led to Spain, my heart breaking a little more with each footstep, knowing that the only thing to do was go on in spite of the beast on our tail.

But that beast was injured, and as every hunter knows, those are the most dangerous kind. Drexler wouldn't give up until we were all dead. Or he was. Out here, in these mountains, with two children and an injured man, the odds weren't looking good.

Well, I'd faced worse odds before and there was no going back now. We had to press on, to freedom, or die in the attempt.

# SEVENTY-FIVE

We rested all that day in the shepherd's bothy Franco had pointed out on the map, high on the col. He was right: it looked semi-derelict and was too remote to attract attention from all but the most determined patrol. Still, I barely slept, instead keeping watch as Guy tossed and turned, the fever once more overtaking him, while the children passed out from exhaustion almost as soon as they lay down on the coat I'd spread on the earth floor. It was bitterly cold but far too risky to light a fire, so we were huddled together, my body lending its heat to theirs.

I tried to picture the route Franco had drawn with his finger, first summiting and then snaking down the mountain towards the treacherous river crossing and Spain beyond. I could hear him now, telling us that was the only place to cross, that the bridge was four miles upstream and heavily patrolled by the Germans. Once over the river, we were to follow the old train tracks and then the tunnels, diverting into the woods once more to avoid the guards on the bridge before scrambling up the bank that formed the final two hundred metres into Spain.

Night was falling when Guy opened his eyes. He looked a

little better, his skin no longer clammy, although he was still grey with exhaustion.

'Let them sleep,' I whispered, indicating the children. 'If we leave at around ten, we should be at the next safe house by dawn.'

He smiled at me, a gentler smile than his usual one. It tied my heart into a knot and sent shards of alarm shooting through me at the same time. 'How are you?' I murmured.

'All the better for seeing you. Come.' He extended his good arm. 'Lie by me. You must be frozen.'

I arched into him, luxuriating in the warmth of his flesh, the way his chest rose and fell, the rhythm of his breathing. Of him. 'You're breathing easier. That's good,' I whispered.

He laughed softly. 'You think I'm going to die on you? Not a chance. I'm not going anywhere, Elisabeth. You can't get rid of me.'

'You think I want to?'

We were so close our faces were practically touching, murmuring as quietly as we could so as not to disturb the children.

'No. At least, I hope you don't.'

'I'm not sure I could bear to be without you.'

There was no point in speaking anything other than the truth now, this close to death. He might not intend to die on me, but we still had a long way to go across terrain that was covered with Drexler's men. Worse, they'd smelled blood now. They knew we were out here somewhere.

All we could do was try to stay one step ahead of them.

## SEVENTY-SIX

### 14 JANUARY 1943, PYRENEES MOUNTAINS

As we crested the mountain, we could see lights twinkling in the distance far below. Between us and them, peaks and valleys covered in snow, a treacherous sea of white that we still had to cross. The wind had died down, although it still whipped around our ears, frosting our faces with its icy fingers. Up here, it was deadly silent. I stared across at those lights.

'Look over there,' I said. 'You can see Spain.'

'Is that where we're going?' asked Robert, pointing with his stick, his face pinched with the cold.

'It is.'

He'd stopped asking about Andrée, apparently resigned to slogging for mile after mile over these mountain paths. He was such a good child. They both were. Endlessly uncomplaining in spite of being tired, hungry and afraid. Guy, too, struggled on without a word, stoically enduring his pain as we stumbled and picked our way along the rocky ridge before beginning our descent to the Col du Poirier and from there to the river below.

The hillside here left us exposed to the frequent patrols, so I sank onto my haunches, signalling to the others to do the same, as we almost slid on our backsides down through the bracken that offered the only cover, finally reaching the sanctuary of the thick oak forest below. All the while, I listened out for any sound that might signal a patrol, stopping dead at the snap of a twig or what sounded like distant voices, staying stock-still until I'd made sure it was safe to continue.

The children walked in my footsteps while Guy stumbled along, bringing up the rear, his head hanging so low it was almost buried in his collar.

*Keep going*, I called out to him in my mind. *You can do it.* In all honesty, I wasn't even sure he would make it. All I knew was that we had to keep going, no matter what.

A labyrinth of pathways ran off in all directions through the woods, mostly used by animals as well as shepherds. And, of course, men like Franco. I couldn't erase the image of that bloodstain in the snow. It haunted me, a symbol of this awful journey, the price we and hundreds of others paid for freedom. In this case, it was Franco who'd paid that price, as so many did who worked for the escape lines. For every life we saved, we lost one of our own. Perhaps, in making that sacrifice, Franco had spared the rest of us from having to do so, but we still had to get across that river raging far below and over the final ridge into Spain.

I chose the path that looked as if it cut down straight to the river, hacking my way through the thick ferns so the others could follow, glimpsing a small farmhouse through the trees as we crossed over a stream and began to make our way along the ravine towards the riverbanks, hearing the roar of the waters as they raced over rocks topped with a mass of spume. All the while, I tried to picture the map in my head and the spot where Franco had indicated we should cross. I knew it had to be to our right, past another farm.

There it was – a farmhouse crouching at the edge of a meadow, slumbering as I hoped its inhabitants were.

I signalled to the others to keep quiet, and we crept as

soundlessly as we could past it, unsure if the people inside were sympathetic to our cause or could be swayed by German rewards.

The meadow sloped gently to the banks, but there was nothing gentle about the torrent that surged in front of us, foaming as it swirled over the larger rocks and boulders that were scattered across the riverbed. I scanned the river, trying to make out the stepping stones Franco had mentioned.

'There,' I muttered, spotting a ridge where the water flowed more smoothly, although the current was still treacherous.

I took Robert by the hand and led our little group into the woods that merged with that end of the meadow, trying to assess the speed and strength of the torrent. It was fearsome.

I looked over my shoulder to see Guy slumped against the base of a tree, his eyes glazed. I crouched down beside him. 'I'll take you across first,' I murmured. 'Then I'll come back for the children.'

He made to protest, but I silenced him with a gesture. 'It's the safest thing to do. You're the heaviest, so I'll need all my strength to get you over. You can then cover us from there while I bring the children. Do you think you can stand if you lean on me?'

He nodded, too weak even to speak. I helped him get to his feet, slinging his bag over my shoulder again so I wouldn't have to go back for it and looping my arm through his as I handed him his stick.

'I need you to look after Robert,' I said to Alice. 'You're both to hide in here until I come back for you. If anyone comes, lie flat among the ferns.'

Alice took all this in. 'Will you be long?'

'Not long at all. See over there? I'm helping Guy to the other side and then coming straight back.'

She seemed satisfied with that, wrapping her arms around Robert as we set off.

The few steps to the riverbank weren't so bad, but the moment we stepped onto the stones, I knew this wasn't going to be easy. The water swirled around and over our feet, the current doing its best to pull us from the slippery stepping stones, and Guy weighed heavy on my shoulder, dragging me down.

We took a step and then another. I felt Guy's feet give way from under him and heaved him upright with all my might, his weight almost knocking me sideways too as I gingerly stepped onto the next stone. Halfway across and the freezing water was up to my knees, lapping at Guy's ankles. A misstep and we were plunging down, the next stone lower than the rest.

The tops of my thighs were now soaked through to what felt like the bone, numb with cold and sheer terror. I could barely see the far riverbank through the spray.

We were walking blind now, the stones completely invisible under the inky dark water, clouds covering the moon so that what little light there might have been from it was completely obscured. I started to pray under my breath, begging whoever might be listening to help us. If anyone was listening. All I could hear in return was the incessant roar of the water and Guy's laboured breathing in my ear. I could feel him slipping from my grasp as, wet through, we scrambled on, feet fighting for purchase, each trying not to pull the other over or to let the river have its way.

Finally, I felt it. The ground rising slightly under my feet. Ground and not rock. We'd made it across.

Still hanging on to Guy for grim death, I forced one foot in front of the other, digging in with my stick, thighs and calves screaming as we scrabbled up the bank, me half-dragging, half-carrying him until, at last, I could let him slide to the ground against a rock. There was nothing to throw over him to keep him warm.

'Get your breath back,' I whispered. 'I'm going back for the children.'

He tried to smile. 'Got you.'

I pulled his gun from his belt and placed it in his hand. 'Just in case.'

Then I was sliding back down the bank, wading into the water, my feet once again feeling their way as I fought the roiling river that, if anything, felt even colder and more terrible in its force. Every step was a fight against a current so strong that at times I thought it might win, the river wrapping itself around my legs and trying to drag me with it to what I knew would be certain death. Only last December, two American airmen had drowned trying to cross this river. It was an enemy just as ferocious as Drexler and one I was also determined to beat.

Alice's head poked up from the ferns as I threw the stick ahead of me and crawled out of the water, trudging towards where I'd left them. 'You're back.'

'Said I wouldn't be long, didn't I? Alright, you two. Your turn.'

Alice began to back away, shaking her head violently.

'Alice, what is it? What's wrong? It's only a river. I'll hold your hand all the way. Both your hands.'

She was standing stiffly, eyes blank with terror as she stared at the water. 'I'm scared of water. I can't swim.'

I glanced sideways at Robert, who was gazing at her, his mouth working. Any moment now she'd set both of them off, and then I wouldn't be able to get either of them across. As it was, she was on the verge of hysteria. The last thing I wanted her to do was start shrieking or break into a run.

I thought fast. 'Tell you what, Alice. I'll take Robert across on my back, and then I'll come back for you. You'll see that it's not so scary after all. If Robert can do it, then so can you.'

She flicked a look at Robert and then back at me, indecision written on her face. And then she opened her mouth as if she might scream.

'Alright, alright,' I said. 'I'll take you first.'

I had no other choice. Leave her here and God only knew what might happen. If she gave in to panic, she could bring patrols running. Then again, Robert was so little and so very precious. I didn't want to leave him here on his own. Under my breath, I begged forgiveness for what I was about to do. But there was nothing for it – I had to choose one of them to take first.

Dropping to my haunches, I smiled reassuringly at them both. 'Look at me,' I murmured. 'I've been over twice, and I'm fine. Here, you can get on my back too and close your eyes. When you open them, we'll be there safe and sound. Alright?'

I stayed rock steady as she clambered on, my hands reaching back to grab hold of hers and help her wrap them around my neck. 'That's it. Now wrap your legs around me as well.'

With some effort, I managed to get to my feet. Alice was tall for her age and heavier than she looked. But then, Guy was even heavier, and I'd somehow got him across. 'Wait here – there's a good boy,' I said to Robert. 'Remember to keep your head down, and I'll be back again for you.'

I thought I saw his chin wobble, then Robert squared his small shoulders, sinking down into the ferns as he held one thumb up. I thought my heart might burst at his bravery.

'Hold tight,' I muttered to Alice. 'We're off. Have you got your eyes closed?'

The tiniest sigh in my ear. 'Yes.'

This time it felt so much harder even to lift a leg, never mind move them through the water. Alice's weight pulled me down even as the current tried to take me, turning this into a

Herculean task. I started to hum under my breath, something I only did in the worst of circumstances, a silent song of hope and fortitude that had got me through the toughest of times: 'Le Chant des Partisans', the 'Song of the Partisans', anthem of the Resistance.

As I hummed the final notes, I could feel the slope under my feet, the signal that we'd made it. Thank God.

I climbed out of the water, turned and dropped Alice with her bag and stick onto the bank, my knees trembling uncontrollably. I felt her slender hand take mine and looked down to see her gazing up at me.

'Thank you,' she whispered.

'You're welcome. Now come and sit by Guy here. You can keep one another warm.'

Guy wasn't looking at us, however. He was staring across to the far bank, his pistol raised. I followed his gaze. There were lights coming along the bank, perhaps half a kilometre away. Torchlights.

'Where's Robert?' Guy rasped.

'Still on the other side.'

'What happened?'

Alice let out a sob. 'It's my fault.'

They were moving fast. They'd be on him in ten minutes, maybe less. It took me almost that to get across the river, and I was getting slower each time. But I had to go back for him. There was no other option. If I left him there, they would find him. That little boy had suffered so much already. I'd promised to look after him, and that was exactly what I was going to do.

'I'm going to get him,' I hissed.

'You're mad. They'll be there any minute.'

I gaped at him. 'This is Robert we're talking about. I'm not leaving him.'

Guy wiped his hand across his brow. 'You're right. I'm sorry. I'll go.'

'Don't be stupid,' I muttered as I rose from my haunches. 'Cover me.'

The lights moved closer and closer along that far bank.

'Hang on, Robert,' I whispered. 'I'm coming.'

# SEVENTY-SEVEN

I plunged back into that freezing torrent, my limbs like lead, every part of me shrieking in pain, fighting my way back to Robert step by step, staggering as I lost my footing, falling forward, my face slamming into the water, then spluttering as I regained my balance, forging onwards, ever onwards, to save him. I thought I could hear them now above the incessant roar, the river demons raging at me, demanding my soul. I shook my head, sending water spraying from my sopping hair.

'No. You don't get me. Not now. Not ever.'

A chant I kept muttering under my breath, through gritted teeth, as I watched those torches coming ever closer along the bank, eyes fixed on the spot where I'd left Robert.

This time I half slid back down the bank as I tried to wade up it, grasping and scrabbling with my fingers until, at last, I managed to haul myself out. He was there, lying exactly as I'd left him, eyes tight shut.

'Robert,' I whispered. 'It's me. I've come to get you.'

At that, his eyes flew open, and he reached up his arms. I grabbed them, slinging him on my back too, snatching up his bag as I spun round and slithered back down into that torrent for the last time. Or so I hoped.

A flash of light glanced off my face as I skidded over the stones, reckless in my haste, instantly dropping as low as I could and standing still as a statue, shivers rattling my bones. I could feel Robert clinging on for dear life, his face pressed into my back. We breathed together, in and out, waiting for the shout that would tell me they'd seen us. Or worse, the shot.

Neither came. They were still a few minutes along the bank, threading through the trees that bordered it there. I could see their torches weaving and bobbing, but there was no time to stand and stare. I ploughed on, head down, Robert's arms tight around my neck, his feet dangling, the water trying to take us both as I forged through that deep trough and then up, up, wanting to cry out in relief as I felt the mud under my feet, instead treading as quietly as I could to where Alice was snuggled up to Guy, her arms around him.

'He's cold,' she whispered. 'So I'm warming him like you said.'

'Good girl.'

For one long, horrible heartbeat I wondered if Guy was dead. His face was waxy pale, his breathing so shallow I could scarcely detect it. 'Come on, Guy,' I whispered in his ear. 'For Alice.'

For all of us. We had to move or those flashlights across the river might swing this way, and then all of it would have been for nothing.

'Alice,' he muttered, eyes flickering. Then they settled, focusing on me. He was back.

# SEVENTY-EIGHT

It sat, squat before us, a long, white building out here, in the middle of nowhere, lit up like a Christmas tree. We could hear an electrical hum coming from it. This was the power plant Franco had pointed out on the map. We'd gone the wrong way.

Railway lines. They'd been marked on the map too, along with the power plant. Follow those and they would lead us in the right direction. But first we had to get past this brightly lit building. I turned and gestured to Guy and the children to get down, crouching as low as I could as I scuttled past, beneath the windows behind which Franco had warned us there were guards.

There were bound to be some patrolling too, and if they caught us, they would hand us over to the Germans.

All this raced through my mind while I moved as noiselessly as I could, acutely aware that if anyone looked my way, I was exposed, an easy target against the white of the walls.

The moment I reached the relative safety of the shadows beyond the building, I waited to make sure they all made it, watching Guy laboriously bring up the rear as he urged the children on.

The tunnel was easily visible around a hundred metres from the plant, railroad tracks running through it. They'd no doubt been used for cargo. Now they would carry us along in a different way, towards the farmhouse at Sarobe where we would find sanctuary.

We followed them for an hour or so, one after another, the tunnel walls dripping in the darkness, the tracks our only guide until we emerged into a ravine to see a guard house further ahead.

I gestured to the right, up the steep slope that rose to the road that ran parallel above. It was far too dangerous to try to get past that guard house with the tracks running right by it. We would have to take our chances on the road, although there would be guards there too. This was another border crossing, and it would be patrolled day and night. Still, we'd made it this far. We weren't giving up now.

The slope was gravelly, and it was difficult to get a grip, even with our sticks. I held out my hand to pull first Robert then Alice after me, offering it to Guy too, although he stubbornly shook his head.

That was Guy all over. Proud. Courageous. Doing it his way so I wouldn't have to. I could see what it was costing him, his mouth set, grimacing in determination, as the sweat poured down his face.

At the top of the slope, I held my hand up to indicate they should wait as I cautiously peered over the lip of the hillside onto the road below. There was another building ahead that looked like a border station with vehicles parked outside it. At least one appeared to be a German jeep, although I couldn't be sure.

To the right of the building was a bridge across which searchlights continuously swept. It wasn't yet dawn. Any guards at the station or on the bridge would be half asleep. I knew from experience that the small hours before sunrise were the worst when you were on watch. Still, we had to somehow get past them so we could follow the road to Sarobe.

I blinked rapidly, feeling beads of sweat forming on my brow just as they had on Guy's. Was I feverish too? Possibly. The river crossings had chilled me to the bone as well as taking almost everything out of me. I was still wet through many hours later, but this was no time to be sick. *Come on, Elisabeth. Concentrate.*

Our best chance was also the most hazardous. We'd have to drop back to the track below and negotiate our way past the guard house instead.

I gave the bridge one last look, trying to use the sweeping searchlights to see if there was an alternative. That was when I saw them, standing at the end of the bridge closest to us, not more than fifty metres from where I was hunched on the hill-side, staring at them.

As if he could feel my eyes on him, the man in the middle of the group turned, looking, or so it felt, straight at me. I instantly recognised those ratlike features, the way he strutted, like the gangster he'd once been and the arrogant monster he was.

'My God. Drexler.'

Was I imagining it? No. It was really him, his left arm in a sling. I was already scrambling back down the slope, stones skittering from underfoot.

I stopped; caught myself. If anyone in that guard house heard those stones, they might come looking, and then we would be caught between two evils.

Crouching down beside Guy, I whispered in his ear. 'It's Drexler. He's on the bridge with some of his men. Injured but very much alive.'

'Jesus. What now?'

'I'm going to finish him off.'

# SEVENTY-NINE

'You take the children that way. I'll meet you on the other side.'

'Elisabeth, don't do this.'

'I have to. I can't let him get away with what he's done. Not just to me. To everyone. To Dr George and the others. To Robert and all those other children, the ones we can't save. I have to at least try and take him out.'

He looked at me for a long moment then sighed. 'I know.'

I pointed down to the tracks and the guard house. 'Go on.'

Our eyes locked as he nodded. We both knew this could be it. Alice and Robert were almost spent after hour upon hour of trekking along the tracks, still soaked to the skin from the river crossing. Neither of us had really slept for days. We were all starving. And I was going to kill Drexler.

'Good luck,' whispered Guy, his smile filling me with a renewed burst of hope.

I crawled down the hillside to the road, keeping well under the reach of any lights, then scuttled across it, dropping down over the bank on the other side. If I could just get up on that bridge, it would be an easy shot. There was a maintenance ladder running up to the far end. I could shin up it in seconds.

But there were too many of them, a couple sporting machine guns. They'd mow me down the moment they saw me. There had to be another way.

The minutes ticked past. The longer I stayed here, the more likely it was someone would spot me.

As I watched, trying to work out what to do, I heard a jeep fire up. Headlights flared, and then it turned in an arc in front of the station, racing towards the bridge. Someone must have seen or heard something. I could only pray it wasn't Guy and the children.

Shouts now and arms waving, but I couldn't make out what they were saying. Then they were clambering in, all except Drexler. The jeep swung round once more and drove off in the direction of the border. This was my chance.

I scuttled as close to the bridge footings as possible, keeping low, the overhang concealing me from anyone above. The hardest part was the ladder. This was where I would be fatally exposed. All Drexler had to do was glance down, and I'd be a sitting duck.

I grabbed the first rung, swinging my legs up, hand over hand, just as I'd been taught. The ladder was slippery, my espadrilles slithering on the rungs, but still I clung on, remembering every blow he'd rained down on me, his fists smashing into my skull, climbing hand over hand, gritting my teeth.

I could see the top of the ladder above me. Just a couple more metres.

I stopped, breathing slowly and evenly. There was no sound from above.

As silently as I could, I hauled myself up, peering over the top of the ladder. There he was. Drexler. Maybe ten metres away, with his back to me, having a smoke.

I glanced over at the border station. Too close. If I shot him, someone would come running. I slipped my commando knife into my hand. There was no one else in sight, no movement from the building. It was now or never.

Drexler was centimetres from the parapet, so I padded along it, crouched like a cat, hardly daring to breathe, my eyes fixed on the back of his head.

Another few centimetres. Nearly there. But just as I reached him, he turned.

I struck the back of his head as I slammed my other hand over his mouth and nostrils, then jumped down and drove the knife deep into his kidneys. He doubled over, gurgling and retching, one of his hands reaching up to pull mine away, the other grabbing for his gun.

I kicked him in the back of his knees, wrenched out the knife as he staggered, gasping, and plunged it into his heart. For one long second, our eyes met, and I thought I saw in his the ghost of recognition before they clouded over and he slumped to the ground. I pocketed his gun, throwing another glance at the border station a few metres away. It appeared to be as dead as Drexler, but I wasn't taking any chances.

I grabbed him by the ankles and dragged him as deep as I could into the shadows at the end of the bridge where the searchlight didn't quite reach. When I let go of his legs, his boots landed with a dull thud.

I froze, looking towards the station. It was unlikely anyone had heard that. Even so, I was already swinging my legs over onto the ladder and sliding back down it, dropping onto the ground below and running as hard as I could for the road, where I paused, scanning in all directions. Nothing. Crouching low, I crossed and headed back up the hill before tumbling back down the other side, forcing myself to go slower so as not to dislodge the stones, all the while chanting the same mantra over and over in my head.

'Drexler is dead.'

# EIGHTY

Down on the railway tracks once more, following the route Guy and the children had taken, I stepped into the middle, onto the wooden sleepers where the sound of my feet would be absorbed. As I crept along, I crouched lower and lower, passing beneath the guard house almost on my knees. From inside, I could have sworn I heard someone snoring. Then I was past it, still creeping along, the searchlights now flashing above me, across the ravine.

Two hundred metres further along, I stepped off the tracks, my gaze constantly travelling the horizon, looking for Guy and the children. I was well past the bridge now and still no alarm had sounded. Good. Hopefully Drexler would lie there for hours undiscovered, alone on the cold stone, until his men returned.

Safe now to do so, I headed back up the slope, which grew so steep I had to clutch the bushes to haul myself up, wondering how the hell Guy had managed with the kids and hoping against hope that he had. At last, I was standing on the ridge above. Behind and below me, I could see the flash of the search-lights, sweeping round and round again. I stumbled on in the dark, all the while praying and hoping, passing a copse to my left. That was when I heard it, someone whispering my name.

'Elisabeth.'

'You're alright. Oh, thank God.'

'We're fine but how about you?'

'Job done.'

'That's my girl.'

We smiled at one another, the children looking up at me as if I was some kind of apparition.

'I thought you were dead,' murmured Alice.

'Me too,' whispered Robert, reaching out to touch me as if to make sure I was real.

'Now why would you think that? You know I'm invincible.' I gave them the bravest smile I could manage before turning to the trail once more. '*Allons-y*. Let's go.'

As dawn broke, we plunged down through thick woods, the going easier now with cover all around us and old smuggling paths to follow. Our espadrilles were torn to shreds, the feet within them blistered and sore. Worse were the persistent shudders that ran through me, jolting my head, which felt as if it had a vice squeezing it.

When we came to a crossroads, tracks leading off in all directions, I could barely choose, opting for the widest simply because it looked the most well-trodden, reasoning it had taken many others to safety. Not the wisest strategy but the best I could muster up with my head swimming.

Just over an hour later, though, we broke through from the trees to see a farmstead below us. We were half-running and half-stumbling in our haste to get there, my knees sagging as I staggered, the world spinning before me.

'Are we in Spain now?' asked Alice.

Guy grinned. 'You bet we are. You see that? The sun rising? It's a brand-new day, kids. A day of freedom.'

I stared up at the rising sun. There was someone standing in

front of it. A figure I recognised. I took a step towards her.
'Hélène?'

She held out her hand, laughing just as she used to do.
Another step and then she was turning, walking away from me.
I tried to follow. Couldn't. The trees, the sky revolving so fast,
the sun blinding me now...

'Hélène, wait,' I called.

And then I crumpled to the ground.

# EIGHTY-ONE

## 15 JANUARY 1943, NORTHERN SPAIN

I don't remember much of our arrival at the farm. When I came to, I was propped in an armchair in front of a fire, swathed in blankets, surrounded by concerned faces.

'She's awake!' cried Alice.

A woman placed her hand behind my head, easing it forward so that my lips met a cup. 'Here, drink this. It will do you good.'

I recognised her accent. Basque. Then it started to come back to me. I tried to sit up, and the woman gently pushed me back just as the world started to sway once more. 'You have a fever,' she said. 'You must try to sleep. The medicine I'm giving you will help bring it down.'

Whatever it was, it tasted pungent. Herbal. I waved a hand weakly towards Guy. 'Give him some too.'

'Don't you worry,' he said. 'These good people are taking great care of me. Of all of us. Listen to what the lady says. Get some rest. Paco here is going down to the bar to call the consulate.'

I squinted over at the boy standing beside Guy. 'You're Paco?'

He beamed at me, answering in French. 'I am, madame.'

'And we're safe? We're really safe?'

'We're really safe, Elisabeth,' said Guy. 'All thanks to you.'

I allowed myself to let go then, to drift into unconsciousness, pictures flitting past my eyes. The raging river. Clutching on, sure I would drop one of them into the water. Feet trudging mile after mile. The forest. Drexler lying dead on that bridge. Seeing the moon high over the mountain peaks and Spain beyond. Then the sunrise. Hélène, waiting for me. But this wasn't my time to go, so not waiting. Seeing me on my way. With Guy. Smiling in blessing. The children safe. Alice with her father. Robert to give hope to so many. I sighed contentedly, giving in to sleep.

The next thing I was aware of was lying on a bed of straw in the back of a cart that rocked me gently to and fro to the clop of hooves. Stopping. Someone lifting me down. Then a British accent. Being placed in a car that smelled of leather and cigars. My head resting on Guy's shoulder as the engine started and we purred along a road, the countryside flashing past in a blur, the children chattering louder as they realised there was no need to stay quiet anymore. We were free.

'Where are we going?' I murmured.

'To San Sebastian. There's a British consulate there.'

'And then?'

I didn't hear his answer. I'd already slipped away again into that land where the sun shone endlessly and Hélène called my name.

'I'm so happy,' she said. 'So happy you found one another at last.'

I smiled back at her. 'How did you know?'

'I've always known. You belong together.'

She was moving ahead of me, the distance between us lengthening. 'Hélène, don't go.'

All I could hear was her voice now, silvery, soft in my ear. 'I'm not going anywhere. I'll always be here.'

Not her voice. Guy's. They were one and the same.

# EIGHTY-TWO

## 19 MARCH 1943, SOUTH COAST OF ENGLAND

Far below us, the waves crashed against the shore in an endless, age-old rhythm, white spume topping them as they curled. Out on the sloping lawns, Robert threw bread for the seagulls, darting backward and forward to my father, who was tending to his fruit trees, covered in blossom. Ordinarily, I loved this time of year, so full of promise. Today, though, I was nervous, staring out through the conservatory windows, wondering if he would come.

I looked back down at the book in my hand. All those faces, some of them smiling up at me as I turned the pages, others laughing as they kicked a ball outside or ran across the lawns. One or two of the children were more pensive, gazing back, perhaps, at the lives from which they'd been so cruelly torn. François had captured them all in a few lightning-quick pencil strokes. There was one here of Walther playing the piano, absorbed in the magical sounds he conjured from the keys. Another of that cheeky young airman, grinning as he presented his best side to François. At the back of the book, Eliane's coded list of their real names; tucked between the pages, the letter I'd received only yesterday from Grant, who was in London.

I unfolded it once more, smoothing out the single page that told me Eliane, François and the other two had been released and were back at Chateau Bleu. There was still no word of Dr George and his wife. Unfortunately, no one knew where Andrée's body had been buried, but the Ministry was delighted with the response to Robert's story in the newspapers. It was his face on posters now above the words, 'Mr Hitler couldn't kill this child.' There was talk of sending a film crew to interview him for a newsreel, although so far, we'd managed to resist that one.

I glanced out once more, seeing Robert hand my father his secateurs. What that little boy needed now was a normal life, to rebuild his own sense of hope and not just represent it for others.

I tucked the letter back between the pages of the book. Once this war was over and we'd decoded Eliane's list, I'd make sure the families of those depicted in it each received a copy. Then they could remember their loved ones as they'd been, alive and full of hope too. François and Eliane's gift for them. She'd written a few words about each person, something they'd said or done while at the chateau. Those who'd made it out could read Eliane's words for themselves. Others wouldn't be so lucky. Their faces still filled my dreams, as did those flames shooting from the deck, the sea claiming them. I leafed through the book every day, trying to replace those images in my mind with happier memories, but still they cried out to me, begging me to save them.

I put the book aside and wandered to the window, pressing my nose against it, breathing on it so that the world blurred. Maybe it was better that way.

'Elisabeth, should you be standing up?'

My mother, fussing around me, bearing with her yet another bowl of soup. I thought I might drown in the stuff.

'Honestly, I'm fine. The doctor said I should try a little exercise.'

'A little exercise. Not all this pacing around. You've had pneumonia, my darling. That takes a long time to get over. Now, come on, just a little soup.'

I took a spoonful to keep her happy. 'That's enough. We're having dinner shortly.'

She looked at her watch, a gift from my father, its fine gold filigree setting off the olive tones in her skin, warmed too by her red sweater. 'It's barely three o'clock, Elisabeth. What time is Guy supposed to be here?'

Before I could respond, I heard my father answering the door.

'Well, well, look who's here, Elisabeth,' he cried in that hearty tone he used whenever he spoke to me these days.

My parents were still trying to absorb the shock of discovering their only child had been engaged in the kind of work that forced her to escape over the Pyrenees, taking a couple of children with her. I was just glad they knew nothing about the price on my head. The price that was still there, according to Grant's letter. That might have about finished them off.

I stayed where I was even though I knew exactly who was at the door. I'd known he'd arrived almost before he rang the bell. For a long moment, I carried on staring out of the windows, down to the sea below, remembering that river, the mountains. The way he'd looked at me. Then I turned. He was looking at me like that now.

'Hello, Guy,' I said.

# EIGHTY-THREE

At last, we managed to escape my parents, picking our way down the hill to the beach below, my mother's admonitions ringing after us as we went. The moment we were out of her sight, I ripped off my shawl. 'My mother thinks I'm an invalid,' I moaned.

He reached for my hand, his fingers entwining with mine. 'You do look a little delicate.'

'Delicate?' I stopped on the path, hands on hips, finally looking at him, really looking at him, taking in that devilish grin I'd missed so much, the mouth I longed to kiss. I could tell by the way he was looking at me that was exactly what he wanted too. But first there were matters to discuss and things to settle.

I spied my favourite rock ahead, poking out of the sand. 'Race you to it,' I cried.

Moments later, we slammed our hands in unison on the rock, panting. 'Beat you,' he crowed.

I threw back my head and laughed. For the first time since my feet touched English soil, I felt truly free. 'I don't think so,' I said, smiling. 'As far as I'm concerned, I win.'

'Oh really?'

His arms snaked around me then, leaning me back against the rock as his lips descended on mine, and I tasted it once more, that sweetness, setting me alight with the fire that was Guy. My God but I'd missed him.

'Wait.' I put a hand up, pushing gently back against his chest. The chest that was all but fully mended thanks to the doctors in the military hospital where he'd spent the best part of a month. I'd spent a couple of weeks in one too before conva-lescing here, by the sea. Although it felt as if a part of me had been missing all that time. Now, as I looked at him, that piece fell into place.

His brow puckered. 'Wait what?'

'I have something to tell you. I wrote to Peter and called off our engagement. I think it came as a bit of a relief to him, if I'm honest. I got the feeling he's met someone else too, from his letter. So as of now, I'm a free woman.'

I watched the kaleidoscope of expressions that flitted across his face, trying to read them. 'Aren't you happy?' I mumbled. 'I thought you'd be happy.'

He raised my hand to his lips and kissed it. 'I am happy. So very happy. There's just one tiny problem.'

'What's that?'

'This finger here – it looks naked.'

With that, he pulled off his ring and slid it on to my wedding finger.

I stared at him. 'What does this mean?' I whispered.

'It means you're a fully paid-up member of the Devil's Brigade. Oh and my wife too, if you'll have me.'

The ring burned into my skin as much as Guy had seared himself into my heart. 'Of course I will. You know I will.'

He took my other hand too, looking deep into my eyes. 'All I know is that I love you more than anything or anyone, Elisabeth. Except, of course, Alice, but that's different. It's not the same way I love you.'

He was fumbling for the right words, trying so hard to say the right thing. 'It's alright. I know what you mean. And I love Alice too. She's a part of you, Guy, in the same way Hélène was a part of us. When are you next seeing her?'

His face lit up. 'Tomorrow. Her grandparents have invited us both down. I told them I wanted them to meet you. They're lovely people, Elisabeth. Sometimes I wonder how they could have had a daughter like Charlotte.'

A shadow passed between us. 'They've all been released. Captain Grant told me.'

'I know. I saw him the other day. We're going to be working together, he and I, running the lines from London, coordinating aid. There's a job for you there too, if you want it. A proper one. I know you don't want to sit out the war here, so why not come and join us? We can be together, helping to save lives, just as we did in France.'

London. With Guy. It was a tempting prospect. I gazed out to sea, over his shoulder, thinking of all those people we'd lost, the ones who, unlike us, never made it out. 'I wish she could be here now – Hélène. She'd be so happy for us.'

'Me too. So let's be happy for her, wherever she is. Some day, perhaps, we'll have a daughter we could name for her. One who already has a big sister.'

I smiled, thinking of Robert helping my father. 'A brother too. It looks as if Robert will be staying with my parents for now.'

Guy laughed. 'You want to get started that quickly? Don't you think we should have a wedding first?'

I punched him on the arm. 'Behave yourself.'

'I'd rather not. Not where you're concerned.'

His mouth nuzzled my neck, working its way up to my lips, and I melted into him, all of him, full of that glorious sense that I was coming home, finally, to the place I'd always belonged.

# EIGHTY-FOUR

## 30 APRIL 1943

The tiny church was packed as we entered, Alice walking ahead of me holding the bouquet my mother had made just that morning – pastel roses and peonies along with anemones and hyacinths. Flowers from my father's garden, his pride and joy. His other pride and joy.

'You're absolutely beautiful, my darling,' he'd murmured as we set off up the aisle. 'I'm so proud of you. He's a very lucky man.'

I'd squeezed his arm.

That lucky man was standing by the altar with Lionel, beaming at me. As I took my place beside him, I slid him a glance. 'Hello, you.'

A tear slid down his face as he took my hand in his, and I knew he was thinking of Hélène and his parents, none of whom could be here, although behind us, in the pews, we had so many friends, including Captain Grant, down from London, and even one or two of those we'd saved, billeted now in this country. All of them here to share our wedding day.

I barely heard the priest as I recited the words, staring instead at Guy's mouth repeating them. The mouth that met mine in a triumphant kiss the moment he pronounced us man and wife. On my finger, a new ring replaced that of the Devil's Brigade, although I would always wear the other in my heart. I felt like an honorary member now, catching Lionel's eye as we finally broke apart, his smile welcoming me into the fold.

Then we turned, hand in hand, to walk back down the aisle together. A burst of Mendelssohn, and the church doors opened, sunlight streaming in. I took a step. Then stopped, gazing at the apparition standing there. Not an apparition. Hélène. Looking just as she had when she was alive, smiling at us both with such love that I knew she was giving us her blessing.

'You see her?' I whispered.

'I do.'

Guy, too, was staring at the spot where she stood, his face awash with emotion. There was love and longing there but also acceptance.

As we both looked back at her, Hélène gave us a final smile and was gone. I could feel the entire congregation holding their breath, waiting for us, wondering what was happening.

'Come on,' I murmured. 'Let's follow her.'

The music swelled as we moved in tandem once more, processing down the aisle into the sunlight. As we walked, I could see that mountain path, the river we'd crossed, the lights of Spain twinkling before us. We were walking into the light again now, a different light, one that illuminated our life together. A life we could share with the children we already loved and the ones we might yet love, knowing that whatever happened, whatever lay ahead of us, we had one another.

# A LETTER FROM AMANDA

Thank you for reading *If I Can Save One Child*. If you enjoyed it and want to keep up to date with all my latest releases, just sign up at the following link. Your email address will never be shared, and you can unsubscribe at any time.

*www.bookouture.com/amanda-lees*

There were so many ordinary people who did extraordinary things to help others during the Second World War. It's those people who fascinate me and about whom I love to write. Always at the back of my mind as I do is the question: would I do the same? The answer is that I don't know, but I hope so because their sacrifice, courage and generosity of spirit saved so many lives.

Among them were, of course, the agents of SOE and the Resistance, as well as those who ran the escape lines that helped downed airmen, agents, escaped prisoners of war and civilians to flee the occupied territories by sea, land and air. Helping those lines were hundreds of ordinary people who risked death if they were caught but who nevertheless took strangers into their own homes, hiding them for as long as necessary, in some cases months and even years. There were also those who escorted the escapers and evaders they called their 'parcels' across France and Belgium, as well as the guides who got them across the Pyrenees into Spain.

Many of those helpers and guides were executed by the

Nazis or died in the concentration camps where they were sent for their supposed crimes. The escape lines calculated that they lost one person for each one they saved, and yet we only know the names and stories of a few of those who gave so much to help others. In my research, I came across numerous accounts of their kindness and courage. I wanted to pay tribute to them in this book, especially as this year is the eightieth anniversary of D-Day, a day of liberation in which they played no small part.

As ever with my Second World War books, the characters in it are based on people who actually lived, loved, fought and died for our freedom as well as their own. I deliberately haven't given their real names out of respect for their privacy and that of their families, as I have, of course, imagined much of what happened too. I would, however, like to name two who particularly inspired me among the many, chief among them Eliane Plewman, who was born in Marseille and returned to the city to serve as a dedicated SOE agent. The Gestapo arrested her at a safe house there in March 1944. On 13 September 1944, she was executed by them alongside Noor Inayat Khan, Madeleine Damerment and Yolande Beekman at Dachau concentration camp.

The other person I want to mention is a guide named Florentino Goikoetxea, a Basque who was a smuggler by profession and who worked for the Comet Line during the Second World War, guiding over two hundred Allied airmen over the Pyrenees and into Spain. For that, he was honoured with the George Medal and the Légion d'honneur, although, as a wanted man in Spain until Franco died in 1975, he had to wait until then to receive them. During the ceremony at Buckingham Palace, he was asked his occupation and replied that he was in the 'import-export business'.

With millions of people today still having to flee war-torn countries for freedom, I wanted this book to remind us that courage isn't confined to a particular time or place and that kindness is something we can all extend to the dispossessed. At the heart of it there is, of course, a love story. Love so often flowered in the extremes of war, as it still does today. It was also love that inspired people to do what they did to fight back: love of their country, of freedom and of the rest of humanity. It's a love I hope we can all still find.

The children in the book represent that love, especially little Robert, whose story is loosely based on the horrific raid carried out by the Gestapo on the orphanage at Izieu in France. I say loosely because, in that case, none of the children survived. All forty-four of them were murdered at Auschwitz. I wanted Robert to stand as a symbol of hope in their memory and to highlight the obscenity of children caught up in war.

Above all, hope pervades this book, even at the darkest moments. It's how people survived, and it's why we're all here today, free to read a story like this. To have hope even when things appear hopeless is, in my own experience, the lodestone that leads us out of the darkness. It's what people refused to give up during the Second World War, and it's something I hope you hold on to just as the characters in this book do. May we never forget the real people and stories they're based upon, and may we always remember the extraordinary things those ordinary people did. We owe them so much.

Thanks,

Amanda

www.amandalees.com

facebook.com/AmandaLeesAuthor
x.com/amandalees

# ACKNOWLEDGEMENTS

Writing a book might seem a solitary endeavour but it does, in fact, take a team and mine is one of the best. First, there is my agent and friend, Lisa, who is as extraordinary as any of the people in my books and would no doubt have made a brilliant SOE agent too (trust me, she's fierce as well as fabulous). Alongside her, she has her own equally amazing team in Patrick, Zoe, Jamie and Elena.

Then there is my brilliant editor, Susannah, and the team at Bookouture, who not only get my books out into the world but make sure they do so in style. Behind the scenes, they crunch data, perform publishing wizardry and weave marketing magic. There is a list of them at the back of this book and I am grateful to each and every one of them for their brilliance in bringing it to life.

I'd also like to mention my fellow author buddies who keep me going through the long, chocolate-fuelled days – Karin, Vanessa, Anne, Victoria, Lisa, Martyn, Susi, Anna, Diane, Vicky, Sam and, again, too many more to mention who have been endlessly supportive. As ever, there is my constant inspiration, my daughter. I love you and I am so proud of you. Next, the friends and family who have been there for me through times dark and light – Julia & Phil, Andrew, Josa, Guy, Helen, Ed, Jackie & Sam, Claire and Sean along with so many others. Thank you.

Above all, thanks to the women and men who served, and

gave their lives in service for, their countries and our freedom. We will never forget you.

# PUBLISHING TEAM

Turning a manuscript into a book requires the efforts of many people. The publishing team at Bookouture would like to acknowledge everyone who contributed to this publication.

## Commercial
Lauren Morrissette
Hannah Richmond
Imogen Allport

## Cover design
Debbie Clement

## Data and analysis
Mark Alder
Mohamed Bussuri

## Editorial
Susannah Hamilton
Nadia Michael

## Copyeditor
Laura Kincaid

## Proofreader
Anne O'Brien

## Marketing
Alex Crow
Melanie Price
Occy Carr
Ciara Rosney
Martyna Młynarska

## Operations and distribution
Marina Valles
Stephanie Straub

## Production
Hannah Snetsinger
Mandy Kullar
Jen Shannon
Ria Clare

## Publicity
Kim Nash
Noelle Holten
Jess Readett
Sarah Hardy

## Rights and contracts
Peta Nightingale
Richard King
Saidah Graham

Made in the USA
Columbia, SC
18 September 2024